MW00573215

THE
BUTCHER
GAME

ALSO BY ALAINA URQUHART

The Butcher and the Wren

THE
BUTCHER
GAME

A Dr. Wren Muller Novel

ALAINA URQUHART

NEW YORK

The characters and events in this book are fictitious.
Any similarity to real persons, living or dead,
is coincidental and not intended by the author.

Copyright © 2024 by Perimortem LLC

Zando supports the right to free expression and the value of copyright.
The purpose of copyright is to encourage writers and artists to produce
the creative works that enrich our culture. Thank you for buying an
authorized edition of this book and for complying with copyright laws
by not reproducing, scanning, uploading, or distributing this book
or any part of it without permission. If you would like permission
to use material from the book (other than for brief quotations
embodied in reviews), please contact connect@zandoprojects.com.

zandoprojects.com

First Edition: September 2024

Design by Neuwirth & Associates
Cover design by Evan Gaffney

The publisher does not have control over and is not responsible
for author or other third-party websites (or their content).

Library of Congress Control Number: 2024935876

978-1-63893-124-9 (Hardcover)
978-1-63893-125-6 (ebook)
978-1-63893-231-4 (B&N Black Friday Signed Edition)
978-1-63893-220-8 (B&N Signed Edition)

10 9 8 7 6 5 4 3 2 1
Manufactured in the United States of America

For John. You simply hold my entire universe together. I will hyperfixate on you (and probably lemon popsicles) way past forever.

For my three magical babies, you continue to be the greatest things in my life. You are magical, hilarious, brilliant, and incredibly kind. This is why it pains me to tell you that you still can't read this one. Please put it down. Let's start with some *Goosebumps* and see where we end up.

THE
BUTCHER
GAME

PROLOGUE

The manhunt for suspected serial killer Jeremy Rose has become a nationwide search. Authorities in Louisiana believe Rose may have left the state and they are working with local authorities in Mississippi, Arkansas, and now Texas to locate him.

The breaking news sounds mundane when delivered with the anchor's standard broadcast lilt.

Philip leans back in his blue chair. He rubs his chin, letting his gaze fall on to the fire that burns strong in the hearth. For days, he has been following the torrent of news concerning his childhood friend and his nightmarish misdeeds. Lurid details of Jeremy's crimes had been splashed all over the national media. The Bayou Butcher finally had a name and the world could look at the face of the man responsible for the vicious serial killings that had terrorized Louisiana for years.

Earlier in the week, Philip had watched a press conference with the lead detective on the case. It was clear Detective Leroux was trying to keep things close to the chest, assuring the public that updates would be provided whenever they deemed it safe and of no hindrance to their investigation. He clearly didn't want the ruthless enthusiasm of armchair detectives and cutthroat reporters following his every move.

Philip is sure everyone is speculating about Jeremy's upbringing, deciding whether it was nature or nurture, and where the blame *really* lies. Next, the world would decide whether he *looks* like a serial killer and then there is a chance everyone will unintentionally compromise the case on social media.

Whenever news of another Bayou Butcher victim made its way out of Louisiana, Philip found himself morbidly curious—part of him always wondered if the killer was Jeremy, but he never had any proof. All he recognized were the names of a lot of the dumping grounds, and he still felt a sense of connection with the community he'd been born into, even if he'd lived in Massachusetts for most of his life. Of course, Philip knew Jeremy was a monster long before the rest of the world.

Finally, his time to be publicly judged has arrived, although no one else knows the half of it. Only Philip knows where it all began. He witnessed the depths of Jeremy's depravity when they were only teenagers, barely old enough to drive.

Philip watched the shift take place that night, saw the brittle threads of humanity in Jeremy's eyes dim like a low-burning flame and then snuff out. People talk about being able to pinpoint the exact moment when something changes. Philip doesn't usually take that kind of thing seriously, but that night, he saw it. He knew Jeremy wasn't finished. He recognized that something primal, something wicked, had sprung open, and there was no way to bury it again.

When Detective John Leroux had contacted him almost a month ago to inquire about a library card in Louisiana, one connected to a serial murder case, Philip immediately thought about Jeremy. The call had been intense. Philip had felt he was under a spotlight.

"Philip Trudeau?" A stern voice with a buttery Louisiana accent came through the line.

"Who's asking?" Philip had replied.

"Detective John Leroux, New Orleans Police Department. Are you Philip Trudeau?"

He'd hesitated. "Yeah. I'm Philip. What's this about, Detective?"

"Have you visited Louisiana recently, Philip?"

His blood had felt as if it had turned to ice. "I was born there, but I moved away pretty early. Haven't been there since."

"Any reason you can think why your name is on a library card at a crime scene?"

"Well, I *did* live there for a few years as a kid. I'm sure I took out a library book."

Detective Leroux scoffed on the other end. "You think I'm looking for a cute reply?"

"Listen, I haven't been in Louisiana at any point in almost thirty years. So, whatever crime scene you're referring to, I wasn't there."

"Still talk to anyone down from the area, Philip?"

"Not really, no. I moved up North when I was twelve. My whole life is up here."

"Think you can tell me where you were on a few dates this summer?" the detective had asked.

"Sure. I work almost every day, and I have my son every other weekend. I haven't taken a day off in months."

"And your employer would confirm this for me?"

"Of course. I'll give you the num—"

"You're a pastor at Covenant of Grace Church, right?"

Philip had laughed. "Right, you're a detective."

"I'll give them a call and touch base with you again soon. Stay available, Philip. I'll have more questions for you."

The line had dropped without a goodbye.

The call had been unnerving, but Philip knew there was only one person who could possibly have had his childhood library card and also have a detective hot on their trail.

As far as Philip knew, Jeremy Rose had never left Louisiana. They were close to eighteen when they stopped talking, their summers in Massachusetts with Philip's family coming to an abrupt end. It was never lost on him that the Bayou Butcher killings started not long after Jeremy returned home after that final summer.

Now, seeing confirmation of Jeremy's degeneration into a true psychopath, Philip wonders what comes next. It's bad enough to have someone out there who holds intimate knowledge of his deepest indiscretions, but it's truly disconcerting to have that person be as unpredictable as Jeremy, especially when he has very little to lose and a lot to destroy.

Philip knows the library card was meant to be a message. To make sure Philip remembers his past, no matter how deep he's tried to bury it. And with Jeremy Rose on the run, Philip fears there's only one direction he's heading.

CHAPTER 1

WREN WEARS THE DARKNESS like a straitjacket. It confines and suffocates without mercy. She struggles to claw through it, but its purpose is set in permanence. The more she fights, the more it refuses to relent.

Her breath comes in short, painful bursts, her lungs raw and wounded. Each puff of air prickles through them like flames licking at bare skin. The sound of her heartbeat thunders in her ears. She can almost feel the blood rushing into her limbs as her system performs its primal fear response.

Panic threatens to overtake her, flooding every inch of her body. She closes her eyes against the dark, still attempting to regain control.

Do not allow your body to control you, Wren. Don't give in.

Her racing mind implores her to take the wheel, but she's lost in the rushing waters of fear that have flooded almost every inch of her body. A faint SOS call sounds in the distance, and she answers it, squeezing her eyes shut.

You are in control, Wren. Harness it.

Her sharp breath begins to steady, and she slowly opens her eyes to the night sky. Suddenly, her surroundings start to make themselves known. They appear slowly all around her, reaching out to her in a familiar way. She reaches back. Wren grasps at a hanging piece of moss and weaves it between her fingers. The soft texture immediately soothes her. She rubs it across her hand like a beloved blanket.

The cicadas scream. A hidden conductor has struck up an orchestra and the silence has turned into a nocturnal chorus. She wiggles her bare toes, feeling warm mud ooze beneath them. It smells like rich earth and swamp. She's been here before.

Propelling herself forward, she almost trips on the exposed cypress roots that twist in every direction. The hanging moss caresses her face as she moves through the swamp, and she relishes the soft touch on her skin amid this bombardment of sensations. She stops and closes her eyes again, spinning slowly to let the wisps tickle her cheeks.

"Wren."

Without warning, his voice breaks through the cypress trees. She stops suddenly, not daring to open her eyes.

"Wren."

He says it again, louder this time. She can still hear the crooked smile in his voice. His presence draws closer, stalking her like a predator. Still afraid to open her eyes, she wills the environment to swallow him up, for the bayou to finally turn against him.

"Emily."

He snarls the name, letting it hit the left side of her like an arrow. In response to her slight movement, a piece of moss slides across her cheek, startling her. She raises her hand to brush it aside and instead feels something else entirely. Her hand doesn't connect with the kind offerings of an ancient tree; what she feels is a human hand as it brushes against her face, mimicking a comforting gesture. She grasps on to the cold, threatening hand and digs her nails into it.

Anger pulses through that hand. She can feel it ignite, infusing fear into every part of her. It reflexively grips her throat, throwing her body like a rag doll. She crumples into the soggy ground, trying to reclaim the breath that was knocked out of her. Her eyes fly open and are met with his unmistakable blue eyes. They appear to boil in their sockets, filled with hate and eager to inflict pain. He crouches and grabs her again, tightening his grip on her airway. She kicks at his legs, claws at his hands. They are a vice. Each kick seems to only tighten his hold. The terror of asphyxiation takes over.

I'm dying.

Her vision begins to blur as Jeremy calmly watches her suffocate. She can feel the picture going dark, the edges collapsing inward. As death begins to place its full weight upon her, it's both nauseating and calming. Sound fades out, bringing her back into the loudest silence.

Then he begins laughing, a genuine laugh that cuts through the swamp. He lets go and she falls like a discarded toy. She coughs and heaves, grabbing the ground as if it will return her embrace. He leans away, trying to stifle his laughter. Finally, she feels oxygen come again, and she gulps it in greedily. In response, her body backs up against a tree. She stares at him with wide, teary eyes.

Crawling toward her on all fours like a wild animal, Jeremy presses his forehead against hers.

"Run."

Wren hesitates, feeling the instinct to stay. Her eyes search his own. At this proximity, they appear brilliant and dangerous, an unfair biological advantage.

"No," she says, her voice a hoarse whisper.

His eyes widen slightly and his eyebrows lift. He presses against her forehead harder, bone slamming into bone, a growl forming deep in his throat.

"I said, 'run.'" He maintains control, but his voice is menacing, enough to cause her breath to hitch and her body to shudder. She steadies herself before pressing back into his forehead with her own.

"No!" she yells. A bird startles nearby, screeching and flapping off into the night sky. From each direction, she can hear an alarm start to wail, lending itself to the defiance she feels. She wonders if help is coming at the perfect time.

"No?" he asks quietly, slowly pulling away. He's unreadable, conveying looks of anger and confusion in equal measure.

Wren keeps her eyes locked on his, shaking her head slightly in confirmation. A crooked smile plays at his mouth, and he produces a hunting knife from his boot.

"As you wish," he says, before plunging the knife into the ground between them. As soon as he drives it into the earth, a fiery pain shoots through Wren's back. It's a hot poker of familiar pain that shakes her resolve and floods her mind with excruciating memories. Instinctively, she tries to pull her knees in to her body, but they remain numb and heavy. She hits them and rakes her nails against her legs, but she feels nothing. The alarm wails louder and louder, but it's too late.

"Wren." She hears another voice call out.

"Wren."

She tries to reach for Jeremy, but he remains just out of reach, grinning widely.

"Wren!"

Suddenly she sits up, covered in sweat. Something between a sob and a scream cuts off in her throat as she looks around her bedroom. Her phone alarm trills. Richard grasps her face in his hands, gently brushing the wet hair from her forehead.

"Wren, you are home. You are safe." Her husband's blue eyes are kind and concerned, a far cry from Jeremy's hateful gaze. With Richard's comforting hands soothing her forehead, she feels immediate relief. She rubs her eyes, then switches off the alarm. She hasn't been at work since the incident . . . since Jeremy got away—but she's kept her six a.m. wake-up to stop herself from sleeping the days away. Two weeks, and her open-ended medical leave still feels strange.

"I had another nightmare." Wren takes a long breath, trying to stop the images from replaying.

Richard nods, tilting his head as if to make sure she is really with him. "I know. Was it the same?"

"I refused to run this time." She answers dryly, swinging her legs over the side of the bed.

"Well, that sounds like progress," he offers.

Wren chuckles, running her fingers along her thighs, feeling the sensation of nails on skin. "Yeah. I suppose."

"He's gone, Wren. He's not going to come back." Richard rises, pulling Wren into an embrace.

"He's not gone, but I appreciate the sentiment." She smiles softly into his shoulder. Richard seems to genuinely believe that Jeremy is gone. He isn't placating her with false hope. He means every single overly optimistic word that he says. That's what she loves about him. But Wren knows better. Jeremy's trail has gone cold, but that is his specialty—going into hiding when he cuts too close to the bone, exposing too much of the truth. After Wren's own escape from his twisted playground, it was seven years before the Bayou Butcher crossed her radar again.

The New Orleans PD has put out a nationwide search for him, but nothing's turned up except a few more cold cases to possibly add to his tally. Wren isn't surprised. Jeremy is reckless, but he isn't stupid. With him, there is no safety in time or distance. He's like a virus. You can put distance between you and this virus, but it will eventually find you.

Almost every night since he disappeared under their nose, leaving a decoy body in his place, Wren has fallen into deep and twisted nightmares. It's as if he ran away to her mind, so he could torment her freely. Every time she closes her eyes, he's there. Sometimes she feels as if it's up to her alone to stop it all. There's a compulsion in her to be his undoing. She may have promised Leroux that she would let the police do their jobs, but Jeremy's nightly visits to her subconscious are becoming harder to ignore.

Richard sighs, planting a kiss on the top of her head. "You aren't doing this alone anymore, Wren. Now come on, I'll make coffee."

He gets up to leave, but she pulls him closer for a moment. They've been through so much together, more than they ever could have imagined; it's as if Richard could read her mind. "I'll meet you downstairs," she says, releasing him.

Wren makes her way to the bathroom and starts brushing her teeth, staring at her flushed cheeks in the mirror. As she does a final rinse, she touches the tired skin under her eyes. An unhealthy mixture of anxiety and lack of sleep has caused purple circles to form. It's like looking at Bloody Mary's reflection and it's just as distressing. If she keeps it up, it will be Wren's name they chant in the mirror at sleepovers. At least no one sees her these days except her decade-long therapist, Dr. Roy.

She passes a closet full of untouched work clothes as she heads downstairs. It feels strange not to be heading into the morgue. She misses confronting the unknown of the day and the constant workout it gives her mind. A disruption in routine feels lightly catastrophic to Wren, a true creature of habit.

She wants to see Leroux holding a coffee and talking shit. She misses his humor and his sideways pep talks. John also took off time for his injuries, but now he's back on the job, working Jeremy's file with Will, and texting Wren daily updates.

Wren's forensics team has taken over her caseload; she hasn't touched a dead body since she left the crime scene of Jeremy's compound. And she misses it—the routine, the heady rush of a new victim, all of it—but she's been told this break is for the best. She needs to heal, to let go. Wren knows it's not her job to find Jeremy—it's to get better. Or at least that's what everyone keeps telling her. But in the back of her mind, it still feels as if those two assignments are linked. She's tried to forget him before, to turn herself from Emily into Wren, and where did that get her? She's not sure anymore, but she's not ready to admit defeat.

As she shuffles into the kitchen, Richard hands her a steaming coffee mug. She takes it eagerly.

"Hero," she says, slipping into her new favorite seat at the table and tightening her robe around her body.

He smiles, sipping his own mug before placing it on the counter. "Hitting the shower." While Richard rushes to start his day at work, she is tasked with "taking it easy" and "trying to heal."

Wren just nods, looking out the window next to the kitchen table. It's a view she hadn't ever noticed before, but now, after staring at it for the last two weeks, she could compose a dissertation on the subject. After all, it offers an unchanging performance each time she takes her seat. It always starts off with the same sticky morning and a view of the same tired tree hanging haphazardly over the porch. There is an empty nest in that tree. It's perfect and seems hospitable but remains vacant. Its strangely abandoned state does offer some dramatic tension, but so far, no wayward bird has come to shake things up.

She doesn't feel healed by watching the view outside her window. Healing isn't even *her* goal; its everyone else's. She desperately misses rushing around with somewhere to go. It's hard to just allow time to pass without purpose. And as much as she struggles with leisure time, everyone keeps telling her that it's an important step to healing.

There's that word again, she thinks to herself.

After all, isn't that what everyone wants? Everyone wants Wren to take a beat, to distance herself from the trauma she clamped off for so long. To *heal*.

No one wants to consider that there's no moving forward without a conclusion. There is no temporary lid that can be placed over Jeremy's escape. It's reality.

Everyone wants slow and deliberate recuperation, like a set fracture left to fuse over time. But Wren doesn't want a process. She wants swift and incautious justice.

CHAPTER 2

J EREMY LISTENS TO THE TWIGS crunch under his boots and counts his steps.

Thirty-four, thirty-five, thirty-six . . .

When he reaches fifty paces, he glances to his right and sees the large boulder he's been searching for. He touches the stone and runs his hand over the crude carving of a rabbit. Using a screwdriver and another rock, he'd chiseled the marker the last time he was here, a few years prior. The deep indentation feels sharp under his fingers.

Full of adrenaline, Jeremy feels a surge of encouragement. It's been a couple weeks since he left home and making it to West Virginia is a feat and a relief. He knew there was always the possibility of needing to flee from Louisiana, and when things went south, he would have to go north. This is where he had to get first for everything else to fall into place.

He looks down at his feet. His boots are almost hidden under dead leaves. Bending into a crouch, he pushes the natural debris out of the way to expose the raw earth. He produces a small garden trowel from his bag and begins to cut the ground open. The earth splits like skin and it somehow bleeds too. Soil and water from recent rains pour back into the hole. Deeper and deeper he cuts, bringing the trowel down like a knife. After several minutes, he finally stabs something foreign and inorganic.

Clearing away the remaining dirt, he pulls the blue bucket out of the hole. It takes some shimmying from side to side, and he swears the dirt almost gasped as he removed it. Inside he finds everything he needs to continue forward. He pulls out a length of piano wire, two different guns, and extra bullets. Stashing them into his bag, he reaches back into the bucket and finds an extra knife. It's shorter than his bowie knife, but it's sharp as hell and curved. Alongside it is a scalpel in a clear plastic container, three boxes of dark hair dye, and a bunch of zip ties. He tosses it all into his bag.

Finally, there is the plastic bag at the bottom. Opening it, he reaches inside and pulls out a stack of cash, about $10,000 in all. The bills look brand-new, still in the wrapping from the bank. They are flat and clean as if they were taken out that morning.

After his mother's tragic death, Jeremy was the beneficiary of her life insurance payout. After using some of it to renovate his living conditions, he took the rest of the money and hid it here, as a last resort. It was always a backup plan.

His bag is heavier now, but he weighed out the contents and knows he can carry it the remaining distance. That's why he chose this place. It was all planned out, all calculated to the minute, to the pound, to the mile.

The chemical stench of recently box-dyed hair is burned into Jeremy's sinuses. His naturally blond hair is dark brown now, disguising one of his most recognizable features. He tilts the brim of his hat forward to cover his eyebrows and scans the room from under it, picking at his fries. It's just a sea of things and people he doesn't want to look at until he notes a young man with dark hair sitting at a table across from him. Immediately, Jeremy is interested. This stranger looks exhausted, like someone who works with his hands all day. He's got grime under his fingernails, but he gratefully eats his cheeseburger, stopping only to remove his filthy baseball hat to rub his greasy hand over his hair. Jeremy studies his features without blatantly staring. He suspects hard labor has aged this man beyond his years, and Jeremy imagines the age on his driver's license is a better match for Jeremy's own. All things considered, he's a decent double.

Jeremy leaves the plate of fries on the table and gathers his things. Taking out his burner phone, he carefully pantomimes calling someone. Holding the phone to his ear, he walks past the man, feigning anxiety and speaking loudly.

"I swear I am going to find a way to get home to you, darlin'." He pauses, waiting for his invisible partner to respond on the other end. "No, don't say that. You won't have to have this baby alone." The man is listening. He lets his eyes wander, clearly trying not to fall directly on Jeremy and his conspicuous conversation. No one can resist prying when they hear human suffering, even on this scale.

Jeremy knits his brows together, stopping near the man's table and bringing as much emotion into his words as he can muster. The man's eyes dart over to him, but he quickly returns to his meal. "Hang in there, Brit. I will get there. I love you so much." He allows his voice to crack a bit, pausing in dramatized silent reflection before hanging up.

Jeremy moves toward the door, appearing to busy himself with more fake phone calls. He waits only a few minutes before the man walks past him out to the parking lot. He follows, stopping just outside the door to watch which vehicle the man heads toward. A pickup truck is parked nearby and Jeremy's sure it's the winner. It's red with faded, unreadable bumper stickers, but it has a set of brand-new oversized tires. As the man walks closer to the vehicle, Jeremy starts after him with a quickened pace. He begins wringing his hands and sighing loudly, occasionally looking up at the sky in simulated desperation. He brushes the man lightly as he crosses near him. This small contact alerts the man to his presence and he spins to look at Jeremy.

"Man, you scared the shit out of me." The man shakes his head, clearly startled at the sudden invasion of his space.

Jeremy puts his hands up in a show of surrender, stepping back a bit. "Sorry, didn't mean to sneak up on you like that. I am really in my head right now."

"Yeah, I overheard you in there. Ya ought to take it easy. I mean, don't walk into traffic or some shit, Jesus." He is still shaking his head, turning to open his door. Jeremy detects a slight drawl to his speech. It's subtle but hits deeper on certain words.

Jeremy nods, chuckling lightheartedly. "Good advice, thank you." As he says this, he looks down. He makes a show of looking bothered and distracted again. Letting his expressive face do the heavy lifting. He's sure this guy can't leave well enough alone and within a few seconds, he proves Jeremy right.

The man pauses before he opens the door of his truck. There is only a moment of hesitation before he walks straight into a situation that doesn't have to involve him. "Are you in a bind, man?" He rubs the back of his neck apprehensively. "I wasn't eavesdropping, but you were talking pretty loud in there and it sounded like you need to get to your girl." He's reluctantly kind, but stupidity wafts from him like department store cologne. It immediately makes Jeremy feel nauseated.

"You heard that, huh? Yeah, my girl is about to pop. I need to get back to meet my son and my car died back on I-79."

The stranger looks Jeremy up and down, probably evaluating the risk as quickly as he can. "Where are you headed, man?" he asks.

"She's doing a home birth. We live in Strange Creek. It's about a ten-minute drive off the highway." Jeremy keeps the look of anxiety on his face, hoping he's sealed the deal.

"Well, listen. If it's a ride you need, I can get you home. I am going right past that exit anyways."

Jeremy grins, desperately trying to keep it friendly. "Wow, are you sure? That's—I really appreciate it, man. Seriously."

The man keeps a straight face, clearly already regretting the commitment to spending time alone in his truck with an emotional stranger. "Yeah, it's no problem. I can't let you miss the birth of your kid." He starts to turn toward the truck but stops, extending his hand. "I'm Tom," he says gruffly.

Jeremy shakes it firmly. "David."

"Hop in, David. Don't touch the radio." Tom opens the truck door and slides into the driver's seat.

"Thank you." Jeremy rushes around to the passenger side.

Country music fills the truck's cab and the engine roars to life. Jeremy scans the interior of the truck as they leave the parking lot. There is a center console, but it's not oversized or acting like a wall between them. Less of a barrier means easier access to Tom's neck and a better chance at incapacitating him without a fight.

As they pull onto the highway, Jeremy wants to kill him just to make the music stop. Instead, he lies, "You don't have to worry about me touching the radio. I love this song."

Tom doesn't respond. He doesn't even nod. Jeremy looks out the window, clenching his teeth very nearly to dust as the music twangs on. It's an unbearable mix of awkward silence and overstimulating noise. He hates small talk under normal circumstances, but he can always fake it. Something about this situation is harder to choreograph.

"Do you ever pick up hitchhikers?" Jeremy asks.

Tom looks a little caught off guard, but he recovers and clears his throat. "Not often, but I guess every now and then I'll help someone out." He pauses, glancing quickly at Jeremy. "Why?"

Jeremy shrugs, scanning the road in front of them. "I guess I was just wondering when it stopped being safe to give someone a ride."

CHAPTER 3

S HE PICKS A SPOT on the wall and becomes entranced by it almost immediately. This office has a calmness to it, with plenty of books and healthy plants scattered around. The walls are a deep but vibrant blue. There's something about that color that must make people want to sink in and reveal all of their secrets to a stranger. Wren wonders if the color was chosen purposefully. Was it a researched choice? She doesn't like the idea of being manipulated by a color, but she doesn't like a lot of what's happening to her lately.

The couch is incredibly uncomfortable, too soft thanks to years of use. It wears the trauma that it has seen and heard too. It's shattered from the inside out, like many of the unfortunate souls that have sunk into it before her. She absentmindedly picks at a twisted fiber that sticks out of the cushion and she can't help but shiver.

It's too cold in the room. It's the cold that makes you feel a little sick. She can see the air-conditioning unit working hard out of the corner of her eye, and she swears it's colder than the morgue in here.

Why can't these places ever get the temperature right? she thinks to herself.

"It's the only way to truly begin to heal, Wren." Dr. Roy knows she is disassociating, so she punctuates the sentence with her name.

Wren blinks, finally looking at her.

"Wren?"

She's probably not talking about the temperature in here.

For a moment, they just look at each other, the hum of the fan saving them from the vastness of true silence. Wren's brain runs through a series of sentence starters. It's very similar to being stumped for small talk at a social gathering. Sometimes the conversation goes stale and it's like a defunct slot machine in there. Pull the lever and nothing but duds flash by. So you say nothing, with panic in your eyes. This time Dr. Roy is the first to start gambling.

"Wren, I can see you're checked out." Dr. Roy says it with a hint of a smile pulling at her mouth. She has a kind way of speaking. Even when she should be frustrated, she never lets on that she's anything other than patient.

"I'm sorry, I can't seem to focus today." Wren throws her head back, taking in the view of the ceiling. She begins counting the holes that dot the tiles but quickly refocuses. "I can't help but think that I'm just taking up space here—space you could fill with someone you can actually help."

"You think you can't be helped?" Dr. Roy doesn't miss a beat. She counsels right through the bullshit.

Wren laughs, bringing her head back down. "I don't know." She picks at the fibers of the couch more. "I don't even know if there is anything that needs helping. Maybe I am supposed to just move on and pretend he's dead."

"But he's not dead, Wren." She launches the assumption at her like a missile.

"Can't prove that beyond a reasonable doubt, right?" Wren forces a smirk.

"We can't prove either side of that argument beyond a reasonable doubt, can we?" Dr. Roy answers pointedly.

Wren bites at her lip, finally extracting the fiber from the couch. She hates this part of therapy. It's the part where the doctor starts pulling at your thoughts and actually makes headway. It's a strange feeling, like being towed by a speedboat. You yell at them to slow down but they power on, the roar of the engine too loud for them to hear your pleas. All you can do is hang on tight and go where they lead you.

She wants to allow this brilliant woman to help her, hoping to avoid wasting her expensive time at the very least. But ironically, she is consistently having trouble opening herself up to be dissected like this. It almost feels like something *is* wrong with her, but she's certain it can't be fixed with some words.

Dr. Roy herself was a massive part of her becoming Wren in the first place, but it all seemed easier back then. In the beginning, she allowed the tools to be taught to her and was eager to use them to become the strong, healthy person she once was. Wren was born out of years of work and perseverance to become whole again, so she knows there is a lot to gain from therapy.

Now she just wants to be Wren again. There's no grand shift in perspective at the end of this anymore. She wants to step back into her own broken-in shoes instead of crafting new ones from scratch. It's different this time.

"Touché," she finally responds, twirling the fiber between her fingers. "But I am already sick of playing this game."

There is a beat of silence, as if Dr. Roy is contemplating her response. "Does it feel like another game? Is the entire situation maybe a bit triggering for you because of that aspect?"

Wren smiles, shaking her head at the question. "Honestly, is it though? I don't know if that's it."

"You may feel like he's still looming, ready to chase. It's very likely this is bringing up your past trauma in a much more specific way."

"I really didn't think of it that way, but maybe you're onto something. Like, the arena has gotten larger, but the dread is still very familiar." Wren drops her eyes to the ground, focusing on the area rug.

Dr. Roy nods. "Sometimes trauma is a lot more focused than we can perceive. Of course you will have trauma from what you have endured, but that doesn't mean it's *all* coming back. You don't have to go right back to the beginning and start again." She captures Wren's gaze and holds it. "Your mind has been able to work through a lot, but there may be specific aspects of the situation that haven't been resolved, and this is pressure-testing those a little bit. That's all."

Wren can feel tears start to form, but she blinks them away. She nods slowly, bending the couch fiber back and forth in her hand.

"We will get those parts resolved, Wren. You will get control back. You're still right at the top of the mountain. This is a stumble, but I will help you get there again."

Wren lets her tears fall freely now. It breaks through the numbness, the exhaustion of her fight-or-flight mode. She has wanted to fly away, to let this all go, to forget. But at her core, Wren is a fighter. And she keeps bracing for the monster to jump out from the shadows.

Stopping in the restroom on her way out, she swipes concealer under her eyes, patting it to cover the evidence of a not-so-cathartic sob. The face reflected at her in the mirror appears foreign and tired. She touches her cheek, remarking at the delicate lines that have appeared in the corners of her eyes. Stress and exhaustion do a good job of writing a horror film on your face.

Her phone buzzes in her bag.

"Hey, John," she answers.

"Muller. Have you thought it over?" Leroux asks.

She sighs.

Leroux asks again. Even though she's on leave, he thinks it may be a good idea for her to tag along on their final sweep of Jeremy's home. Dr. Roy thinks it's a good idea too. Wren isn't so sure.

"Ugh," she moans, "I guess I should bite this bullet, huh?"

"Yes. I really think you should. Walk through that place and take the control back and shit."

She laughs, rolling her eyes.

"All right, *Dr.* Leroux. I'll join you. Just let me do something first."

"I'll see you at one thirty." Without waiting for a proper goodbye, he hangs up.

He always does that.

She heads onto the street outside Dr. Roy's office, squinting in the bright midmorning sun. The office is in a crowded part of town, so she always takes an Uber to avoid the parking situation. A black Jeep with an older gentleman in the driver's seat pulls up. He lets the car idle, saying nothing. Wren doesn't break the silence, instead choosing to stare at him through the passenger-side window until he presses the button to lower the glass.

"Good morning, did you call for a ride?" he asks pleasantly.

"Do you have a name on that ride request, sir?" Wren asks, bending slightly to meet his eyes.

He looks slightly embarrassed and swipes his phone screen quickly. "Oh yes, Wren? Are you Wren?"

She smiles, nodding and opening the rear door to slide in behind the passenger seat. "Yes, thank you. Sorry, I am just a nut with ride-share safety." She changes her tone, shifting into a slightly friendlier disposition.

He glances into the rearview mirror to connect with her gaze. "No need to apologize, miss. It's a scary world out there."

As he pulls away from the curb, she looks out the window. Everything blurs by and she rests her head back on the seat to watch it.

"It sure is, Paul." She uses his name from the app. "It's kind of wild, I was taught my whole life to never get into a car with a stranger, and now it's the only way to get anywhere."

He laughs, genuinely amused. "Ya know, I always think that whenever I pick someone up. Things sure have changed."

She nods. "They really have."

"We can just do our best to keep up." His eyes scan the road in front of him.

Wren wonders if Paul has children or grandchildren. He has kind brown eyes and an authentic smile. It's the face of a grandpa who would give you too many cookies behind your parents' backs. He has a comforting aura about him that is incredibly nonthreatening, possibly disarming.

Abruptly, she realizes she has shifted her gaze to him in the rearview mirror and has been absentmindedly staring as she analyzed him. She finds herself in this awkward position a lot, staring like a toddler would while dissecting someone internally. She quickly brings her eyes back to the window. To her, Paul just looks like a sweet man.

Of course, Paul could also be a serial killer. Now she notices the small teddy bear tucked into the corner of his dashboard. It's cute and disarming. It's something a lot of monsters do to make it look as though they have children, to bring a false sense of safety to their intended prey. He has a whole grand-father vibe working in this car, and it could all be an elaborate trap. She hates that she always thinks in dichotomies, but she grips the mace on her key chain tightly anyway.

The car rolls onto Coliseum Street and comes to a stop out-side of the powder-blue Commander's Palace restaurant.

"Here we are, miss." He smiles, putting the car in park and getting out. In an instant he appears at Wren's door and opens it, stepping aside to let her out.

"Thank you, Paul," she says. "It was nice to meet you."

"The pleasure was all mine." He says this without even a hint of artifice.

She smiles and turns to walk down the sidewalk, slinging her bag across her body as she does. She takes a step but turns around.

"Hey, Paul," she calls out, stopping him in his tracks before he can slide back into the driver's seat. He pops his head over the door.

"Do you have kids?" she asks.

He grins again, shaking his head. "Nope."

Wren nods, putting a hand up to wave. "Have a great day, Paul," she says as she walks toward Washington Avenue. *I knew it. Serial killer*, she jokes to herself.

Not unlike St. Louis Cemetery, Lafayette Cemetery resides behind a white fortress. The walls keep it safe from the bustling world outside, sealing in secrets and the warm reticence inside. The entrance on Washington Avenue is imposing yet beautiful. The intricate wrought iron gate both welcomes and warns visitors as they cross through to the silent world of the dead. Wren likes that world. It's a world she knows and understands to an extent. It calms her mind and helps her sort her thoughts in a way that no therapist can. Today, she quietly asks this place to help her heal.

As she crosses through the gate, she passes a tour group waiting outside. They stand, sweating together in a clump.

They hold papers in their hands and giddily look forward to the macabre adventure that awaits them. It's a thrill to hear the sordid history of these souls and their final resting places. But what the tourists won't readily reveal to you is that they are looking for a plot twist. People love turning death into something other than the ultimate horror show they believe it to be. They romanticize it to turn a historically documented death by tuberculosis into a jilted lover dying of a broken heart. The tourists' voices are loud as they mill around the entrance, but they almost always instinctually drop to hushed whispers as they cross the threshold into the cemetery. It's like an unspoken agreement between realms.

Wren glides past the small tour group and saunters down the path in front of her. It's a long, roughly paved trail lined with tombs of various shapes, sizes, and conditions. The pavement beneath her feet is broken but walkable. As she travels the well-worn path, she wonders how many bones are beneath her feet. Lafayette was proclaimed to be "full" at least twice in its lifetime. Whenever the walkways are disturbed for renovation or repair, it's like a bat signal to forensic anthropologists to converge upon the unclaimed burial plots. A bone here, a bone there. The cemetery sextons soon saw these rogue grave discoveries as just another workplace quirk.

Today, cemetery ferns reach out from every crack, infusing life into death. Wren always heard them called resurrection ferns, and they live up to both names. They are hardy enough to lose 97 percent of their own water and still seamlessly resurrect from a small splash of hydration. Wren touches the brown end of a fern that bursts through the side of a tomb to her left.

The dried-up tip of the tendril crumbles between her fingers, blowing away in the slight breeze. It's comforting to know this is only a pretense before its inevitable resurrection. She feels more connected to these plants than she ever has before. Their presence signals a delicate message, showing that something can thrive and adapt even if it's surrounded by death.

Wren can't help but feel a pang of jealousy. The ferns probably never have to explain how comfortable they are with the world of the dead as much as she has to. They never have to apologize or avoid acknowledging death's omnipresence. They merely accept it as a part of their vibrant life, a vital piece of their show. As a result, they are celebrated and left to prosper in their strange world. No one asks them to heal. They just do.

She gazes around her, taking in the peculiar landscape. Anyone could get lost in this place, with similarly hued tombs and crypts lining every conceivable aisle. But if you have chosen to cross into this labyrinthine world, it's best to take the time to not only appreciate the architectural beauty but to use it to your advantage. Notably intricate tombs can become homing beacons in a sea of decaying stone. For Wren, she always notes the Karstendiek tomb as her home base. Its deliciously Gothic structure drew Anne Rice to create a similar resting place for Lestat. As it is the only cast-iron tomb in the cemetery, it is easy to spot.

She pauses, feeling her heart race and cold sweat drip down her back, and watches the world around her bend and wobble as she is hit with the memory of digging into soggy earth to retrieve a body—someone's daughter who never went home again. Emma was one of Jeremy's victims, only a few short weeks ago. She had clawed at her prison deep in St. Louis Cemetery, and Wren had failed to save her in time. The memory of it continues to haunt her, but it's especially fraught when she finds herself in a cemetery. It's maddening that a place that has always given her so much serenity has become tainted by Jeremy's vicious scent.

Wren lets herself take a second. She breathes and feels the cool air hit her skin, calming her stomach and bringing her back to the present where she belongs. It's an exercise of release, by way of amateur exposure therapy. Exposing herself to these memories is difficult, but doing so is necessary for her to conquer them. She knows she will never see real peace until she dismantles the source of them. His continued existence remains her most challenging vexation.

Once she feels steady enough, she continues, farther into the rows of tombs. It's easier and easier as she propels herself forward, letting tranquility take control once again.

As she heads toward the southwest corner of the cemetery, she passes tombs whose textures beg to be touched. These graves are like miniature cobblestone cottages. Wren's hand impulsively snakes out to run her fingers across the stones. There is a strange dichotomy in the construction. Two disparate ideas fight for supremacy among her senses. As her fingers connect with the wall of one of the tombs, it feels organic and familiar. A body encased in stone just feels right. Surrounded by stones that were quarried from the ground, a body is reclaimed. But to the eye, these cobblestones appear like bulging flesh bound too tight. It's an unnatural pattern that feels like a trap. Still, she touches them, tracing the ligature as she walks past.

Finally, she spots it. An area of the cemetery known as the Secret Garden. It's her favorite thing about this place, if only for the legend behind its existence. In this corner sit four almost identical tombs. The area stands out because of its simplistic beauty. The four graves are neat, uncomplicated designs that sit side by side. Surrounding them is a green, lush hedge of boxwood that signals something unique is happening here. Etched atop the four markers are the names Dupuy, Ginder, Palfrey, and Griswold: four lifelong best friends who wished to be entombed together along with their families.

In life, it was said that they formed a secret society called the Quarto and together would perform random and anonymous acts of kindness around New Orleans. The legend goes on to say that they made a promise to one another: in the end, the last one alive would destroy all records of the Quarto, forever assuring its existence in mystery. Wren imagines this pact of friendship sealed with blood. Of course, there's no historical evidence of a blood pact, but it's the truth according to Wren.

There is something about the Secret Garden and the Quarto that makes Wren feel like a kid again. Instead of thinking about murder, she can lose herself in a fairy-tale legend. It's a story of secret societies and mysterious pacts, punctuated by an eternity of fellowship. This is what Dr. Roy means when she tells Wren to do what fills her cup. This fills it up. It makes it overflow.

She understands what Dr. Roy was getting at now. Wren lives. Wren survives. Wren has an entire life she has built, filled with success and love and discovery. She doesn't have to ignore what is happening. Leroux wants her there, wants her mind, her sharp eyes, her keen intuition. That's what she does best and that's what she will continue to do. No one will shatter that part of her.

Shake it? Yes.

But no one will shatter it.

CHAPTER 4

Tom is uncomfortable. He shifts in his seat, not quite knowing what to say to Jeremy. When he does speak, his voice is softer. The gruffness is still there, but Jeremy can almost feel the man's fight-or-flight response kick in. "Are you trying to say it's not safe for me to be driving you right now?" Tom lets out a shaky breath. It's subtle, only detectable to Jeremy because he is causing the response. A connection has been made, and Tom's nervous system is acting like an umbilical cord, feeding Jeremy all the necessary information he needs to move forward with his plan.

Jeremy hides the rush of excitement he feels, allowing a genuine smile to cross his face. He glances over at Tom, who eyes the road with anxiety-filled focus. Jeremy chuckles lightly, acknowledging Tom's question as a joke instead of a real concern. "Well, I suppose that wouldn't apply here, because I'm not a hitchhiker in the classic sense."

"You didn't answer my question." The touch of fear is still detectable in Tom's voice, but with it now is a hint of anger.

It's clear he's a simple man who doesn't appreciate games. He couldn't have chosen someone less suited to his personality and patience to help tonight.

"Honestly, I'm just looking at history here. It feels like in the fifties and even the sixties, people hopped in cars without a second thought, made some small talk, and then got to their destination richer for the experience." He pauses, glancing slyly at Tom, who listens stoically. After only a breath, he continues his train of thought. "Was it sometime in the seventies that it just got rocked? Like it finally became clear that maybe naivete and blind trust should be punished, instead of rewarded or ignored?"

Tom shakes his head, almost scoffing. "It doesn't have to do with blind trust, or whatever the hell else you just said. Think about when it started here. The seventies. It's when this country lost its way. Society strayed from Christ, that's the real problem here. People are angry and bathing themselves daily in their sins." A bead of sweat forms on Tom's forehead.

It's only then that Jeremy notices the rosary hanging from the rearview mirror. He somehow hadn't seen it before, too focused on what was between himself and the driver's seat to notice the small details of Tom's personality scattered around the vehicle. The interior of the truck is not dirty, but it's cluttered.

Empty coffee cups lie scattered at his feet, there's a handful of change in the console, and random napkins and wrappers are stuffed in cup holders and in the door pockets. It's obvious that he is in this truck an awful lot. Propped up on the dash in front of him, stuck in the area next to the odometer, is a prayer card. Jeremy can't make out what it says, but it's obvious religion is part of Tom's personality, even if he doesn't seem to adhere to the notion of cleanliness being next to godliness. After a moment, he decides to play Tom's game.

"Well, Tom, I'll give you that. People are definitely angrier nowadays, and that may play a role in how acts of service can be confused for acts of stupidity." He licks his lips, ready to change the tone. "But I'll have to disagree with you on the whole sin thing. People have always been sinners. Proximity to Christ doesn't change that."

Tom frowns. "You're wrong. We lost our way as a country. You talk about hitchhiking being unsafe? That's because everybody forgot their place."

"Next exit." Jeremy directs him off the highway. "Tell me more about that, Tom." Jeremy can't help but experiment a little. Creatures like this one always fascinate him. Before the ride ends, he wants to dissect his prey.

"It's about respect. Women need to respect men, people need to respect the church, and families should be normal." Tom shakes his head. "Sure, people have always been sinners, but they used to keep it behind closed doors."

Jeremy can't help but laugh. "Yeah, I can see what you're getting at there, Tom. But regardless of whether it's an infiltration of the devil like you say, hitchhiking and picking up hitchhikers has become a pretty reckless thing to do." He sees a look of trepidation cross Tom's face before he continues. "Maybe you're right though, Jesus probably would have given people rides. If he was doing that now, we'd probably find his head in a creek somewhere."

The words hit Tom hard. It's an uncomfortable, almost blasphemous notion. Jeremy can see the man struggling internally. "You never did answer my question."

Jeremy fights back a smile. "Come again?"

"Are you trying to tell me it's unsafe to be driving you?" he asks, adjusting what is surely a gun in his waistband.

Jeremy lets the question linger, no longer treating it like a joke. "Realistically, yes. But I guess the more important question would be *who* is unsafe?"

Tom isn't prepared for that answer. A mix of fear and confusion dances across his face as he prepares a response. "Well, I'm no freak." He grips the steering wheel, his knuckles turning visibly white. "I'm starting to think you might be, though." His eyes flick briefly to Jeremy, warning him.

"No, not me." Jeremy shifts in his seat, turning his attention out the window. "But I think it's important to consider these things. After all, it's not the fifties anymore, right?"

Tom scoffs, resting his elbow on the window. "You're fucking weird, man. You're seeming more and more like one of those hitchhikers that you're claiming to be worried about."

"I'm not a hitchhiker, remember? I didn't even ask for a ride. You approached me." Jeremy lets the last part of his statement hang in the air. He means it exactly like it sounds. In a few minutes, he wants that reality to flash in Tom's mind like a marquee. He wants it to hurt later. The punch line will hit him just as the lights go out.

Tom feels it now. That nervous system starts to fire again and the air in the cab becomes thick with tension. The silence that follows is intentional. He struggles with it but Jeremy feels comfort in it. Whether there is any truth to that notion that meat loses flavor when it experiences fear before slaughter, it's fun to think about.

"Where's your place, man?" There is a hint of aggression in Tom's voice. When he offered the ride, he certainly never saw it going like this. He likely thought he would get a quiet drive to suburbia, or at the very least an excited father-to-be. Instead, he got Jeremy.

"Right down this road." Jeremy gestures in the direction of a dark street. Upon first glance, he spots a single streetlight illuminating a dark corner. The light weakly sprays down onto a small area of the sidewalk, allowing only enough visibility to have a last-minute view of what waits for you in the inky black on every side. It's not entirely unfortunate as far as neighborhoods go. The few houses that line the street are dark too, but most of them seem lived in and decently maintained. It's perfect. Isolated but not abandoned.

As the truck crawls down the street, Tom bends forward. He strains his eyes to see through the seemingly endless darkness that stretches out in front of him. "Jesus, haven't they ever heard of streetlights?" he asks, a look of annoyed concentration stretched tightly across his face. "What number are you?" The words come out terse. He just wants to get to their destination. He doesn't know he should be running from it.

Jeremy looks straight ahead, allowing his breath to fall into a steady, even rhythm. "Thirty-three."

"You're gonna have to direct me, 'cause I can't see a damn number on these houses if you paid me." He sits back, allowing Jeremy to navigate him blindly through the neighborhood.

Jeremy nods. "Sure, just keep going straight for a minute and then bear to the left up ahead." He points forward as if there is any other direction to go. Tom creeps the truck along, not asking any more questions or making further attempts at small talk.

As the houses begin to appear farther apart, Jeremy goes over the plan in his head. It's not lost on him that he only has one shot at this. One wrong move, and it could all come crashing down. He runs his fingers over the pocketknife at his side, sliding them over the intricately etched hilt and tracing each groove as if it's precious. His breath is still measured, never betraying his anticipation.

As they continue to drive, the vibe changes dramatically. It's not quaint suburbia anymore. It's ominous. The streets look sparse and neglected. Neighbors aren't borrowing sugar from each other in a place like this, and it's certainly no place for children. The sidewalks are cracked and overgrown with weeds. Broken chain-link fences do nothing to keep things out.

"It's right up here." Jeremy gestures to a home sitting up on a hill. It looks as if it was once beautiful, but it's now run-down with an overgrown yard and vines that threaten to swallow the house whole. It exists in almost complete darkness with only one single light shining from a second-floor window. Jeremy can see the trepidation on Tom's face as he pulls up the hill. The only sound is the hum of the engine and the heavy buzz of dangerous air. He's sure Tom is revisiting his earlier question about the safety of picking up hitchhikers, likely trying to picture a young couple about to become parents in this dilapidated dwelling.

"All right then." Tom doesn't even look at Jeremy as he says it. His eyes stay glued to this strange home on the hill, a home that he would've never known existed. As his instincts implore him to run, his hands grip the steering wheel like a lifeline. For a moment the silence hangs in the air. Jeremy doesn't immediately respond, and Tom doesn't look for a response. Jeremy sees his eye flick very subtly over in his direction to see if he is making a move to leave.

"Listen, I appreciate the ride." Jeremy unclicks his seat belt and pushes his open hand toward Tom for a handshake. It hangs there, unshaken for several moments. Tom recoils very subtly at the invasion of his space and rubs his stubble-covered chin. The fingers of Jeremy's left hand dance over the blade under his leg. He keeps his eyes trained on Tom, willing him to either look at him or answer the handshake. For what feels like several minutes, Tom remains silent and still. After one deep breath in, he grabs Jeremy's hand and gives it a strong shake. That's all it takes to seal his fate.

As Tom attempts to pull his hand back, Jeremy uses the leverage to yank him toward his body. Caught off guard, Tom slumps over the center console with a jerk.

"What the fuck!" Tom growls out, his breath bordering on hyperventilation now. Instinctively, he reaches up to grab Jeremy's neck, slamming him back into the headrest. Tom's strength comes as a surprise. Even using his left hand, he holds Jeremy with a conviction that comes only from desperation. Jeremy can't help but smile at this new challenge.

He locks hard on that right hand, not allowing Tom to free it, but Tom still tightens his grip on Jeremy's neck, baring down hard with his nondominant hand. Still holding the knife at his left side, Jeremy quickly brings it up, stabbing it into the underside of Tom's bicep and tearing the flesh open in one quick motion. With a primal yell, Tom moves to grab the wound with his right hand and Jeremy releases it. Before another word can be uttered, Jeremy flips the knife into his right hand and jabs it directly into Tom's heart. He pulls it out and hits again and again as Tom struggles to fight him off. But he's at a disadvantage with his body locked into his seat, and his wounds begin to take their toll.

The sounds are loud at first. They are constant and harrowing, filling every inch of the truck's cab with the music of pain. Jeremy's heart hammers in his chest, like a mechanism urging his arm to move harder and faster. It's warm, this feeling. It flows through his limbs and brings with it a feeling of true purpose.

As Jeremy plunges the blade into his shoulder, Tom releases a growl that originates deep in his chest. After what feels like a lifetime, Tom's defenses begin to wane. The term *fight for your life* means something different to everyone, Jeremy has noticed. Most people do what you think they will do. They scratch and scream and truly fight. It's the end that varies from person to person. Tom is formidable in this sense, refusing to allow even the last flicker of life to drain from his body. He's making Jeremy sing for his supper.

He loses count of how many times he's penetrated Tom's body with the blade, and he doesn't immediately notice when the thrashing stops and the screams go silent. Blood pours out of some wounds and slowly trickles from others. It's a deep color that almost looks black in the dark. Tom coughs out a spray of blood, decorating the driver's-side window with tiny speckles of viscera that glisten like jewels. In his last moments, Tom slumps over the console and his face pushes against the radio. His eyes are open as he dies, and the volume knob jams into his left eye.

It is always strange to see those kinds of things happen postmortem. Things that normally make a person squirm don't matter anymore. Nothing hurts when you're dead.

It's as if the truck becomes a vacuum, sealing all sound outside. It's suddenly eerily quiet, except for the bursts of Jeremy's own breathing. Sitting back in his seat, Jeremy gets his system under control and tries to organize his plan. He's winded.

He intentionally took Tom down this street. No one has cameras or alarms here. They mind their business to keep themselves and their loved ones safe. It's a place where some-one can get away with something, because the lights are off, the shades are pulled, and you didn't see what you saw. After catching his breath and cleaning off his hands and knife, he digs around in Tom's pockets and waistband, taking the gun and wallet. As suspected, his driver's license age and photo will make a serviceable disguise as he continues north. The gun isn't even loaded.

Amateur.

He quickly looks around again, scanning the area and tak-ing note of his options. He sees that the home on the hill has stayed quiet, too high above them to be an issue. To the left, there is a long stretch of overgrowth leading into a deeply dark forest. There is a dirt path heading into the trees and beyond. It's just wide enough for the truck to pass through, and he decides to take a chance to see where it goes.

Leaving the cab, Jeremy swiftly makes his way to the driver's side, opening the door and pulling the lever to make the seat recline backward. He yanks it until the seat is as flat as it can go and jerks Tom's body into a sleeping position.

Jeremy then climbs into the rear of the cab, where there are two seats. He unbuckles Tom's seat belt and pulls the body toward him, allowing him to fall partway between the back seats, with his upper body sloppily draping over one. For a moment, he catches his breath in the dark. The smell of blood begins to fill his nose. The sharp scent of metal attaches itself to his senses and he breathes it in. His entire body is buzzing, electrified by an invisible force.

He shifts into the driver's seat, pulling it back to the upright position, and begins the drive down the narrow dirt road to nowhere. The tires crunch over the uneven ground, and at the first jolt, Tom's body falls fully onto the back floor of the cab. It makes a sickening sliding sound as the blood that still pours from his wounds makes the floor slick.

Jeremy feels full and satiated, even as the thick blanket of night swallows the truck. The headlights bounce in front of him, and the longer he finds himself surrounded by trees, the better he feels. He drifts farther and farther into isolation until the dirt road opens into a vast field of what looks like tall grain. He stops the truck, putting it into park, his eyes scanning across everything the headlights illuminate. He opens the door, listening to the stillness. A star-filled sky threatens to swallow him whole. The lack of light pollution makes the stars shine almost too brightly. They are intrusive to him now, as if they are specifically spying on his little corner of the world. He ignores them and takes note of a sound he hears in the vast swath of nothingness. It's water.

This place is different from Louisiana, that's for sure. But the tactics and techniques to conquer it are similar. If you allow the forest to speak to you, you can start to control what you hear. Grabbing a flashlight out of his bag, he follows the sound, leaving the truck running. Trudging through long stalks of grain, he can sense Tom's final resting place is ahead of him.

The grain gives way to dark woods. Trees become dense and the path closes inward, warning him to turn back. To him, it's like a coded invitation. Still, Jeremy beats on, desperate to find the perfect hiding place.

As he comes closer to the sound of rushing water, he can feel the air change and the breeze swirl around him. Through the trees, the stream comes into view. He trudges toward it like the undead and reaches it in three minutes. He holds his filthy hands under the water, using his fingers to rub the dirt and blood from his knuckles. When his hands are clean, he takes in his surroundings.

On one side, there's a boulder with a handful of smaller rocks surrounding it. The stream flows freely over it, creating the small waterfall responsible for the noises that summoned him here. Between the boulder and the rest of the rocks, there is a crevice. It's dark with a depth he can't ascertain.

But it's big enough for his own body to slip into and be lost forever between water and stone. Which means it's big enough for Tom.

He walks back to the truck, taking care to move any rocks or branches that could block the path. Opening the passenger door, Jeremy pulls Tom loose from between the seats. Once he has him free, he lets the body slam to the ground with a thud. Hooking Tom's legs around his waist, he begins to drag him down the path toward the water.

Each step is like walking through sand as Tom's head and arms tangle with the long stems of grain. Once the water comes into view, he picks up his pace, excited to savor the moment of quiet that follows a disposal. Normally he enjoys the presentation. He likes his victims to be found, to serve their purpose. Tonight, he needs Tom to disappear. He's eager to get this body off his hands and into the dark where it belongs.

As Jeremy nears the crevice, he drops Tom's legs and pulls his upper body toward the rocks. He pushes him headfirst into the opening, cranking his head to the side in order to properly stuff it down. The shoulders slide through easily, with his body and arms following in short order. Tom hits the bottom of the dark pit quickly, but his legs still stick out at odd angles over the rocks. Jeremy maneuvers Tom to curl into himself, pushing his legs over and to the side in a modified fetal position. He is completely hidden now, aside from his right foot, which is wedged in the opening, a work boot stopping Tom from being completely swallowed by the darkness.

Jeremy takes a moment to catch his breath, and then with all the strength he can muster, he wrenches Tom's foot to a horizontal position, breaking it with a loud crack. Using a heavy rock, he pushes it farther, destroying the anatomy beyond repair. The bones shatter with force, with one clean white piece jutting out through the skin of Tom's ankle. The compound fracture is another example of death killing everything. No sound comes from Tom. No expression of pain exits him as his bone cuts through his skin. Death makes it okay.

With a final push, the mangled foot slides down to join the rest of the body.

For a moment, Jeremy allows himself time to appreciate this type of neat disposal. He can remember only one other instance where he hid a body and intended for it to stay hidden. He used the woods then too, and she remains there.

Jeremy looks to his left and sees something hidden among the trees. He startles, immediately launching into a defensive position. He relaxes once he sees that it isn't a person, but an object in the dark. It's brown and shaped like a crude dwelling. Bits of dirty fabric hang over the front of it like a makeshift door. Suddenly his heart begins to beat faster, harder. It's a shack. It's a filthy shack in the middle of the West Virginia woods.

He pulls himself to his feet, slowly making his way closer to it. Again, he listens, trying to drown out the sounds of the rushing stream. He hears nothing and detects no movement as he approaches the structure.

He backs himself against the old wooden slats and logs that have been crafted together to form the bones of the shack. Using this angle, he peeks around the side of the fabric hanging over the front entrance. It's one small room, the size of a walk-in closet. A bit of moonlight streams in, illuminating parts of the room. He can see bottles and shelves, but nothing else. Grabbing the knife from his ankle, he stabs it into the fabric, pinning the makeshift curtain to the side and allowing more moonlight to stream in. He enters, crawling on his knees to do so. Only a child could stand in this place.

Shelves line the perimeter, made from old wood pieces. He uses his small flashlight to get a better look at the items that reside on them. Bottles. Dozens of old, foggy, and dirty bottles line the shelves. Each of them is filled with various natural oddities. There are dead bugs, animal bones, and animal feet. He notes rabbit feet, bird feet, and a larger jar that has two paws, which look like they were taken from a fox. He can smell the decay and the solutions used to preserve these items, and he wonders how long it has been since the builder has visited. Is he returning tonight?

Sliding in farther, the smell begins to take a grip on his senses. His eyes start to water and he coughs out a couple gags. He notes the skin of a few animals tacked to the wooden walls of the structure. An entire fox, four rabbits, and a skunk. Flies buzz around and slap his face every now and again. The buzzing is almost maddening.

He points his small flashlight at the floor and he notices the cardboard under his feet is stained rust colored. Parts of it are black with rot, and it's clear blood has splashed, dripped, and soaked into almost every inch of it. He shines the light on a bundle, wrapped in filthy once-white fabric, tucked into a corner under a shelf. It's stained brown, deep red, and yellow. Jeremy's sure if he touches it, it will feel hard in his hand, not like the soft material it likely once was. Something draws him to it. The stains and the flies that surround it call to him. They implore him to look inside, to discover what darkness coexists with him in these woods.

So he gives in to it. He places the flashlight handle between his teeth and approaches the bundle. As he gets close to it, the smell is almost unbearable, thick and hazy, causing even the flies to look as if they are moving in slow motion through a layer of invisible gelatinous sludge.

Jeremy reaches out, pulling apart the ends of the bundle that are gathered at the top. He does this slowly, confirming that the fabric is indeed hard and crusted into such a state that it feels as if it could crumble in his hands. It opens like a fortune cookie and reveals the contents, which are cast in a ghoulish spotlight from his torch.

He smiles instinctively, letting his eyes roam over everything in front of him. The first thing he sees is a human finger. The skin is still very much attached, but it's decaying in a way that makes it look fake. Maggots slither from holes, tumbling out like candy in a piñata. Next to it are strips of flesh, stacked like deli meat.

Moving the finger aside, three human eyes are revealed. They appear sad and deflated, but they somehow look up at him with judgment, as if he is the one who placed them there.

It's a macabre arrangement that takes even Jeremy's breath away for a second. Among the other things, there are clumps of hair and broken fingernails as well. Blood and flesh are attached to everything, too preserved and odorous to be from long ago. The person who packed this was here recently. They will definitely be back.

When Jeremy casts his light around again, he starts to notice more hidden treasures. In some of the bottles there are clearly pieces of human. Eyes, fingers, ears, and chunks of meat are floating among the animals and bugs. It's a beautifully sick museum of pain.

He is briefly at a loss for clear thought. When the neurons start firing again, he grins to himself. This is what resides in the woods with him. Evil lurks here. Who built this foul little shack by a stream? He pictures a true feral mountain man. In his mind, this man looks painfully inbred in filthy clothing and smells so bad that the air bends around him. His long beard is wired and tangled. Jeremy can see him trudging through the forest, dragging a human by their hair. Taking them back to his shack to slice off the pieces he wants to keep. Jeremy can only imagine what he does with the rest of them. Taking one last look around this small corner of hell, he places the edges of the bundle together again, backs out of the door, and removes the pinned knife. The brown fabric falls back over the door as if he were never there.

How many people have been mutilated by this boogeyman in the woods? How many hikers stopped for a drink in the stream and were torn apart and kept for display? Knowing this sick fuck will continue beyond reproach is powerful. Only

Jeremy knows he exists, yet this grisly dwelling hides in plain sight if you venture deep enough into the unknown.

Jeremy walks on, taking one last glance back at the shack. There's truth to the folklore we all hear and read about. There are monsters in the woods.

Back at the truck, Jeremy begins the cleaning process. He pulls bleach wipes from his bag, and in the glow of the cab light, he wipes down the seat, taking care to get the stitching. It's those little details that matter most.

People always forget that blood flows to the places you don't see. It hides like the secret that it is, that it knows itself to be. Nefarious things always hide in the places where no one will look. Blood that is shed from violence never really disappears. It's never truly clean. Jeremy isn't looking for clean here; he never was.

CHAPTER 5

"HEY, JOHN." Wren answers the phone and takes a sip of her drink, a Louisiana Harvest.

"Muller, you know I'm waiting for you," he says impatiently on the other end.

She sighs, her eyes scanning the dining area of Jack Rose. Her insides don't match the vibrant and beautiful decor around her. The restaurant is bustling but peaceful. She just feels chaotic.

She'd promised to meet Leroux at Jeremy's home for the final sweep by one thirty, but after the visit to the cemetery, she isn't sure if she could face the scene of the crime and Jeremy's escape.

"You're so persistent," she complains. "What if I can't?"

"I don't think *I can't* is in Dr. Muller's vocabulary, at least the woman I know."

Wren laughs, rolling her eyes and taking a bite of cheese. She ordered the shareable cheese board with pickles. She doesn't regret it at all.

"All right. I'm coming. But first I'm finishing my cheese in peace."

He chuckles. "I don't know what that means, but I better see you in thirty minutes."

They hang up and Wren leans back in the wicker-style chair and takes another sip of her beverage. It's a sweet gin drink with refreshing lemon and raspberry. Normally, she doesn't drink alcohol during the day. It was never a rule she set for herself or anything, just something that naturally happened. But lately, she has found her habits changing. Nothing soothes her much anymore, but a Louisiana Harvest comes damn close.

She leans forward, starting to work on her cheese board and catching the conversation happening next to her. It's a young couple, maybe early twenties, and they are fighting.

Wren loves it when couples fight in public. It's an embarrassing quirk, but there's just something about the shamelessness that comes along with it that fascinates her.

This particular couple is fighting over a text message.

Patrick, the young man sitting directly to Wren's right, is in a heap of trouble. Lauren found a text message on his phone from Patrick's ex-girlfriend and *mad* isn't even the word to describe her right now. She is speaking as softly as she can for public decency, but she talks a million miles a minute and with a razor-like precision. Apparently, Patrick has a track record, so Wren doesn't feel bad for snooping. He has proven he is capable of this kind of thing, after all.

Patrick looks to be in pain. He doesn't look as if he regrets what he has done or that he feels empathy for Lauren. No, he looks as if he is struggling to even pay attention to what she is saying. He sits there as if he's being held hostage by an invisible villain. Once Lauren has unloaded all her very well-organized points on him, he shrugs and says he's sorry. That's it. No explanation. No conversation. Just a brush-off.

Lauren isn't having that, and frankly, at this point, neither is Wren. Lauren loses her temper, calling him an "antagonistic little prick" and says she is sick of being put second.

Just as she finishes her tirade, Wren gets the check. She pays it, passing right by the table on her way out. She stops, thinks it over, and decides to lean down to Lauren and say, "You can do better," before walking out of the restaurant and not looking back.

The ride to Jeremy's home is a disturbingly familiar one. She feels carsick, constantly fighting back the urge to retch. The long stretch leading up to his hidden horror house is the worst part. Her mind conjures up images of her unconscious body curled up in his trunk, drugged and about to have her life fundamentally changed forever.

Around one forty-five p.m., Wren rolls up to Jeremy Rose's abandoned home. For a split second, she wonders why the hell she agreed to be here. Fortunately, the moment is quick and dissipates when she thinks about walking through his home, unencumbered by the possibility that he would show up and kill her.

As she walks up the steps, moving past the old police tape and through the front door, it's as if she has stepped back in time.

It's clean, despite everything that happened. She wouldn't expect it to be any different, but it's still strange. It feels as if it's been years since she has been here but it's also as if she never left. She pulls on a latex glove from her kit and runs a hand over a carved doorframe. It's beautiful and haunting, with deep curves that hearken back to another era.

"How do you feel, Muller?" Leroux leans against a nearby wall, propping his crutch against an emerald-green settee.

She jumps at the sound of his voice. She had been mindlessly tracing the lines of the woodwork, trying to get herself out of this chaotic mindset she has been living with. She crafted this life, this identity, and now it feels as if she is shattered into a million pieces again. Her old life has mixed with the new and the colors have bled together. She can no longer separate them and hide some away. It's all in the same jar now, muddy and ruined.

Wren gives him a once-over. It's the first time she's seen him since she paid him a visit at the hospital.

"Better question," she replies, "how the hell are *you* even here? Shouldn't you be in bed or something?" She gestures to his left leg. The wound's dressing is covered by his dress pants. It almost looks as if nothing is wrong, if she ignores the crutch and limp that he will likely hang on to for a while.

Leroux chuckles, sitting on the arm of the settee. "I told you, it didn't penetrate as deeply as it would have from a straight shot." Even through the bravado, he winces when he moves his lower half. There is a medical boot over his shoe that absorbs some of the shock, but an arrow to the calf muscle will really bring the pain.

"You are lucky, my friend." She looks at him, noting that he has lost some weight in the week or so since she last saw him.

"No luck needed." He scoffs, looking around the room. "That idiot is a terrible shot. His arrow grazed a tree on the way to a target that might as well have been a billboard. Experienced hunter, my ass."

Wren laughs, feeling a little relief from the levity only Leroux can bring to a situation. She crosses the room, noting the smell that emanates from Jeremy's once-impressive plant collection. She wrinkles her nose, finding it more difficult to stomach than some morgue smells. As she steps closer, she is struck by the vast amount of botanical carnage laid out before her.

Most of these precious plants are brown, wilting, and seemingly lifeless. A variety of orchids, some creeping devil's ivy, and a once-magnificent monstera are just a few she can spot. She touches the monstera's leaves and they disintegrate in her hand. Wren thinks back to the cemetery ferns that crumble only to resurrect endlessly. Something about this plant tells her it isn't as immortal. It's the smell that keeps breaking her from her silent wonderings. The odor is swampy and sickly sweet, almost like decomposition. As she bends to position her face closer to the plant display, it gets much stronger.

Leroux notices her horrified expression. "It's root rot that you're smelling."

She straightens, lifting one eyebrow. "Excuse me?"

He sighs, gesturing to the table. "My guess is he overwatered all his plants before he left. The standing moisture just sat there and rotted the roots. He has poor drainage on most of these guys too. Shame." He doesn't notice Wren staring at him, mystified. When he finally catches her gaze, he shifts uncomfortably. "So, he doesn't only kill humans I guess."

"I'm sorry, John Leroux, how do you know so much about drainage and root rot?" She can't help but smile, waving her hand to waft the smell away from her face.

He smirks. "I like plants, okay? You'll never catch my place smelling like a swamp."

"Wow, you are an enigma." Wren shakes her head, walking along the table until she comes across one green, seemingly healthy plant. "Oh, look. We have a survivor."

Leroux hops slightly onto his foot, using his crutch to make his way to the table. "Ah, a Boston fern," he says, rubbing the healthy leaves between his fingers. "They love humidity. I would bet his poor, overwatered pals created a nice humid environment for this little guy to thrive in."

"You have taught me a lot today, John." Wren can't help but be impressed by this unexpected torrent of plant knowledge. "I *have* been tempted to become a plant mom. But I thought I didn't have the time." She chuckles lightly. "I have the time now."

Leroux senses the drop in tone as she says this. Seeing Wren uncertain and off her game isn't something he's used to. "Well, you should start with this wayward soul." He gestures to the fern.

Wren's eyes widen. "Take one of his plants into my house? Are you high, John?" She's almost disgusted at the suggestion, turning to distance herself from the plants altogether. The air immediately turns tense.

Leroux blanches a little at her anger but quickly recovers. "I know it sounds counterintuitive, but you aren't looking at this the way I am. This plant survived him. It didn't ask to be in this house, but he brought it in here anyways and despite all of his best efforts, it's thriving. Does that sound like anyone you know, Muller?"

Suddenly she feels as if the air were kicked from her lungs. She tries to argue, but she is stunned by how organically the comparison presented itself. It's the first time someone has made it seem as if she isn't going to shatter like glass. Even Richard sweetly treats her like porcelain lately. It feels good to hear that she still projects strength. After a long beat of silence, she decides to relent. "You are calling me a stubborn houseplant. You realize that, correct?" A smirk plays at her lips even though she tries to hide it.

He lets out a relieved chuckle, looking down at his foot and steadying himself against the table. "Take the plant, Muller. He couldn't kill it. The symbolism is too good."

She hesitates, eyeing the pop of green among the dead.

Leroux rolls his eyes again, throwing his head back. "Come on, don't make me say some flowery shit about the plant not succumbing to the death that surrounds it. God, I spend too much time with you."

Now she laughs. A full laugh that she feels in her chest. How she can laugh while standing in his living room must be an act of pure magic, she decides. "All right, all right. It's not the plant's fault. I'll take him."

"Good, because I couldn't leave it." He grins widely.

"Oh, so you used my trauma to make me take it instead. Really nice, Detective." She playfully smacks his arm, knowing he's right despite her reservations. This plant didn't ask to be here any more than his victims did. Jeremy brought things into this house to watch them die.

"All right, leave your rescue plant here and follow me." The serious tone to his voice makes Wren's senses go haywire. She nods, stopping herself from helping him as he clumsily gathers his crutch. He has been extremely irritable about his own healing process, and she knows when to offer aid.

They walk across the house and into a lounge area. It's decorated like an old movie set. Green velvet curtains cover the windows and drape lazily from gold rods. They form inviting puddles on the floor, and she wishes she could dive into them and be in a reality far away from here. Maybe that reality would have less murder and more pizza.

There's a settee in the corner. Like everything else, it's from another era, intricately carved with satin and velvet pillows threatening to spill over the edge of the cushions. The well-worn fabric has faded delicately.

A curio cabinet contains a myriad of oddities, mixed with vintage finds. If this were anyone else's home, it would be uniquely beautiful. But it's not someone else's home; it's his.

Nothing looks out of place in this room. It's all very thought-out and orderly, albeit dusty as hell.

"Take a look in the cabinet." Leroux's voice breaks through her thoughts. His tone is serious, and it makes her nervous.

She looks at him for a long moment, trying to read his features. He betrays nothing.

"You're confident I can handle whatever it is in there?"

He nods, leaning his hip into the settee. "I know what you can handle."

She squints, allowing her eyes to scan the items in front of her. Vintage perfume bottles, butterflies and moths pinned to velvet-backed frames. On another shelf, there are a few bones, clearly animal, displayed in a line. She looks them over until she spots an outlier. Her gaze comes to rest on a series of finger bones that are distinctly human. Her breath hitches as she pulls back a bit.

Before it can truly set in, she sees hair. Blond, brown, and ginger-colored hair, all tied in ribbons, laid out on the shelf beneath the bones.

"John, didn't I tell you he would be a trophy guy?"

He lets an uncomfortable laugh escape. "Yes. Yes, you did," he relents.

She keeps looking, and her eyes land next on a porcelain bowl. It's ornate and clearly antique, filled to the brim with rings and necklaces. Gold, silver, and everything in between. It's a lost and found of women's jewelry. There is something monstrous about a bowl overflowing with rings stolen off dead girls. It's macabre.

"This is a lot of jewelry," she says, still staring. "Do we have—"

"Unidentified victims?" he finishes the sentence while scanning the room. He doesn't wait for Wren to answer. "There are items in that case that we haven't been able to connect with known victims. But I looked in my dad's files, and there are some cases he was questioning that maybe we can finally put to rest."

She smiles weakly, turning to face him. "Making lemonade out of napalm."

"Always," he responds.

"Take me outside," she says flatly.

"Muller, I don't know . . ." he starts to protest, but she's already on the way to the back door. Walking down the steps, her foot hits the backyard with a thud. The ground is dry and uneven, but it's just a backyard. Nothing triggers her fight-or-flight response, nothing feels different.

She stops for a minute to look around. From the back, the house looks normal, if mildly run-down. But a closer look reveals the spiderwebs, broken glass, and weeds that hint at the depraved fiend that dwelt inside.

Leroux follows close behind, getting steadier in his gait through sheer spite. She never believed he would take time to heal either. He plows through, probably suffering in silence at the end of the day for his hubris.

The ground slopes a bit as she enters the tree line. Her feet take control and guide her farther into the trees, where the ground begins to get soggy. A quick scan of the surrounding area shows it to be treacherous. She knows there are emotional land mines everywhere now. She has willingly stepped into a carnival of trauma, and the regret creeps in like a slow gas leak. The effects hit her in tiny bursts as the poisonous air seeps in from every angle. She spots the broken perimeter fencing that stretches into forever, and as the thick canopy begins to block out the sun, she immediately picks out a dirty speaker high up in the trees.

Suddenly, she's thrust into battle again. She smells the swampy earth and feels the cypress branches scratch at her arms. It's the world of her nightmare. Everything around her constricts and spins. The heat, the sounds, the smells; it's all-consuming and wretched. Pungent waves assault her senses, smelling like rotten wood and death.

She swears she sees a snake slither over her foot but quickly shakes her head and it's gone. A phantom bug falls on her shoulder and she panics. Nothing is there.

But she hears the sounds.

The cicadas scream, louder than ever. The taste of blood fills her mouth, a burst of metal that threatens to make her retch. Her hands clap over her ears instinctively, trying to block out his voice, which she just knows is about to come out of the speakers above her. She's so sure it will come.

Hands clamp down on her shoulders, and reflexively she spins around to punch. Leroux stumbles back, almost losing his balance and narrowly missing her fist connecting with his cheek. Suddenly, she's grounded in place with him. His face is there, comforting her despite her attack.

"Wren, it's John!" he yells, inching back toward her.

She lowers her fists to her sides, suddenly feeling the chaos around her deflate like a clipped balloon. It rushes out, and suddenly all is quiet. The buzz is calming again, the trees tickle, and the sun pokes through the canopy in streams of light. It's not what it was. It's never going to be that again.

Nature came and reclaimed this place. Moss decorates the speakers, and the broken fence keeps nothing in. Fresh air fills her lungs, and she takes a deep, revitalizing breath.

"I'm here. Sorry I almost hit you," Wren says sheepishly.

Leroux smiles. "That would have left a serious mark, Muller," he says, placing a hesitant hand lightly on her back. "Let's get you out of here. You did your job for the day."

"Thank you," she says softly, walking out of the trees and back into the safety of the backyard. "I don't want to ever see this place again."

"I promise. Never again."

After entering the living room again, she pauses to grab her plant, hugging it close to her body protectively. As she presses her finger into the thirsty soil, she can't help but feel like she's not alone. Something else made it out and never has to return. She gets to be an unstoppable fern after all.

As they walk back to the driveway, Wren feels as if the ghosts of the house are clawing at her, asking for her to listen. It's how she feels in the morgue when presented with a new victim. Years of working with the dead to uncover their secrets have taught her that the answers are almost always tucked somewhere in the shadowy parts of someone's life. But they're not in this house. All that's left is rot and decay.

For the past two weeks, she thought she could sit by and watch things unfold. But that's not what Wren needs to heal. After today, this episode in the swamp, she knows the nightmares won't disappear until she does something. She isn't built for this life of passive participation, regardless of the emotional collapse she is currently digging her way through.

Her monster isn't going to disappear on his own. He won't let her be. He'll let the dust settle, let another story dominate the news, and wait until everyone has forgotten those battered, swamp-sodden bodies. Everyone's attention spans, or the lack thereof, will be his collaborators. If she waits long enough, she knows he will crawl back out, but she isn't willing to wait for that.

She pulls off her latex gloves and stuffs them into a pocket.

It's time to get her hands dirty.

CHAPTER 6

H<small>E HID</small> T<small>OM'S</small> <small>TRUCK</small> in the woods after a nine-hour drive north, knowing he'd need it later. Now, Jeremy walks past the row of houses that line Lake Garfield. Most of them are massive and well-maintained, appearing like palaces at the ends of long driveways. He ducks past motion lights and takes note of the sporadic sounds and sights that indicate a currently lived-in home. He passes by some smoking chimneys and muffled conversations heard through a casually cracked window and ventures to an area where there seems to be an almost alarming silence.

Vacant homes hold their breath. They stay quiet, not daring to speak their vulnerabilities aloud. But a quiet home isn't the only qualifier he is seeking tonight. He passes by a large white beauty of a place, peaceful and dark against the water. To anyone passing through, it would appear empty. Another look with a qualified eye tells a different story. A well-manicured lawn and healthy plants indicate a groundskeeper, or renters at the very least. He trudges on, looking for the telltale long grasses of a purely seasonal dwelling.

The darkness is tantalizingly scary. He feels unsettled and paranoid. It's as if every cell in his body has snapped to attention. They buzz and set his entire system on fire, leaving him momentarily feeling like a homing beacon for particularly attuned predators who troll these woods alongside him tonight. A twig snaps to his right and he cranes his neck to follow the sound. His eyes slightly adjust to the darkness, but only enough to somehow make the woods look more ominous, with shadowy shapes twisting in every direction. Luckily, there are many of the same foes that he faced in the forests of Louisiana. Black bears are always a fear, but they aren't a threat unless threatened. As he silently lists the characters out there tonight, he begins to feel his fear dissipate. Bobcats and coyotes are a familiar sight. The only potential shocker would be a moose sighting.

He takes a deep breath, vaguely remembering his visits to Massachusetts as a child. His former best friend Philip's family was split in two back then. Philip would spend his time visiting his father's side up north and sometimes he would take Jeremy with him.

These trips were the only times Jeremy felt any sense of a controlled family environment. Philip's family was big, loud, and outdoorsy in a way that Jeremy's family wasn't. Jeremy's mother barely saw the outside world, and his father was a hunter, but that's all the outdoors meant to him. In Louisiana, Jeremy was taken outside only to kill or prepare to hunt.

Philip's family went hiking, they went to the lake to play, and they just enjoyed each other's company by a firepit. But as safe as it should have felt, it was all so foreign to Jeremy. He managed to find discomfort in the comfort.

It doesn't take long before a quiet dwelling comes into view through the trees. It's almost completely camouflaged in the dark. The black paint job is chipping and aged, but it's elegant, nonetheless. He stalks along the perimeter, carefully scanning the area for motion lights or the small pinpoint sensors of a camera. Seeing none, he ventures closer to the structure. The lawn is overgrown, as if a mower had been there about a month before and had not seen it since. Spiderwebs have formed across the entry to the wraparound porch, undisturbed by any visitors to the front door.

He walks around the house slowly, taking in all the entry points and trying to find a weakness. He spots one almost immediately. Passing through the dry grass that bites against his pant leg, he nears the sliding door at the back of the house. It leads directly into the living area, and he can see from where he is standing that the latch is not down. He pulls it open with force, in case it catches and needs to be encouraged to open. It unlatches easily with a deep breath, allowing the fresh evening air to pour inside. He pauses for a moment, letting his eyes scan the inside of the room, confirming that it has been empty for weeks. The dust is settled and undisturbed.

He lets himself in, dropping his bag with a loud thud, and waits for someone to startle. He hears nothing, as expected. He flicks on a light switch, illuminating the room like a showcase.

The room is red. The walls are a deep shade of maroon and the couch and chair set centered around a coffee table are also red. The shades aren't the same. The furniture is a brighter shade than the walls. It's maddening.

Interesting choice.

He walks now, running a gloved hand over surfaces and sitting on the couch for a minute. He leans back, taking in the comfort. He lets the throw pillows swallow him up and he looks at the ceiling fan above him. It hasn't been dusted while this house has sat vacant. It had maybe never been dusted.

It's always interesting to see what people prioritize in their lives and homes. This house is clean and orderly. It's lived-in, and someone takes pride in this place even if their decorating is questionable at best. They keep it tidy, but they just don't give a fuck about that ceiling fan. He wonders if they use it at all. If he turned it on, he would catch his death with the amount of dust that would fly off it.

He stands up, stretching and making his way over to the impressive fireplace at the center of the room. It's the show-piece. It's designed to be the thing everyone would comment on when they enter the home. This one is ugly, but it's expensive-looking. He has plans to use it. He thinks about this family finding a used fireplace upon their return, the ash and burnt logs teasing them with a sense of violation. A burned log in the fireplace is so subtle but so menacing. He can feel their vulnerability, their fear. After he leaves, this place will never be a place of secure refuge for them. It will all be permanently altered. He likes that.

His eyes soon look up, now taking stock of the collection of photos that sit along the mantle. One frame shows a middle-aged couple, standing in an embrace. They look happy. Photos don't usually show reality; they show a curated version of it. You would never guess that these people don't at least pay someone to clean their ceiling fan; with their plastered-on grins and clean-cut clothes, they seem like the all-American, wealthy family.

Another photo shows that same couple with what appears to be their young adult children. They pose together in an open field, wearing cowboy boots and buttoned-up shirts. The wind blows their hair and their hands rest on one another's shoulders. It's all very apple pie and ignorance.

Other photos show a birthday party and a black-and-white picture of a young couple from what looks like the 1950s. He's drawn to it, admiring the man's slick suit and combed-back hair. The woman in the photo is striking, her hair curled into a bouncy bob. She wears a dress that he can see only the top portion of, but she looks classic. It's as if they were created from an ideal.

He shakes his mind away from the photos and walks into the kitchen. It's big and open, with lots of random shit piled on the counters. It's still tidy, but they love to show off all their poor design choices. The theme of the kitchen is pea green. The refrigerator, the bowls, and even the tiles on the back-splash of the stove are Regan MacNeil green. It makes his stomach turn a bit and he can't help but think about demonic vomit painting this whole room. He will never quite under-stand the choices people make.

Continuing through the house, he opens drawers and cabinets. He's looking for personal touches that make this house someone's home. It feels good to touch people's things, the things they never want touched. He finds a man's wedding ring. Either he is missing one or he has two, but it's shoved behind some takeout menus. He takes it out of the drawer and places it on the counter.

He finds those strawberry hard candies filled to the brim in another drawer. This makes him laugh, it's so stupid. He grabs one and unwraps it, throwing it in his mouth and savoring the taste of childhood. Anyone who ever knew an old person has sucked on one of those strawberry candies.

He opens the stainless steel refrigerator and peers inside. It's relatively empty but there are a few leftovers on the brink of spoiling. There is butter, some baking soda, and a couple questionable deli cold cuts. At a glance, he sees cream with only two days left until its expiration, and immediately he starts looking around the kitchen for some honey. He quickly finds some in a lower cabinet and feels he made the right decision in picking this home.

Walking upstairs, he finds three bedrooms and a bathroom. The main bedroom, what he assumes to be the parents' bedroom, is massive and yellow. It's bright yellow from wall to wall, with a bedspread to match. Even the trim is yellow. When he turns the light on, it looks like the surface of the sun, if the sun was drawn by a toddler. Yellow. Just a shocking shade of yellow.

Shaking his head, he checks on the other rooms, hoping they're more neutral. Surely they wouldn't use that color scheme throughout. No, they are yellow. The entire upstairs, save for the bathroom and hallway, is a putrid hue of dehydrated-piss yellow.

Might as well take the big bed, then.

He's too tired to care much, so he throws his bag into the main bedroom and grabs his toothbrush.

The adjoining bathroom is big. It's almost too big, feeling cavernous and out of place. He stands in front of the mirror in the surprisingly white bathroom and searches for tooth-paste. He finds some in a bottom drawer and hoists it up like a triumphant treasure hunter. As he brushes his teeth, he walks around, opening drawers and surveying the contents. He pulls one open and shuffles through the items inside. It's almost empty, with only some floss sticks and extra razor blades in it.

As he searches the drawer, he presses slightly on the bottom, feeling it give way a bit. He pulls up on a corner and peels it back to reveal something rolled-up underneath. His gloved hand pulls at the object, unraveling it into its original shape. He smooths it out on the counter, stifling a laugh.

It's what his mother would have referred to as a dirty magazine.

On the cover is a busty gal wearing a nurse's outfit, or what society has deemed to be a nurse's outfit. Jeremy has never seen a real nurse wear an exposed garter belt and a minidress with a red cross stretched across her chest. It's all very exag-gerated and so far from reality. But what's funniest to him is the cap. Every sexy nurse's costume is complete only with a tiny cap with a red cross on it. If you don't have it, you aren't immediately recognizable. Hell, you could be a member of any sexy profession without that cap. The thing is, those caps used to be real; they were originally created before the 1800s for the purpose of modesty. It's all very ironic.

This woman, whom he imagines must be a founding member of the Daughters of Charity, is holding a comically large syringe. By the looks of it, she's ready to provide some healing.

He spits out the toothpaste into the sink and tries to keep a laugh from escaping. The edges of the magazine are frayed and curl in on themselves. The reader has even dog-eared some pages for easier and quicker access. It's all so sad. He smooths it over the counter, picturing a middle-aged man crouching in his own bathroom and jacking it to an illicit magazine. Is it always when the wife isn't home, or is this sometimes an activity done while she sleeps a few feet away? He has a lot of questions.

Jeremy takes a long, hot shower, finally ridding himself of the dirt and grime that has been caked on his body for weeks. Swirls of filth snake their way down the drain. He drops his gaze to watch it all disappear, cleansing him completely. It feels like a reset button. He doesn't stop until the heat becomes too much.

He changes into borrowed pants and takes a long look in the mirror. His clean face is mostly recognizable to him again. His new, unintentional diet has sharpened his features a bit, exaggerating his cheekbones and making his face look menacing.

Grabbing the dirty magazine, he makes his way downstairs with it. He stops in front of the mantle and slides it behind the photo of the family, displaying it proudly behind them. They seem like a family that respects medical professionals.

With his good deed done for the evening, he settles into the couch to look at the reading selection, or at least the books that have been deemed acceptable for public consumption. His eyes are drawn to a coffee table book boasting an unparalleled look at the best hidden gems in the Berkshires. Intrigued, he flips through it and stops at the scene of the Berkshire UFO Incident.

He delves into the topic and can't help but be interested. It happened around this time of year, in September 1969. Over 250 people reported the same UFO on the same night. There is a bridge in Sheffield called Old Covered Bridge where a family alleges they were chased and pulled into the ship.

He doesn't believe in alien abduction stories. Why would sophisticated, otherworldly beings pull dirty Earthlings onto their ships? Of course, this doesn't mean he doesn't think it's all fascinating. These kinds of stories provide a glimpse into the human mind, if anything at all.

He reads that there's a plaque commemorating the abduction in Sheffield. It acknowledges the UFO incident and confirms that it should be treated as a historic event. It's amazing what humans will commemorate, but 250 people seeing the same alien spacecraft? He can't deny that's strange.

Flipping farther into the book he learns of an ancient waterfall and then another, even more interesting hidden gem. It's something strange that begs to be disturbed. The more he reads, the more positive he becomes that this is the place to begin. He didn't even know what he was looking for until this moment, until this place found him. Everything up until this point has reached out and grabbed him, leading him where he is meant to be. Now, here in this house, in this book, a location reveals itself again. It's spooky, beautiful, and purely fascinating. The site feels like a spectacle already. It's a blank canvas of disturbing backstories and local lore, and it's just waiting for him to paint it red.

CHAPTER 7

WREN LEANS BACK in her desk chair, chewing on the end of a pen. She crunches down on it, relishing the feeling of plastic crushing beneath her bite. She's been staring at her computer screen for hours, ever since she returned from the final sweep of Jeremy's compound.

It's one thing to believe he's still out there, still breathing. It's another to take the first steps to finding him. For days and weeks, she has wished and hoped that Jeremy was dead. But tonight, sitting in this room, she can feel him.

Rising to her feet, she paces around the room. She's in the home office she shares with Richard. The walls are a mix of framed degrees, a *Silence of the Lambs* poster, and a map of Sweden, where Richard's family is from. It's a perfect representation of the two of them in one space. She shuffles across the hardwood floors, desperately trying to search her brain for pathways. She begs an unknown force for a string to pull or a door to peek behind. For hours she has come in and out of this room, unsuccessfully manifesting an answer.

She was sure after everything that happened, she would be able to let go of the reins and allow justice to let her know when it was complete. It was all such a show. She played the part of a compliant victim, ready to heal. She pretended to be comfortable existing far away from the trauma and the constant gridlock of new information.

But she isn't comfortable with it. She's known that all along and she knows it now. As soon as she convinces herself to stop watching, she starts doing. She begins to sift through it all, carefully disinterring the darkest parts of her story and analyzing each of them closer than she ever wanted to before. It sounds scary, but anything worth a damn usually is.

So off she goes, into the gloom with nothing but scars and a dull axe to grind. She pushes aside the sweet miasma of death and finally sets out to track him down. She's done waiting for horrors to find her, waiting for them to get too close to extinguish. It's time to force his hand.

"Think, Wren," she says out loud, stopping in front of a bookcase and hoping it will offer her some advice. She scans the titles and authors that line the shelves. Richard's and her collection is a true melting pot of interests ranging from thrillers and romance to biographies and horror. She runs her fingers over the spines of several books. She feels the different textures against her skin, preferring the feel of the leather-bound and hardcover tomes to the paperbacks. Her fingers dance over *'Salem's Lot* by Stephen King, then make their way to *Ethan Frome* by Edith Wharton. She skips down one shelf to touch *The House of the Seven Gables* by Nathaniel Hawthorne, and as her hand moves to another book, she begins to see a uniformity in her casual touches.

She notices that, unintentionally, her hand has hit only books based in Massachusetts. Initially, she smiles to herself, thinking she must be some kind of witch to be able to pull that off among countless titles without a plan to do so. But as she identifies the novel where her hand currently rests, there is a strong feeling of connection. She doesn't know why, but she pulls the book out, turning it over in her hands.

The book is *American Pastoral* by Philip Roth. She almost laughs out loud at the fortuity of the random selection. On their third date, Richard had feigned heart failure when she revealed that she had never read it. He brought her a copy on their fourth date, insisting that she crack it open as soon as possible and expand her dismally inadequate literary repertoire. She told him that it was an arrogant and presumptive move on his part and that she was perfectly capable of choosing her own reading material. She remembers clearly how he had laughed and held his arms up in mock surrender. Then, he promised to hold on to it until *she* asked to read it. He was sure they would be together long enough for her to come around. He was right, and she read it by their first wedding anniversary.

Suddenly she feels calm. Everything has become so serious and dire lately that she's almost forgotten she has already created plenty of carefree memories and that there are plenty more waiting to be made. It's true what they say about missing the forest for the trees.

It's strange, but she knows. She pretended to believe everyone when they said he could never survive this long, or he would have been caught by now. She nods when they tell her to move forward, to act as if it's all over. After all, she learned how to play the role of survivor before and she still remembers the lines.

She opens the shade, looking out into the darkness. She sees nothing but her own reflection anxiously staring back at her. Her hand absentmindedly strokes the Boston fern she adopted. It occupies a special place on the windowsill, waiting to be healed too. She glides the leaves between her fingers affectionately, infusing strength with each touch.

If someone *is* standing outside her window, they can see her and everything around her perfectly. Slowly, she reaches over and pulls the cord to click the floor lamp off, and suddenly the world opens up. She can see lights in the distance and the wide expanse of trees. Other than that, there is nothing. No one.

Wren wonders if this feeling is just massive amounts of unchecked trauma, or if he's really out there. It doesn't feel realistic that he would stay in Louisiana. He's too smart to keep himself close to the fire. But where is he? Whenever she is stuck with a problem, it usually helps to eliminate possibilities first. Sometimes that gets her brain to a better place to problem-solve.

She slides into the desk chair and stares at the screen, wondering where to start. She types in some cursory searches that lead to nothing but nonsense. More than three decades on this Earth, and she still can't figure out how to cobble together a proper internet search. Realizing she is searching too broadly, she gets more specific with her word choices. This is when some troubling results pop up.

Suddenly, she sees his face. His driver's license photo is at the top of the page. He smiles at her from years away. Initially, she feels assaulted, as if he is somehow in the room with her. Her inner sanctum feels violated. This is *her* office. He can't be here. She breaks herself from the panic, but her senses remain engaged.

She clicks the article associated with the photo and begins to read. There is nothing new, just the same regurgitation of the story and a half-baked theory of where he may be.

The reporter is sure that he's dead, writing that he will likely be found in the belly of some beast or floating lifeless in a swamp somewhere. They are determined to get a poetic ending for Jeremy. He hunts in a swamp; to the swamp he must return.

They don't get it. No one gets it. They toss these thoughts around like facts and offer nothing to cling to. Reporting that he is *probably* dead is not helpful. It tranquilizes the wrong people and takes their guards down. That's where Jeremy built his playground, in the land of well-meaning fools. Everyone with a pulse should be scared, but misinformation is starting to work like a sedative.

She switches her focus to scrolling through social media, and it's there that she finds a host of even more fascinating opinions. One user swears they saw Jeremy at a farmers' market in California. They say he was stealing mangoes and looked as if he had been through hell and back.

Nope. He would never go west.

Another post alleges that he is probably holed up in Wren's basement. The comments theorize that everything was all an elaborate hoax, and some kind of strange relationship is occurring with the blessing of the police and apparently Richard somehow. No one is quite sure of the details or logistics of this theory, but they perpetuate it all the same.

She shakes her head, clicking the window into oblivion and returning her screen to her desktop. She leans back in her seat with a sigh.

No more theory diving, she tells herself.

The truth is, none of them are close to reality. This fishing expedition to eliminate ideas was a successful one, because she feels even more resolved in her gut feeling. Wherever Jeremy is, he is likely still alive. She just feels it now. He's also too confident to try a fake-out and head somewhere like California or Texas. Neither would suit him, and he doesn't do anything that makes him uncomfortable. It's his own needs above all, and he won't sacrifice that part of himself in order to blend into the crowd and disappear. He doesn't want any of that. She is sure he is somewhere familiar, lying in wait before he strikes again. This cooling-off period was forced on him, and that fact is likely pissing him off. Again, he doesn't sacrifice his own needs for much of anything.

A chill runs down her spine, shaking her from her thoughts.

She looks to her right, noticing *American Pastoral* still lying on the desk beside her. She glances at it without a second thought until she reads the author's name again. The name *Philip* suddenly triggers another avenue to travel down.

She types "Philip Trudeau Massachusetts" into the search bar, then scans the results quickly. A few social media sites come up and she decides to start with Facebook.

The profile isn't completely private, but it's not completely public either. She can see a few pieces of information that lead her to believe this is the Philip that Jeremy knew. She learned from Leroux that he is a pastor at a church in the Berkshires, and this profile's Philip has that title public on his page. In his profile picture, he, his wife, and young son all wear flannel and smile at the camera as though nothing could ever trouble them. A look farther down the timeline shows that something obviously did. Philip is listed as single now, with the notable status change occurring only a couple months ago.

Wren clicks through to his now-ex-wife's profile. Her name is Kathryn, and to Wren's delight, her page is public. She spends the next twenty-five minutes digging through Kathryn's posts, analyzing cryptic poetry and song lyrics to conclude that something very nasty happened between them. The blood is bad. Kathryn won't come out and say exactly what happened, playing the role of the pastor's wife even after their marriage had ended, but whatever went on between them was significant.

After a while, Wren forgets her original purpose of hoping an old name from the original Butcher investigation would help her pick up his trail. Instead, as she clicks over to the public page for Philip's church, she wonders how there was even a friendship between these two men at all. Looking at Philip's social media presence, she has a hard time imagining how he and Jeremy would connect in any life, past or present. Philip's faith is front and center, although he wields it a bit like a weapon. He's got a quiet strength in his convictions, but his sanctimonious nature comes through even in his typed words on a screen. He has a family, however dysfunctional, and he seems to spend a lot of time helping people in his community, or at least bragging about helping. He appears to be a very well-liked pastor.

The only thing that raises Wren's eyebrow a bit is seeing how many women seem to appreciate his . . . guidance. They fawn over him like a rock star, leaving hearts on photos and gushing about his proximity to the divine. It makes Wren consider Kathryn's position a little more carefully. It seems as if there is something a little dirty about this shepherd.

She sighs, closing out Facebook. She has wasted too much time going down the rabbit hole of some stranger's personal drama.

Wren remembers how, just a few weeks ago, they were so hopeful that Philip Trudeau would be the lead that took them straight to the Butcher. When it led to a dead end, it felt as if the only thread to pull had been cruelly clipped. It's still strange to her that Jeremy planted Philip's name on a body for the sake of a red herring. Jeremy rarely did anything without a complex purpose.

She taps out a text message to Leroux, knowing that he won't hide the truth.

Am I losing it?

That's a loaded question.

Be honest with me . . .
do u think he's alive?

Oh, this is a serious
conversation?

John.

Well, I think it's entirely possible.

Do you really? You're not
just placating me?

When have I ever just
placated you?

True.

I think you know it better
than most. He's a cockroach.
He's looking to be around
for the end times.

Yeah.

You okay?

I just hate unfinished work.

I hear you.

He does too . . .

We are going to get him,
Muller. Focus on you.

She stares at the screen, feeling the day finally catch up with her. She's exhausted. A yawn escapes, dramatically.

I scared u today, huh?

She waits, watching his reply pause over and over. She knows Leroux is worried. Even *she* wasn't expecting to have an experience like she did in the bayou woods earlier. It was just something about that familiar air and that suffocating space. It was as if suddenly she had strings attached to a mad puppeteer. She lost all control. Her mind went into system override, leaving her helpless. It's a feeling she never wanted to experience again. She could see the fear on Leroux's face.

You couldn't scare me if you tried. But despite what you believe, you are a human being. It's okay to falter a bit.

Everyone keeps telling me he's dead.

It's already falling out of the news cycle.

Everyone sucks. Are you looking for confirmation that I am on your side? Consider this it.

Thanks, John.

Andrew says he really liked that band you suggested.

She smiles, recognizing that Leroux has done all the heavy emotional lifting that he can stand for the evening.

> Ha! Tell him to listen to the new
> album. It's a little different but
> still has the same ingredients.

He doesn't respond, but she's not bothered by it. It's not a slight, it's just how he works. He's never good at goodbyes or long texting conversations. She is honestly impressed that she kept him going for as long as she did. She gathered the important information; he is on her side. Leroux knows Jeremy isn't gone. He knows this isn't finished.

She stands now, taking one last look outside at the night world, searching for villains in the dark. Nothing out there scares her anymore.

CHAPTER 8

THE TYTUS MANSION RUINS stand immense and powerful in an open field. Hidden away in the Berkshires, they represent a whisper of wickedness that suits the biblically significant address. As Jeremy hikes up to the site from the parking lot, he admires the four large stone pillars set against the late-afternoon sun. They are the only things left of the once-magnificent estate, and they don't disappoint.

Last night, he read that the home was built for Egyptologist Robb De Peyster Tytus in 1910 and burned to the ground in the early 1950s, after years of already enduring rumors of a bona fide mummy's curse.

After a short hike through a dense forest, Jeremy emerges through the trees, hypnotically following the undeniable lure of suburban ruins. They don't disappoint. Although they are breathtaking to see, they feel as if they are out of place in the quiet, boundless expanse of nature that surrounds them. Four inorganic, injured objects hover there among the wildflowers.

The tops appear charred, forever a visual testament to the disaster they withstood.

It's almost impossible to grasp the home that must have been attached to them and even harder to imagine the blaze that turned it all to ash. He has never seen them before. Even after he spent years visiting the Berkshires growing up, he had never heard the story. This was the one hidden gem he was compelled to visit.

He approaches the pillars as if they're a mad king. Somehow, they feel royal and almost bewitched in some way. There is something in the air around them that makes Jeremy's body buzz. He can almost feel the warning, the scream that was ignored before an entire estate worth of memories was reduced to four pillars in a field.

In the couple hours that he remains there, he sees only three people. They trudge in wearing visors and snapping photos on their phones. Most of them are immediately distracted. He mills around nearby, pretending to take in the ruins alongside them. They all tell one another the history, adding various embellishments along the way. He follows a couple into the decrepit foundations, keeping a safe distance but monitoring how they move and what draws them in.

He decides this is the place to begin. He is ready to make his presence known, but only to the right people. The local police won't have the resources or the experience to deal with a crime scene of this magnitude. It will allow him to remain completely invisible while sowing discord. He wants massive confusion. He can just feel her heart sink.

Has she already considered this? Has she considered that he may run *to* his past, as she runs from her own? If she hasn't thought of it already, he will have to force her hand.

The ability to take someone by surprise is important. It's imperative that he switch up his process a little bit until he is settled. This area seems as though it reached out to him. Surrounded by dark, deep woods and still a relatively quiet attraction, it lends itself nicely to an unplanned event.

The sun tumbles closer to the horizon and the evening golden hour takes hold. Long, spindly shadows fade into darkness. He waits, watching a couple in their twenties finish taking photos of each other, using the last of the light. They have been here for a while, moving all around this place. He immediately locked on to them when they arrived and now finds himself unable to shake that familiar feeling. It electrifies him, curing him. He feels ready.

While keeping to the perimeter, he studies them, tracing their movements. They are highly choreographed, making him think this is something they do often. The photos are entirely curated moments in time, without even a hint of authenticity. They set up the camera and pretend for a moment to dance as the sun fades out of view. But as soon as the shutter stops, the dance abruptly ends too. They break apart like magnets of the same polarity, rushing to check the images of their farce. He finds himself becoming angrier with each passing moment, absurd pose, and click of their camera. In a place of such solemn air, their indifference is vexing him, to say the least.

So he sticks around, not letting them see him. Crouching behind the broken remains of a once-grand fireplace, Jeremy quietly readies himself. After taking his small pistol crossbow from his bag, he inserts a bolt in it for ease of use once he is within range. He impatiently waits for his moment, listening to their conversation, fueling himself further in the darkness.

"We should get going back." The young woman has an edge to her voice. She looks around nervously as the light dims, realizing they're the last visitors.

"I just want to get one more. Can you take one of me with the heart again?" The man doesn't even look at her. Instead, he tears his eyes from the camera only long enough to position himself next to a pillar vandalized with a red, spray-painted heart. He poses next to it, looking off into the disappearing light. Another sign of his unflinching ignorance.

"Craig, I already got some of you and the heart. Let's go before it's pitch-black. We have to walk through the woods to get out of here." She holds the camera at her side, refusing to snap a shot.

Craig sighs, throwing her a look that he has no doubt given her many times before. "We can cut through the field, Taylor. Just take a couple more."

Taylor shakes her head, holding the camera up and snapping a few quick photos. With each shutter snap, he changes his head position ever so slightly. "There. Now I want to leave."

He laughs, walking toward her and gathering her into his arms for a forced hug. "See? That wasn't so bad. Took you two minutes." He plants a kiss on her forehead. "Let's go. I want to get these edited."

They gather up their equipment and he slings the camera bag over his back.

She hesitates a moment, noticing just how dark it has become. "I don't know which way out is worse. I feel like the woods at least has a trail. What do you think?" She turns to look over the open grass in front of the ruins, scanning the darkness with squinted eyes.

Craig looks there too and then glances to the trail that leads into the woods. "Honestly, we are fucked either way." He says it seriously but then breaks into a grin.

"Shut up!" She can't help but smile at his teasing, playfully slapping him as he pulls her closer to him around her waist. Suddenly, they both flinch as if they dodged something, looking out into the darkness together. "What the fuck was that? Was that a bat or something?" she asks, horrified.

Craig moves his arm from her waist, a look of confusion crossing his face. Jeremy watches as he scans the field, trying to force his eyes to see farther. After a second, he shakes his head. "Probably. It was wicked fast. It almost hit me in the head, I swear."

She rubs her arms, shivering noticeably. "Okay, that's our cue to get the fuck out of here now. Let me wear your sweatshirt, I need a hood for this."

He throws his arm around her shoulder, kissing her head again. "Come on. I am here to protect you, right? Any animal that wants to get to you has to get through me." He jokingly flexes his other arm, and before he has time to register it, a cascade of blood sprays across his face and into his mouth. He reflexively removes his arm from Taylor's shoulder, only to see her drop to her knees.

She gasps and sputters, holding her throat, blood spraying in great amounts onto the marble below and onto his jeans.

"Taylor!" Craig screams, grabbing her hands and finally noticing the medium-sized crossbow bolt sticking out of her throat. Her eyes are wild, the whites are like lights in the dark. She sucks in air greedily, but it does nothing, escaping out of her throat instead of making its way to her lungs. Craig kneels beside her and yells. It's a primal yell that makes Jeremy's core radiate warmth. The feeling of a real hunt has eluded him for a while. This is where he is meant to begin again.

Craig grasps at her, not knowing whether to pull it out and not yet considering where it possibly could have come from. He fingers it gently, unable to even comprehend what it is. He pushes her hair back and tries to calm her, oscillating between primal yells and calm whispers.

Jeremy stands, watching and knowing they can't see him yet. He can't help but be pleased his first missed shot was mistaken for a bat. Craig fed him the perfect line to facilitate the perfect shot to his intended target. He observes Craig's confusion and fear. It meshes with grief and shock to create a stunning visual on his face. Taylor's sputters have almost completely stopped, making way for wet gurgling sounds instead. He holds her limp form over one knee, soaked in her blood and staring into her dead eyes. They aren't bulging anymore. They are sleepy and hooded, not focusing on anything.

Then it's like someone hits a reset button, as Craig realizes danger is nearby. Craig's eyes suddenly dart around frantically. He gently lowers Taylor onto the concrete and stands slowly, backing away from her as if she's on fire. Dropping his bag, he takes off running, jumping over a retaining wall and into the woods. He's smarter than Jeremy gave him credit for. He had been sure he would run into the field.

"This way is more fun," he says to himself as he breaks into a sprint through a back exit. He's on Craig quickly, running parallel through the trees as Craig runs down the path toward the parking area below. It's a long, winding, and sometimes treacherous hike with fallen trees to trip over.

Jeremy stops short. He waits, knowing Craig doesn't see the large log in front of him as he glances back over his shoulder. Craig hears Jeremy's running suddenly fall silent, and that small distraction costs him his footing. He hits the log hard with his shin, toppling over it and landing partially on his face on the rocky path. His cheek tears open and he skids to a stop, before lifting himself up as quickly as possible with his injuries. Jeremy takes the opportunity to shoot the crossbow. He misses again, reloads fast, and takes another shot. This time the bolt hits Craig's ankle, eliciting a satisfying snap as the bone fractures.

Craig is on the ground, grasping at his leg and howling like an injured animal. Jeremy observes the way his face distorts with pain and fear. It's dark, but Jeremy's eyes quickly adjust. He walks out from the tree line and makes his way closer to Craig, who fights to stand. He senses Jeremy's approach and starts to move forward, dragging his injured foot with him. He grasps his thigh, trying to propel himself down the path and away from this place as quickly as he can.

Jeremy doesn't run. He doesn't even pick up his pace. He follows slowly behind him, giving the man space to fight for his life. Finally, Craig looks over his shoulder and sees Jeremy's dark form following him. The whites of his eyes are visible as they open wide with terror. He sputters, pulling himself faster down the rocky terrain. The path slopes downward. He pulls himself over fallen limbs and rocks, now keenly aware of the predator stalking him. Jeremy never gains on him, though. He lets Craig work. Jeremy lets the fear build. It feeds him. He feels the panic in the air, so thick he could grasp it in his hand. It's such a clear, unseasonably warm night and when the moon shines just right through the trees, he can see the sheen of sweat on Craig's face.

"Who are you?!" he yells, growling in pain.

Jeremy smiles. "Don't worry about that. Worry about what you are going to do if you get to the bottom of this hill."

Craig spits, grabbing a tree trunk for balance, and spins to face his pursuer. "You sick fuck, why don't you face me like a man, huh?" He leans down, grasping a rock in his hand and holding it, ready to throw it at Jeremy's shadowy form.

"That's an interesting way to phrase that, Craig." He grins, knowing Craig can't see it. He stands just far enough for his features to be obscured in the darkness. "Should I act more like you? The kind of man who makes his nervous girlfriend take another photo as the sun sets?" He steps closer. Craig stumbles back. "The kind of man who gets so much satisfaction out of an image of his own face that he allows someone to impale his girlfriend with a crossbow bolt?"

"Fuck you!" Craig snarls, launching the rock at Jeremy. He attempts to dodge it but it hits him hard in the shoulder. A searing pain shoots down his arm. Jeremy's amused fascination turns to blinding anger. His rage blooms like a brush fire. It's quick and unstoppable. Craig senses the switch and he takes off, leaving the path and rushing into the dense brush that lines it. Jeremy races after him, no longer interested in leaving any distance between them, and gains on him easily.

"Oh, I get it!" Jeremy yells, sliding his knife from his ankle holster. "You're the kind of man who won't be found until the fucking maggots hatch!" He easily grabs Craig from behind, pulling him down hard as Jeremy readies the knife at Craig's throat. Craig reaches up, fighting with whatever strength he has left. He pulls the back of Jeremy's shirt up, trying to hood it over his face. For a split second it works, and Craig wriggles his body free from Jeremy's grasp.

Jeremy recovers quickly, using his ability to work in the dark to his advantage. He reaches forward as Craig struggles to stand. Enraged, Jeremy grabs the man's hair, twisting a handful of brown curls with one hand. Grabbing a stone in his other hand, he brings it down hard on Craig's temple. The sound is a sickening crack. Now a crumbled heap on the forest floor, Craig coughs and sputters, reaching out to grab anything around him, unable to focus.

Jeremy sits on his knees for a moment, catching his ragged breath. After he has calmed himself, he places a palm on Craig's forehead, dragging the knife quickly and deeply across his throat. Jeremy makes sure he hits bone.

Like a man.

Blood soaks into the ground and Craig's eyes flutter as he chokes on his last breaths. There is a strange throat or chest rattle that occurs before the final lament. It's subtle, but it's there if you listen for it.

Jeremy was once surprised to find out that the death rattle was real. He didn't hear it clearly with his first victim. Maybe he wasn't prepared to listen for it back then. It was his third victim who revealed the sound. She lay there on her back, in the middle of his guest room, as she had been for hours. He walked into the room to observe her and that's when he heard it. It sounded like someone spilling a load of beads onto a plastic dish.

He remembers the excitement and intrigue he felt, crouching next to her to hear it closer. He wanted to bottle it up and display it. It's such a uniquely horrific sound. Every ragged breath sucked in, there it was. Now, it catches him off guard every time, but it is always a welcome jolt.

He listens for it, whenever someone is tumbling into that delicate place between life and death. He can spot it now. He sees them go there, and he follows them whenever possible. Like a visitor sneaking through a briefly open but typically secured door, he enters a place he shouldn't have access to otherwise. It's a uniquely voyeuristic experience, watching someone turn into the husk we all eventually become. He learned there is no pain in this place, just a ghastly sound and a body finally giving up. Although the lack of pain frustrates and confounds him, it's that helplessness that pleases him in the end.

The human body is a wonder. It's a perfectly imperfect machine that embodies both exquisite fragility and indomitable strength. Hearing something that formidable finally give up and bend to his relentless will? Well, it's the closest he has ever felt to a god. Once he felt it, he knew there was no going back. It's imprinted in his DNA, and he will chase it forever. Lucky for him, he doesn't have to do a lot of chasing.

This time, it doesn't take long before the rattle comes to a whispered stop. It's a welcome silence. Jeremy sits back on his heels, taking in the stillness of the forest. He finds himself almost meditative, listening to an owl nearby. The sound is comforting but haunting. It's a slow, deliberate call that sends a chill up his spine. Usually, that sound is a warning to animals around the owl that a predator is nearby. It's an emergency siren to those who wish to heed it. Jeremy can't help but close his eyes and smile. He's the predator they are sounding the alarm for.

He stands, pulling the bolt from Craig's ankle and putting it back into his bag. He leaves him there in the underbrush and makes his way back up the short distance to the ruins.

There, lit by the moonlight, is Taylor. He stops, looking up at her crumpled figure from below. From this angle, she almost looks like an ancient sacrifice. The visual is something out of Greek mythology, with the crumbling pillars standing above her as crimson tendrils of blood drip off the sides of the stone. She looks beautiful and tragic. Her skin, no longer blushing, appears porcelain and fragile.

"Now *this* is a photo worth taking," he says to himself as he climbs up to approach her body. The silver light allows him to see every detail before him. Her hair is splayed out around her head like a halo, her eyes stuck open and not yet milky. They look to her right, as if she is gazing over the open field.

He puts a hand on her head, bracing her against the ground as he pulls the bolt from her neck. It isn't easy and exits with a visceral sound of ripping muscle. Her mouth falls open slightly, as if she wants to yell. He puts the soiled bolt with Craig's and takes a small scalpel from his kit, lifting one of her wrists to the moonlight. The blade glints as he lightly cuts into her flesh, making deliberate movements and varying the depth of each stroke by design.

When he is done, he manipulates that arm to be outstretched next to her on the white stone. He makes one last cut to her wrist and stands, admiring his work. He smiles, looking from her body to the open field on which her empty gaze still falls.

He takes one last look at Taylor before making his way down the path from the opposite side of the ruins. It's a quicker, easier way back to the road and parking area. If only Craig had taken the time to notice his surroundings, he may have outrun his death. Jeremy's sure that Taylor would have enjoyed the gardens from this path too.

As he makes his way back to his stolen vehicle, he knows this is the beginning of it all. This is what will bring Wren out.

CHAPTER 9

THE CALL COMES in the middle of the night. It always comes in the middle of the night. As her phone rings louder, Richard snorts. He sits up, unceremoniously roused from sleep. Wren yawns, flopping her arm out to the side to shut off the sound.

"What the hell? Is that an alarm?" His voice is just a mumble as he rubs his face with his hand.

"It's Corinne." Wren says the name almost in the form of a question.

"Corinne? Should I know what that is?" Richard's patience wanes as he pulls up the covers.

She sits up, unplugging the phone. "Corinne Matthews, from the Salem PD."

"I'll just wait to be filled in later." He relents, turning over.

"Hello?" Wren answers, trying to clear the raspy sleep from her voice.

"Wren? Wow, looks like you haven't completely abandoned your nocturnal life, huh?" Corinne chuckles. Her voice is the kind that always translates a joke better. Everything Corinne says sounds like a stand-up routine.

Wren smiles. "You know I can't resist a good two a.m. phone call. It's in my blood at this point."

"I heard about everything, but I should have known you could never truly take time off," Corinne responds. "Give it to me straight, would you self-destruct if you stopped moving?" Wren can hear the grin in her voice.

"Corinne, is everything okay?" Allowing her eyes to adjust to the dark, familiar room around her, Wren steers the conversation back to its original purpose. She can hear some bustling in the background on the other end of the phone. Muffled voices and sirens make this call seem important.

"Right to business, I see. Look, I know you are trying to take time away, but there is something happening up here that may be of interest to you." Corinne pauses, letting Wren's silence encourage her to continue. "We have an attempted homicide that looks like it could fit your guy."

Wren flinches at the choice of words. "My guy?" she asks, already knowing the answer.

"Listen, you have a missing and very capable killer. I have a barely surviving victim that fits the profile and was left soaking wet near a New Orleans–themed bakery named Fais Do Do."

As soon as the location is mentioned, Wren's mouth goes dry. "No one saw the drop?"

"A worker at the bakery saw someone about an hour ago. The bakery is open all night and sometime around one a.m., they saw what they believed to be a man skulking around the establishment. Didn't catch a drop, but it's a promising lead."

Wren furrows her brow. "Why would they pick a place that's open all night?"

"That's exactly my question. There aren't a ton of all-night places around here. He picked one of the only ones and it happens to be a New Orleans–themed bakery? I gotta be honest, I don't believe in coincidences." Corinne chuckles to herself.

"Neither do I. What are the injuries? It doesn't look like an accident?" Wren asks.

"She's got evidence of prolonged torture. Ligature strangulation around the neck. It's a clear attempted homicide."

Wren rubs her temples. "It sounds familiar, that's for sure."

Corinne speaks to someone on her end of the phone before returning to Wren. "It seems like a bit of a long shot, I know, but he's on the move and has ties up here, right?"

Wren's response is silence as she struggles with the idea that someone is clinging to life after meeting him. It's all feeling too familiar. It's all feeling too much like a horrible new beginning. The wheels in Wren's head begin to spin. Too much is falling into place for this to be a coincidence. She knows Corinne wouldn't bring this to her without cause to believe it's connected somehow. Wren finally breaks through her silence: "He's a survivalist of sorts, so it's possible he could be there. Hell, he could be on Pluto."

"I'm thinking he hasn't made it to Pluto just yet. Again, I come to you on my knees here. I was hoping you could catch a flight to Boston tomorrow and give us some more insight into the similarities?" she asks with clear desperation in her voice.

Wren shakes her head at the request. Something is pulling her away from Louisiana to finish this. It feels as if the universe has plans that she is trying fiercely to ignore. But the more she shuts it out, the harder it comes calling for her. She silently reminds herself that she is in control.

"I'll see what I can do. Is she able to communicate?"

"Unfortunately, no. We are hoping for a miracle, but short of one, we'll be relying on your expertise."

"Okay. Give me some time to think this over. I'll let you know as soon as I can."

Corinne sounds relieved that the option is still on the table. "Great. And I'm sorry for waking you. Old habits and all that."

"Not a problem. I'll talk to you soon, Corinne." She hangs up without waiting for a proper goodbye.

Richard has sat up now, looking at her in the dark with worried eyes. "What's going on, Wren?"

She turns on the bedside lamp. "He may have failed in Massachusetts," she says, her voice tight.

"Failed? There's a survivor?"

"Barely. But Corinne needs some insight. Remember Corinne Matthews? We went to undergrad together." Wren pulls a sweater over her T-shirt, smoothing it out over the fabric.

Richard squints. "I think I remember her. Was she like, a random lab partner that kept in touch or something?"

"She came to our wedding." Wren tilts her head in disbelief.

Richard shakes his head, puffing out air. "It's unfair to ask me to remember anything at two a.m., Hun."

She allows herself to chuckle lightly, putting her hair into a casual bun. "I will give you that."

"Where are you going?" Suddenly he's alert and full of questions.

"I am just going to sit downstairs for a bit. I need to clear my head before trying to go back to sleep."

"Ah, no need for new nightmares, right?" He smiles, rubbing the back of his neck. "Mind if I join you?"

"Please," she says, already heading down the stairs.

When Richard enters the kitchen, she is already washing out her favorite coffee mug. Coffee helps her think. It's a smooth way to transition from brain fog to clarity for her.

"Of course he can't lay low. He can't cool down." Wren scrubs the mug, holding it over the sink and punishing it with a sponge.

Richard leans against the counter, watching the assault happen. "You want to tell me what that mug did to you?"

She stops scrubbing, staring up at him. "Richard, I don't know what to do."

He relents immediately. "I know. We knew this was a possibility, but we couldn't have prepared for it."

"I am so sick of his presence." Wren slams the mug down, wiping her hands with a towel.

"I fully resonate with that feeling." Richard sighs.

Wren braces herself against the counter, looking through the window into the darkness. The sound of the coffeemaker is loud and intrusive. It sputters and spits before finally start-ing a steady stream. "I am unsure how to feel here."

"Well, what exactly did Corinne say? I know you said Massachusetts, but what did she say, exactly?" he asks.

Wren sighs, knowing she owes him more context after giv-ing him the truly vague rundown in their bedroom. "She told me there is a body in Massachusetts that matches his particu-lar brand of brutality."

"I'm sure you have already considered this possibility, but couldn't it be a copycat? Or even just someone as fucked in the head as he is?" he asks.

"I initially thought that was it, but they were dropped out-side of an all-night New Orleans–style bakery. There's also evidence of torture with ligature strangulation. I would bet my life that she was strangled and revived several times." Wren pours coffee for both of them.

Richard recoils. "I'm sorry, what?"

Wren chews at her lip and slides into a chair at the kitchen table, cradling her hot mug. "Mmhmm. It's not a common way to try to kill someone, but it's one of his favorites."

"I would love to argue this, but it seems too disturbing to be anyone else." Richard sits down with a heavy exhale.

"Yeah," she says quietly.

For what feels like an eternity, they sit together in silence. Wren can see the thoughts turning over in Richard's mind. Inside, they fight for his attention. She can't even slightly blame him. After all, she can't decide which of her own take prece-dence over the rest, either. There is too much to figure out and not enough information to conjure up an appropriate reaction.

"Where in Massachusetts?" Richard finally asks.

Her eyes flick up at him. "Salem."

Richard can't help but laugh uncomfortably. "That seems pretty on the nose, doesn't it?"

"He *is* theatrical. It makes sense. Maybe it makes too much sense, but he has never let that stop him."

"You're thinking about going, aren't you?" He's staring off into the window above the sink.

Wren pauses, thinking it over before answering. "I have to be a part of ending it. I can't sit by passively, or I will always feel a little uneasy."

"You don't feel like you have done enough? You survived him, twice. You walked into the line of fire to try to end it. It isn't you that he outsmarted; it was the police." He points to emphasize his words. "If it wasn't for you, they would have believed that dead decoy. You tipped them off immediately. Every second counts in those scenarios, Wren, you know that."

She looks at him. "He got away, right in front of us. It wasn't just them; it was me too. I hesitated. If Will hadn't been there . . ."

"Will was there. But it was their responsibility to finish the job."

"I just have to know if it's him, Richard."

He nods, finally relenting. "I know."

"I have to decide pretty quickly. But I'll think it over some more."

"I'll come with you. I have some vacation days to burn. Let's make it a trip."

Wren smiles weakly. "Thank you."

"Someday we'll go on a vacation that doesn't involve death, at least not intentionally." He smirks.

Wren chuckles, rubbing her eyes with her palms. "Man, I wonder what other people talk about over coffee at three in the morning."

"I am sure it's nothing we would be interested in."

"I'm sorry," she says, unexpected tears beginning to prick at her eyes.

Richard quickly turns to face her, knitting his brows together. "Why are you apologizing?"

She bites at her lip again, darting her eyes back and forth as memories start to crash through her brain. "There's so much that I regret."

"No way. Stop that. You have absolutely nothing to be sorry for. Do you hear me?" He taps his hand on the table to get her to meet his eyes. When she does, he locks her gaze there. "Nothing," he repeats.

She half smiles and looks down. "I feel like I could have done a lot of things differently." She absentmindedly runs her fingers over the wood grain under her hand, tracing the grooves over and over. "I know that kind of thinking doesn't help now that I can't change it, but it doesn't mean I don't regret a lot."

"I know what happened, Wren. It's part of your story. I accept every part of you. You know that." Richard's eyes really look at her. He always really looks at her. It is the kind of gaze you receive only from someone the universe placed on Earth for you. That's why it hurt her somewhere deep to reveal that he didn't know the whole story.

"I know. I just . . ." She stops, taking a deep breath in and slowly letting it go. Richard is now on high alert, sensing something is wrong. Right on cue, he clicks his tongue. It's his tell. His poker face is disastrous. "What is it?" he asks softly.

Wren pauses before the words can come. "It's just, there's another layer here. It's weird, and it's shameful, and I haven't reconciled it yet. So I think that's why I haven't told you about it."

Richard smiles uncomfortably, shifting in his seat. "You're kind of freaking me out a little here. But just tell me what it is, and we can talk through it."

"I'm sorry." Her eyes can't stay on him for long. They anxiously dart around the kitchen as she tries to find the words. "Jeremy and I were close."

Starting there doesn't feel as ghastly, so she lets her eyes meet his own briefly to get a sense of his reaction.

He nods slowly, waiting for more. "I know that, Wren." He quickly drops his gaze to his folded hands in front of him, then flicks his eyes back up to her again. "How close?"

She lets her eyes scan the cabinets to the left of Richard's head again. "It wasn't just a friendship . . . not really. I mean, we never truly dated," she says slowly, "but he seemed infatuated with me. He almost courted me, if that makes sense." She closes her eyes, shaking her head to clear the strange memories that march through it.

Richard's lips are pursed as he tries to take in the information she clumsily relays to him. "Sure," he says softly.

Wren is struggling to keep up with the emotions that fight their way in front of the facts. "No, of course that doesn't make sense to you, it's horrific." She says this fast and smiles as she always does when she doesn't want to cry.

It's only now that she realizes she may never have been ready to talk about this. No one knows this part of the story. She has never even spoken these feelings or questions aloud before. It feels as if she opened an ancient door only to let a fast-acting virus loose on her alone.

"I suppose it was just him wanting to hunt me, though? I was a worthy adversary, maybe. I don't know," she says with an uncomfortable laugh as tears start to fall. She wasn't expecting to feel like this, to work through all this in real time.

Richard is still looking at her. He rubs his chin, then drops his gaze as he presses his hand to his forehead. After a moment of what Wren assumes is a sudden stress headache, he returns his hand to his chin. "You're upset because you were interested in him too. You were attracted to the person he was pretending to be." He throws the prediction on the table with confidence, but it's clear he is hoping to be wrong.

A bit stunned, Wren lets her breath fall from her mouth all at once. "Yeah, I mean . . . I guess that's an accurate way of describing the situation." She wasn't expecting the truth to be launched at her like that. "You actually said it much better than I could. It wasn't him; it was a character he crafted for me." There is a strange sense of relief before her overactive mind smothers it back down. "But I fell for it."

"Listen, I get why you didn't tell me this part before." Richard takes her hand in his. "He's not human, Wren. He could manipulate anyone. It's not your fault a monster was fucking obsessed with you." She can feel his anger and protectiveness pulse through his fingers.

But it isn't Jeremy's previous feelings that haunt her; it's her own. Her mind races and she squeezes Richard's hand before pulling her own back abruptly.

"No, it's shameful, Richard. I let him touch me. I let him kiss me. The things he has done, I can't believe it was the same person." She uses her hands to cover her face, feeling tears spill over onto her cheeks.

"Wren." Richard's voice softens, attempting to tear her out of her memories.

She's too deep now, swimming in the damage. "That day in the woods. He used it. It's like he thought he could bring me back to that place with him. It's so bizarre and unsettling." Wren can taste the salt from her tears, and she finally lets them flow freely. She remembers back to that night at the bar. A whole group of students had gone out to celebrate after midterms. She and Cal had been in this nebulous flirtation for months.

As Cal, he was always mysterious but made his interest in her known. She liked that she had captured his attention. Even if he was a little odd, he was undeniably handsome. They were alone at some point, watching their friends dance and laugh. They sat together in the dark corner and just talked. They talked about school and books and outer space. It felt different, as if it were all building to that moment. After some liquid courage, he tucked a stray hair behind her ear and kissed her.

It was brief, but she felt chills as he gently held the back of her neck. It was a move of possession, but it didn't register back then. She remembers every single movement, now understanding how calculated they were. He knew he had her where he wanted her.

Richard doesn't speak right away. He lets the emotional tidal wave recede before he breaks the silence. "It's obvious that he is a great actor, Wren. He figured out what he needed to be for you, and he became it." He takes a sip of his coffee before continuing. "You have moved so far past that. Frankly, your taste in men has never been better."

She moves her hands away from her face and he gives her a cheeky grin. Richard's smile is perfect, not crooked or cruel. She shakes her head, giving into a cathartic laugh. "Thank you," she says.

He leans back in his chair, still wearing a smirk. "This is the first time I've seen you cry since that day. I know you're fighting hard against the whole 'healing' notion, but this is a good start."

CHAPTER 10

Jeremy wakes up in a stranger's bed again.

His body moves against the stiff vacation-bed sheets, picked for the intermittent holiday and certainly not for comfort. They are made of the kind of fabric that never truly gets soft, and he wonders if they came right out of the package and onto the bed without even being washed first. The sunlight snakes through the blinds, and he sits up, looking around the room for a moment before swinging his legs over the side of the bed and standing up. It's still yellow. It's still piss yellow, just as it was when he crawled into the bed the previous night.

His sleep was deep after such a chaotic evening. He had stood in the shower for a long time. He watched the water around his feet turn pink with blood as it poured off his body. It swirled around as if he were dropping dye into it. He spent some time just staring at it until the water turned clear again. It was soothing. When he left the bathroom, he was calmer than he had felt in a long time.

Now, as the sun creeps through his borrowed window, he resists the urge to pull the blinds up and instead peeks through them. A mourning dove coos a tragically somber song. Over and over, the high trill is followed by three low moaning sounds. When he was younger, he was sure the sound was an owl. The vocalization has the same haunting quality, but there *is* something that distinguishes it from its more traditionally spooky winged counterpart.

As he wanders into the kitchen, his boots clunk against the floors, shattering the silence. He didn't want to take them off. He even thought about wearing them to sleep. His plan was to live in them 24/7 to reduce the possibility he would be forced to run or fight on a wooden floor with only socks on, but he decided to take his chances for a good night's sleep. There is just no way he can bring himself to lay his dirty boots on a bed. As an act of self-consolation, he instead slipped his feet into them as soon as he woke up. He will spend every waking moment with shoes on now. There are a lot of things he can do barefoot, but he's not looking to make his life harder. He's looking for ease of movement. Otherwise, mistakes get made and corners get cut—two things he wants to remain unfamiliar with.

The house is cold this morning and his skin feels like the touch of death. He runs his hand over the back of his neck, feeling the icy sting as he tries to use friction to warm it up. He glances at the thermostat on the wall but doesn't bother with it. They are all different and he would rather stay cold than risk throwing the temperature into an erratic place. He wonders if it is on a timer, because the chill wasn't as significant the night before.

His thoughts have been focused on simply getting from one place to another without detection. He has had to be consistently vigilant. He has been taking in nothing else, allowing his brain to block out everything except thoughts of survival. But he's never been someone who could push off tasks and plans. His mother always called him *obsessive*, curling her lip into a disgusted snarl as she spewed the word out at him like venom.

"People are going to think you're stupid, Jeremy. You *obsess*." She would draw out the sounds like a serpent. "No one wants to hear you talk about the same thing all the time. Jesus Christ." His mother would always punctuate a sentence with something biblical. It was her way of shaming him, but it just confused him more than anything. Being a sinner was never something he felt compelled to avoid. Even through the constant guilt and the sermonizing, it felt like nonsense.

From early on, he wasn't willing to subscribe to a method of thinking that involved actively shaming yourself on a daily basis. Shame is a waste of energy, a waste of emotional bandwidth. It's rare for people to truly even feel it when they are "supposed" to. The degradation that woman would heap onto her son always surrounded situations he didn't feel a lick of shame about.

See, part of her problem was that she was a lousy saleswoman. She evangelized and insulted, throwing her self-righteous dog shit in every direction, but through it all, she never even slightly sold the idea of shame to him. There wasn't ever a reason behind it; it was just something he was supposed to inherently feel because she said to. Well, that wasn't good enough for him.

Poor selling skills aside, his mother could expertly cut someone down with her hateful tongue. She housed an arsenal of razor-sharp weapons behind her teeth, and when she started wielding them, it was like a good old-fashioned public stoning. Yet for her, the words never held any type of weight. She tossed them around easily, never caring that someone else might struggle under their burden. She was the strong man in a freak show, routinely forcing a one-hundred-pound emotional dumbbell on her child.

But she's dead.

Now he finds it easier to trail off a bit and allow his attention to shift, even when he has a task that needs to be completed. Her absence has afforded him that, but only for brief moments that feel as if they are there purely out of spite. Because his mind always snaps back to attention, never straying from its true purpose long enough to relax.

That's why it hits him hard as he walks into the kitchen trying to rub the cold from his neck. The magnitude of this suddenly plows into him and he begins to wonder if Wren is here. There is something crackling in the air, but he can't identify it yet. Whatever it is, it feels important, as if everything around him is begging him to take notice.

Wren can't be here, he thinks to himself. *I would know it.*

He spoons the weak coffee into a filter, overfilling it and beginning the brew. As it coughs to life, he leans against the counter to let the air speak. Although he is sure she isn't near, he's confident she will be soon. It's taken years for him to listen to his gut. For most of his life, he ignored it.

He smiles to himself, appreciating the way he feels branded onto her. There's an unparalleled bond between a killer and a victim, whether they survive or die. It's like how one twin will know that the other is suffering or sense when they are nearby. Jeremy held Wren's life in his hands once. He twisted the knife that was intended to snuff it out. Although it may be unwelcome, she can probably sense him too. She is surely beginning to know where she needs to go, and he is beginning to feel that shift in her. She's like a dark soulmate, tied to him despite their current distance.

His plans must start pushing forward, but once the distance closes, he'll need to redirect his attention as much as possible. It may be time to call in a favor from years ago. Jeremy always told himself he would never bring someone else into his world, that he would never share this work. People don't ever deserve trust. He learned that hard truth a long time ago. If his mother taught him anything at all, it was that finding someone to trust would likely elude him his entire life. Without realizing it, she delivered that lesson perfectly and almost daily. Aside from expressing her revulsion toward her only child, providing a harsh reality about deceit was one of the only consistent things she did.

But sometimes, with the right bit of coercion, people can be useful. Most can be guided to set off in a specific direction, like a toy top with purpose. It's all about power, and information is *real* power. Once you gather a bit of curious information about someone, they are pushed below you almost immediately. You have something they want or something they don't want to be released. Tangible things are feeble in that way. They don't hold up to the power of information, of words. Fortunately, Jeremy has held on to a slice of information for all these years, long enough for it to mature into a beneficial tool for him to use.

This is a new place, a new playing field. It makes sense to bend the rules a bit. You don't start a new page by drawing the same thing you always have.

After pouring some fresh coffee into a mug, he spoons the honey in with a splash of the cream that teeters on the edge of spoiling. Stirring it together and taking a slow sip, he thanks this home again for already having honey and cream still in date.

It's time to make bigger moves here, and as he opens the book on the coffee table again, he feels the same way he did the night before. He feels drawn to some of the places listed, but nothing can match his own memories. Nothing can take the place of his own nostalgia. And who better to share it with?

CHAPTER 11

WHEN WREN WAKES UP the next morning, the world feels scarier.

She tossed and turned all night before finally giving into exhaustion for only an hour. It was thankfully a dreamless sleep, but she woke up feeling completely drained. He's making his way out of her nightmares and into her real life again.

She keeps replaying it in her mind, trying to somehow erase pieces of it and analyze others. She swings her legs over the side of the bed and taps her bare toes against the carpet. She feels panic when she thinks about everything she told Richard after Corinne's phone call. It brings the same sick feelings back to the surface and she taps her toes harder and faster, watching them as she does.

Dr. Roy had suggested she look at something innocuous when she feels rising panic or stress. The idea is to stare at something, something like your toes, and just appreciate that they're ordinary. Sometimes dissociating into an uncomplicated thing is calming; it reminds you that everything isn't as bad as it seems.

So she stares at her toes. They are painted. Well, they *were* painted. The dark red polish from three weeks ago is chipped and almost completely gone. It's polish from before. She painted these nails before she knew anything about Jeremy Rose returning to her life. She had painted them with ignorance and its best friend, bliss. She would give anything to go back to that place, so she looks at her toes and thinks about that innocence.

After a moment, her heart slows down and she can breathe slowly. She takes a deep inhale through her nose and releases it through her mouth. After checking her phone, Wren rises to her feet and heads downstairs.

The smell of fresh coffee greets her and she quickly fills up her mug.

"Morning." She forces a smile.

Richard leans back in his chair, folding the paper. He's a morning person, always has been. "We heading to Massachusetts?" he asks.

"Can I have some caffeine first?" she asks, completely caught off guard by his greeting.

"Of course." He places the paper down and sips his coffee. "How did you sleep?"

She sighs, rubbing her hand over her tired face. "Not great."

"I figured as much," he responds.

She looks at the news playing on the small kitchen television. Her nerves feel as if they are on the verge of collapse, but the world is just beating on. It's another one of those dis-associating moments, only this one isn't comforting. It's even worse. It's unbelievably irritating to watch war and politics surge forth with no regard for her problems.

Shaking her head away from the doom cast on the screen in front of them, she looks back at him. "I guess I should start packing."

He purses his lips, taking his phone out. "Are we going to be in Salem proper?" he asks without missing a beat. If there is anxiety inside of him, and Wren knows there is, he is hiding it completely. He appears calm, cool, and totally unbothered.

She nods, making a mental packing list.

Richard nods too, his eyes scanning his phone screen. "Essex County?"

"Mmhmm," she answers, still making her checklist.

"If this is him, he's going to do a lot of damage up there." He scrolls through his phone, clearly scanning through some search results related to crime rates.

She sighs. "I know. There's no way that department is ready for someone like him."

A heavy silence settles between them. She knows what Richard is worrying about. He's thinking about Wren jump-ing back into the fray. He's looking up crime rates in areas of the country they never would have thought to visit. Richard's alarm bells have begun to sound, but he's going to play it off for now. It's Wren who breaks the silence this time.

"There is another way to look at this, though," she says.

He doesn't look up, still glued to internet statistics. "What do you mean?" he asks.

"Well, he doesn't have the cover there. He can move a little freer here, counting on other monsters to make the water murky. Up there, he's going to stick out like the demon he is."

He nods, finally putting his phone down on the table in front of him. "I guess that makes sense. Isn't that kind of scarier, though?"

She raises an eyebrow. "Not sure what you mean."

"Let's say this is really him. He went up there knowing what you just told me. He went in knowing that, but he still went for it." Richard leans forward, absently playing with his wedding ring like he always does.

"I suppose you're right. But it's to his own detriment," she says.

He nods in agreement. "It's definitely reckless."

"It's hubris."

"Whatever it is, it's still concerning. Hubris or balls, he's got nothing to lose now."

She knows Richard is right. He's looking at the situation the way it should be looked at, through the lens of concern. Wren has become so competent in the art of evisceration; she even does it to things she can't physically touch. She pulls situations apart and dissects the pieces she feels she can critically handle. She wants to do the same now. She doesn't want Jeremy to have that power over her anymore. She wants to release the hold he has on the part of her that fears him. But that isn't what is going to make this go away. He won't stop just because she wants to move on.

CHAPTER 12

H E WALKS UP A DIRT PATH, leading to his destination. The sun is just now setting, bleeding out across the sky like a beautiful wound. Oranges and pinks leak through the clouds, staining everything he can see. It's a slow weep of color before darkness smothers it completely.

The crumbling Great Barrington Fairgrounds lie lonely and forgotten next to bustling Main Street. There's a busy grocery store across the road of passing cars, but even with the buoyant civilization a stone's throw away, the fairgrounds, pushed back off the road in a beaten field, feel isolated. Mountains loom above, dominating the abandoned relic, and the thick fog rolling down them threatens to swallow the grounds whole. But the remains still exist, even as the world closes in around them.

He steps past the NO TRESPASSING sign, forcing his way through the overgrown weeds that snake out of the cracks in what's left of the concrete pathway. It leads to the decaying skeletons of six ticket booths. In the distance, a watchtower hovers over him. For a moment, he stands staring up at it. There is something imposing and authoritative about it. The aged wood flakes and cracks, bending in treacherous ways, threatening to come tumbling down at any moment. It's too big. It feels as if it will tell his secrets, but something about that excites him.

"One ticket, please," he says to the ghost in the booth as he saunters through. He chuckles to himself, letting the crisp air bite at his skin. As he walks in farther, that watchtower does what its name suggests. He wonders if people ever go up there anymore. He and Philip used to sneak up the old steel ladder in the summer. It was always at night, away from bees and the obvious threat of a trespassing charge. They would look out over the town, casting judgment over everyone and everything as they drank beers and ate whatever delicacy their combined change would buy them. Many Ouija board portals were opened up in that watchtower, and he feels as if he stands under the watchful eyes of all the spirits they conjured up. They judge him tonight, but he doesn't mind at all. He likes the feeling of existing for their amusement. It's another world out here where time has halted, but nature carries on.

The grandstand lies ahead of him now, though. It's a massive structure, stretching open above what was once a grand staircase. As he climbs to the second floor, he passes decades of graffiti. At the top of the stairs, he casts a flashlight around the space, igniting the emptiness and scattered debris in an eerie shade of yellow. This place is good. It's vast and unnerving in the best way. There is a lot working to his advantage at the fairgrounds, which are abandoned and cocooned by noise on all sides. There is a hum created by the traffic that consistently hurries by, and life continues to thrive in every direction. No one is paying attention to the long-forgotten carny village that forms its nucleus. He's hidden in plain sight.

Scanning the space, he notices piles of ancient papers and dead leaves strewn almost everywhere he can see. He swings his bag down off his shoulder and it hits the floor with a thud, sending dirt and dust into the air. Millions of tiny particles come into view in the flashlight beam. He can't help but think about his lungs. They must be screaming at what he has breathed in tonight.

He takes two things from his bag and quickly buries them under a pile of debris in a corner for when he returns. He takes note of a spray-painted pentacle on the wall above the pile. Even if he doesn't use it as a locator for his tools, it adds to the theater of it all. Throw a pentagram on anything, and simple-minded people go right off the deep end. Satanic panic never began, and it certainly never ended. It's always been around, and it always will be as long as there is a demand by red-faced preachers to fund their private sins. If parishioners' cups continue overflowing with a heavy dose of bullshit and fear every Sunday, satanic panic is here to stay. Personally, Jeremy loves it.

Grabbing his bag, he makes his way back out of the grandstand. He descends the stairs slowly, allowing his eyes to adjust. The air has changed, and the light has disappeared completely. He walks toward the perimeter, taking a spool of thin wire out of the bag. This arena reminds him of his compound back home. The message will be clear.

This is where he will bring his next victim. He intends to bring chaos to this place of quiet reverence.

Only a few people are left milling the sidewalks of Great Barrington. It's close to midnight, and everything is closed for the evening, just how he wants it. He crosses the road onto Railroad Street, holding a bouquet of flowers in a tight grip. Two dozen all-white Southern magnolias threaten to spill out of his hands.

The florist in Connecticut had tied fall-colored ribbons around the bouquet, and although they have started to wilt from their journey, they haven't lost even a bit of their charm. As he walks through the dark center of town, the flowers' sweet citrus scent wafts up to touch his senses. It's refreshing and strong, reminding him of home. His house was always surrounded by magnolia trees, and he had specifically loved the long-lasting blooms that carried into the autumn months. They were always one of the last ones to give in to the seasons' metaphorical hourglass. They stay as long as they want to, and they don't apologize for it. They maintain their beauty and their delicious scent until the bitter end, never bowing to a forced curtain call.

He supposes that all this could be why Wren chose them for her wedding bouquet. After all, she can certainly identify with something tirelessly stubborn and unwilling to die when they are supposed to. A woman who chooses *Wren* for a name is rigidly deliberate. A wren is known for being resourceful, curious, and bold. They will take on bigger birds without hesitation and they will do absolutely anything to survive. Choosing the wren as a namesake makes a statement. Absolutely nothing she does is incidental or a result of chance. There is no doubt in Jeremy's mind that magnolias were a very conscious choice for her big day and not just because of their Louisiana roots. They are who she is, and up until now, she has lived her life in accordance with this character that he wrote for her, though she still tries to live as if they were qualities she was born with, as if she created Wren.

But there is always a chance that he is wrong, of course. Perhaps she chose these flowers to symbolize the hardiness of her impending marriage. Maybe she chose magnolias to represent good fortune and stability for their life together. Regardless, she chose them.

Now, he's choosing them too.

Walking the sidewalks, he pauses at each business that lines the street. He places a magnolia at every doorstep he passes, even the ones hidden down art-covered alleyways. Tomorrow, there will be a subtle smell of lemon in the air and a swath of white at every address. It won't cause panic. It likely won't cause anything, except for some confusion. But it will be talked about.

And it will get to the right people. Cops sure like to talk. Eventually it will make its way to John Leroux and the rest of them. They will bring together the brain trust again to try to make up for their recent failures, but it will be John Leroux who takes it personally. He will be the one to step outside the lines of jurisdiction, and he will drag Wren with him.

Of course, pulling Wren here won't be easy. There is likely a whole army of people tasked with keeping her hidden and docile. Coaxing her out of her safe haven won't be as simple as dumping a body in plain sight. It will require a bit of outside aid as well, but he's already working on that. Bringing her out of hiding will be a slow, meticulous dance that requires patience. Jeremy has the patience.

"Oh, how pretty!"

A voice cuts through the quiet, making him immediately go on the defense. When he turns to see who it comes from, he is surprised to see an older woman, bundled up and admiring the flowers in his hands. She smiles genuinely and waits for him to speak. He doesn't. Instead, he just stares at her.

"Is this for an event tomorrow?" she asks.

He shakes his head, deciding to play along. "Actually, it's for a proposal."

She claps her hands together, delightedly. "Oh! That's lovely! What a thoughtful way to propose."

"Thank you. I hope it will really wow her." He puts emphasis on the *wow*, knowing that it's partially the truth.

"How could it not?" she asks, kindly.

He chuckles, tossing a flower in front of the doorstep next to him. "It's late. You should be careful going out alone."

She waves her hand dismissively. "Oh, I do this all the time. When I can't sleep, there's nothing like a brisk walk in the night air to calm me."

"It *is* very peaceful around here."

"Well, I've kept you too long. You finish up your beautiful display and early congratulations to you!" She places her hand on his arm as she walks by, giving it a friendly pat. It immediately irritates him. He doesn't like an uninvited touch.

He nods, watching her make her way down the street, to the corner of the sidewalk. She takes a right and heads toward one of the smaller neighborhoods, hidden outside the more bustling center of town. It's disconcerting to him that this woman feels so comfortable walking alone at midnight. This place is different. It's challenging to navigate when people act as if there is no danger lurking out in the dark. This community feels remarkably unafraid. He wants to change that.

As he comes back down the other side of Railroad Street, toward the main road, a car stops at the light up ahead with its windows down and music playing loudly. "Dancing in the Moonlight" by King Harvest blasts from the speakers, cutting into the late-night air. The driver moves his shoulders smoothly, feeling the music as he absentmindedly idles at the red light. Jeremy can't help but do the same, putting a sway into his hips as he drops flowers along the way.

He knows now that it's time to make a move. The seal must be broken, because the courtship has begun.

CHAPTER 13

"That was the first time I have seen you sleep soundly in weeks." Richard smiles, throwing their bags in the rental car and jumping into the driver's seat.

Wren sighs, feeling rested as she rolls down the car window and breathes in the crisp air.

"Just stick me on a plane and fly me above it all." She smirks, leaning back in the seat.

Richard chuckles, straining to figure out where to turn and fiddling with the navigation system. "You're like a baby who needs a car ride to sleep. Only, you're more expensive."

She laughs, yawning and helping him enter the address onto the screen. "We can go straight to Salem Hospital."

He nods, turning down a one-way street the minute they pull out of Logan. "Shit!" he yells, immediately throwing the car into a U-turn.

"Just don't kill us before we even get there," Wren jokes.

"I'll do my best." Richard grins back at her.

It's different here. Despite the ominous reason they came, it still feels lighter somehow. She looks back at Logan Airport, forgetting how they even made their way through it and to the car. They walked in silence with each other, knowing they had touched down somewhere possibly tainted by poisonous hands.

As they make their way through the maze of exits and entrances that surround the airport, she allows herself to disassociate. She looks at the afternoon sun dipping lower in the sky, welcoming the lights of the city, and plays her favorite game. Each time they pass a building, with the lights on and most of the blinds open, she asks what the people inside are doing. She wonders who they are and what they are worried about. When they stop at an intersection, she decides to include Richard in the game.

"That window up there." She points to an open one with twinkle lights strung across the top of the walls. "What do you think they are doing up there?"

Richard looks up, taking it in for a second before answering. "Maybe a college kid? I feel like they're probably stressed about finals or something inconsequential like that."

"Inconsequential?" She scoffs. "Since when are finals inconsequential?"

He chuckles, seeing he hit a nerve. "Well, how many times have you been asked your final exam grades as an adult?"

"Well, the med schools I applied to were pretty curious about them," she answers.

"That's not fair; med schools ask for a promise of your first-born too."

She rolls her eyes, looking at the window again. "I don't think it's a college kid. I think she's an artist."

He nods, pulling away from the building as the light turns green. A car behind them beeps almost immediately. "Tell me more," he implores, shooting the driver behind him a nasty look.

"She probably has a new job, the one she has been waiting for. It's a really complex but rewarding situation, you know?"

"Of course," he says. Wren suspects Richard might be lying to keep her happy. He knows this is Wren's way of easing anxious thoughts, so he plays along.

"And she's working her ass off to finish this project up in time for a deadline. If you listen closely, there is music playing loudly. It's maudlin, the kind I always picture an artist creating to. That apartment is probably cool inside. I bet she has a great snack drawer."

"Wow. That weirdly made sense," he answers.

She continues her description, seeing this woman in her head now with curly hair pulled up into a messy bun. Her overalls are sloppy, with paint stains all over, but she looks cooler than Wren has ever hoped to look. She's effortless, even in her anxiety.

"You gonna answer that?" Richard breaks through her thoughts and motions to her phone, vibrating madly in the cup holder. She hadn't even noticed it while she floated through her creative exercise.

"Hey, John," she answers, seeing Leroux's name.

"You in Massachusetts yet?" he asks without any real greeting.

"We just landed and are headed to Salem Hospital."

He sounds irritated. "Well, we have two bodies in another part of the state that are almost certainly Jeremy's victims."

"What?" Wren's blood runs cold and she almost yells her question. "What, um, w-what do you mean?" She tries to recover her voice, take the panic out of it, but it's still there.

He sighs. "It's a man and woman. There are details we need to go over together. I'm catching the next flight I can."

"You're coming up here? Is Andrew?" she asks, her mind suddenly racing in ten different directions.

"No, he can't get coverage this quickly for the restaurant. But I'll be there. There's no way I am leaving you to handle this all yourself."

"Thank you. Text me your flight details and anything else."

"Yeah, I think the town is called Tyringham? I'll send you everything as soon as I can." He seems flustered, not a good sign. Wren always thinks of Leroux like a flight attendant on a plane. If they look scared, you should start panicking.

"Okay, talk to you soon."

She hangs up, letting the information settle. Finally, Richard cuts through it.

"What's wrong? You look like you've seen a ghost." He strains his eyes, making sure he's not turning into oncoming traffic.

"Looks like the *real* deal is in"—she reads through Leroux's incoming text—"Tyringham. It's in western Massachusetts."

"Massachusetts still? *This* isn't the real deal?" Richard's tone is confused and slightly annoyed.

"That's what John said."

Wren reads over the details again, gulping down the feeling of sand in her mouth.

"Oh, this is bad," she says quietly. "Two bodies. Man and a woman. Crossbow wounds, and the man was found in the woods. He's hunting again." Her stomach churns and she opens the window to get some fresh air.

Richard gnaws at his bottom lip. "Okay, wow. All right. And John is coming up?"

She nods, then realizes he is driving and can't see it. "He's booking the next flight."

"Should we figure out a rental in this Tyringham place?"

"Yeah, we should. This is Jeremy. I can feel it. I had been thinking that maybe this Salem one is a copycat. My gut said it didn't feel right." She feels her whole body ignite in a way she can't describe. It's as if everything is telling her this is it and this is where she needs to be to stop him.

"You seemed so sure Salem could be the real deal. Should we go straight to western Mass?"

"No, I promised Corinne. Even if it *is* a copycat, I need to be sure," she says.

"Got it. We are about thirty minutes away."

As the lights of Boston begin to disappear behind them, she prepares herself for the unknown.

CHAPTER 14

THE BAR IS CROWDED, even for a weekend. Locals collide with "leafers" who converge upon New England like a vicious plague as soon as the first leaf begins its beautiful dance of decomposition. He's already spotted her.

She's a local, that much is clear. She makes small talk with a close group of friends, extending warm greetings to anyone passing by her table. She's striking, with waves of curly blond hair and effortless style. He likes that she stands out and she's clearly well-known. It's the kind of victim that would really cause an uproar. She won't be cast into the bowels of the papers so quickly. She's above the fold, front-page news.

Jeremy hangs back, studying her movements and her conversation style, trying to plan his method of gaining entry into her space. After a few minutes, it's already clear to him that she will be an interesting challenge. She's a fast talker with quick wit, but she's got an irritatingly whimsical sensibility. He sips his drink, listening to her explain the benefits of bee pollen, and it's in that moment that he almost abandons ship. But despite himself, he remains committed. At its core, her argument sounds like nonsense, but there's something about her enthusiasm and delivery that makes her formidable. He won't be stocking up on bee pollen anytime soon, but then again, neither will she.

An hour passes and then two. As the evening trudges forward, her table dwindles in number. Somewhere around midnight, she's left to her own devices while her remaining friends take a smoke break. She doesn't join them.

Seeing an opportunity, and having gained the right amount of information about her, he begins.

"Excuse me." Jeremy lifts his finger in the air, signaling to the bartender at the other end of the bar. The man is speaking to a couple patrons, leaning his forearms onto the bar top and likely counting the minutes until his shift is over. In a place like this, tips get fewer and irritants multiply as the hours get later. It takes him a second, but he notices Jeremy midconversation. He nods an acknowledgment, throwing a rag over his shoulder as you see in the movies.

"What can I get ya?" the bartender asks, appearing in front of Jeremy with his eye on the clock.

"I want to send a drink over to that woman." He points at her without looking back. The bartender's eyes narrow as he follows his finger.

"Blond, curly hair?" he confirms.

Jeremy nods, taking a sip of his old-fashioned. "She seems health-conscious, talking about clean eating and Pilates. What do crunchy people drink? Some kind of wine spritzer?"

The bartender looks suspicious. "You been eavesdropping on her tonight, brother?"

Jeremy wrestles with the urge to break his glass and shove it into this man's neck. Instead he simply looks into his eyes, tightening his mouth into an expressionless line. When he speaks again, his words are measured. His voice takes on a darker tone, a way of usually suggesting to his prey they've waded into dangerous waters. A warning shot. "Eavesdropping? No, friend. I am just interested. Ever been interested in a stranger?" He spits the words out with venom.

"Got it." The bartender shakes his head, not wanting to bother with an altercation this late into his shift. "What about an Aperol spritz?"

Jeremy smiles, adjusting his useless horn-rimmed glasses. "Sounds just soulless enough. Let's try that."

"Got an ID?" He holds his hand out, using the only stalling tactic he can think of.

Jeremy smiles, reaching into his wallet and removing Tom's license. He hands it over, taking a little too long to release his grip on it. It's risky, but he likes the feeling of being this close to discovery. He likes that this man is feeling something come off him, something sinister. The bartender keeps his eyes locked on Jeremy's before dropping them to look over the details on the ID in his hand.

"Tom?" he asks.

Jeremy nods.

"Can you tell me your birthday, Tom?" he asks, trying to remain authoritative.

Jeremy grins, glad he memorized the information necessary for this kind of useless interrogation. "July 5, 1984."

He can tell the bartender is fighting with the part of himself that feels something is off. He hesitates briefly before handing back the ID and turning to make the drink. Jeremy watches him battle silently to make the right decision, but instead, he finishes the cocktail with an orange wedge. Before he can slide it over to him across the bar, Jeremy slips a twenty in front of him.

"Do me a solid and bring it to her?" He grins widely, keeping one hand on the cash.

After a moment, the bartender grabs the money and slips it into his pocket. He is reluctant, but money talks. Carefully weaving his way to the table just behind Jeremy and to the right, Jeremy watches him place the drink in front of her. He says something quiet and points in his direction. As he does, she begins to turn, but Jeremy faces the bar, only catching the exchange through the mirror that lines the back of the bottle shelf. She's a little stunned but accepts the drink. She taps her nail on the side of the glass then stands, crossing the room with it and sliding into the seat next to Jeremy. He smells her perfume. It's clean, with a hint of citrus. She's like a glass of fruit-infused water. He doesn't look at her yet.

"Thanks for the drink," she says dryly, placing it on the bar in front of her.

"You're welcome," he replies, still not looking at her, but allowing a crooked smile to play at his mouth.

She lets out a short chuckle of a breath. "Yeah, I wouldn't look so smug. You didn't nail it."

His eyes, which had dropped casually to look at his own drink, flick back up angrily. He turns to look at her face. She looks distorted and more unappealing than her mirror counterpart. He supposes everyone looks better with the aid of inversion. "Is that right?" he asks, not caring about her response.

She shifts in her seat, flipping her hair back over her shoulder. "I don't really do spritzers. I'm a gin and tonic girl."

"Wow, I was that off the mark, huh?" He tries to say this with a strictly playful tone, but a little bit of anger colors the words as they roll off his tongue.

She feels it but tries to salvage the moment. "Yeah, I guess you were." She holds her hand out. "I'm Charlie."

He shakes it firmly. "Tom."

"Bad drink instincts aside, it's nice to meet you, Tom." She smiles, showing nice teeth.

He smiles back, not because he feels it, but because he knows that's what she wants. He flags down the same bartender, who eyes them both. "Can I grab a gin and tonic?"

Trying to assert herself, Charlie begins to pass her card across the bar as payment. Jeremy stops it, placing a gentle hand on top of hers and throwing her a reassuring grin. "On me." He slides another twenty to the bartender.

"Thanks." Charlie smiles.

"So, are there any other surprising aspects of your personality, Charlie? Are you a yoga girl?"

She raises an eyebrow, not knowing whether to be offended or amused. "Um, I like yoga, yeah. What made you ask that?"

He laughs, sliding the fresh gin and tonic in front of her. "I heard you mentioning it earlier."

"You were listening to my conversation?" She's half kidding but wears a look of slight discomfort.

"Jesus, you know you're in a public place, right? Why is this very normal thing so nefarious to everyone around here?" He's annoyed by the paranoia. Back home, people are much friendlier and willing to meet a stranger. It works to his advantage. He doesn't ever have to break a sweat before the good part. At this point, he doesn't even care if she walks away. In fact, he's feeling recklessly angry and almost welcomes it.

But she stays put, and surprisingly, she laughs. "I overheard the bartender give you shit about it before he even brought me that drink." She takes a sip of the gin and tonic, flicking her tongue out to taste what's left on her lips. "You should lighten up."

He puffs out a breath and shakes his head, smiling organically now. "Cruel woman." He holds his drink up and she clinks it with her own.

"Do you always get so worked up when people challenge you?" she asks.

"People don't challenge me much," he responds flatly, keeping his eyes locked on hers. He's still irritated, but the reckless energy is dissipating. Replacing it is a controlled compulsion.

She raises her eyebrows, almost incredulously. "You asked me if there were any surprising parts of my personality? I'm not entirely sure what that means, but—I like taking risks."

"You drive without a seat belt, do you?" he teases, making sure she feels his patronizing tone.

She smirks, defying his apathy. "I like not knowing what will happen or whether I'll be home on any given evening."

He nods, swirling his drink. "Interesting. So, is it that you like adventure, or you like the possibility of being kidnapped?"

She smiles wide, taking a sip of her drink. "I like adventure. Spontaneity is the best part of life." She doesn't put on any air of flirtation. To her, this is a genuine moment of connecting with another human being. To Jeremy, it's torment. As she talks, he tunes her out, watching her face and taking the moment to study her features up close. Her nose is interesting and slightly crooked, but he likes it. She has lips that remind him of a rosebud, with the top one appearing slightly fuller. As he studies her, she suddenly appears slightly uncomfortable. Her story has finished, and she is looking for an appropriate response.

"Yeah, I am a planner, but I can appreciate the sentiment of spontaneity." He clears his throat, wondering how to keep this conversation flowing without any semblance of common interests.

Fortunately, she likes to talk. She takes another sip of her drink, looking at herself briefly in the bar mirror. "You seem like you need to let loose a little, Mr. Planner." Now the flirtation breaches her carefully curated exterior. She's lost herself for a moment in the idea that he is interested.

"You know, that's exactly what I was hoping you would say. There is nothing I love more than to hear how much better my life would be if I surrendered to chaos and irresponsible whims." He's officially irritated now, but he's committed to punishing her for it.

His shift in attitude catches her off guard. She looks stung by the sharpness in his words. "Let me get this straight, refusing to plan every second of your life means that you are chaotic and irresponsible? Do you know how insulting and generalizing that is?"

He lets out an undetectable sigh and continues to swirl his drink. "Probably about as insulting and generalizing as telling a stranger that they need to loosen up." He looks up at her out of the corner of his eye and smirks.

It disarms her immediately. Her hardened expression melts into flushed cheeks and she shakes her head. She plays with her necklace, a delicate gold chain with a single emerald charm attached. "All right, I guess you got me there."

"How about I guess your sign." He lifts his head up, looking at her with endearing eyes.

She bursts out in a laugh and asks incredulously, "My sign?"

"Yeah, your zodiac sign. Come on, I know you're into that."

"Okay, here you go with the assumptions again." She tilts her head, trying to feign a look of offense.

Jeremy lets a full smile cross his face and gives her a knowing look. He doesn't say anything, but the look says everything.

"Fine. Even a broken clock is right twice a day. Go on and guess." She has shifted her body to face him openly now. Her guard is dropping.

Jeremy takes a moment, pretending to really think it over before answering confidently, "You're a Leo."

One of Charlie's eyebrows shoots up and she leans forward, putting her chin in her hand. "Wow, what makes you say that?"

"Why? Am I right?" he asks.

She bites her lip. "Maybe. But first I want to hear your answer. Why am I a Leo?"

He takes a sip of his drink, breaking their eye contact to look down at his glass. She's looking for a deep, insightful answer. She wants to hear him validate one of her own foolish interests. He won't do that, and it won't matter. She's hooked, even if he continues his subtle assault on her character. He answers, "Honestly? Your hair reminds me of a lion's mane."

She sits back, giving him a look of incredulity. "Seriously? That's it? Just my hair?"

"That's it. You have lionlike hair," he says.

She looks equal parts amused and irritated. "I was waiting for you to surprise me," she says with a tinge of disappointment in her voice.

He smiles. "Despite my whimsical exterior, I have no knowledge or understanding of astrology."

She can't help but chuckle now, leaning in again to close some of the distance between them. "I knew that would have been too good to be true. It didn't fit you." She locks her gaze with his again. "Do you even know your sign?"

He looks at her with a raised eyebrow.

"I figured." She digs in her small purse and produces a laminated card from her wallet. It's intricately designed with metallic flourishes, and it lists all the zodiac signs and their date ranges. "Here. Take a look at this."

Jeremy looks it over quickly before sliding it back over to her. "Apparently I am a Capricorn," he says flatly.

"Wow, that makes sense."

"I'll take that as a compliment. More importantly, was I right? Does your hair foretell your inner animal?" he asks.

She shakes her head. "No. I'm a Sagittarius."

"Nope. Come on, you made that word up," he answers.

"No, I didn't! It's a real sign. Sagittarians are adventurous, optimistic, passionate . . ." She lets the last trait hang in the air for a moment, never taking her eyes off him.

He's suddenly uncomfortable with her proximity, but he knows how to mask it. "Sounds like it fits you well." He shifts back a bit, still maintaining an air of interest. "Or is it the other way around? Maybe you have crafted yourself to be the perfect Sagittarius."

"Absolutely not." She scoffs. "It's just further proof that it's real."

He purses his lips, taking another sip. "Well, I'll take your word for it, I suppose."

"I mean, you knew to guess that I was a Leo. You must have heard that somewhere. Maybe there is a fleeting interest we can uncover?" she asks.

He shakes his head. "I only know what a Leo is because that's my mother's sign."

"So let me guess, your mother is confident, very warm-hearted, and generous?" She smiles, thinking she has started to crack him. She thinks she will get some nostalgic bonding experience. She has no idea what lies behind the door she just opened.

"On the contrary. She is egotistical, domineering, and childish. You know, a real lion." He turns his face to her, keeping his expression blank.

"I'm sorry, that must have been hard for you," she says, trying to reroute this ill-fated journey toward something healing.

He can see her wanting to fix him already. Her eyes are sympathetic, and she reaches out to lightly touch his arm. He rests his gaze on her fingers for a moment before looking back up at her face. "Honestly? It wasn't easy, but we have moved past it. I talk to her every single day," he lies.

She looks moved. "Wow. That's really amazing that you were able to form such a great relationship."

"Yeah." He quietly struggles to keep a laugh concealed. "Life is too short, ya know?"

"So true." She isn't quite putty in his hands, but at least she's intrigued.

The conversation turns to one that is almost wholly focused on Charlie. They talk about her hairstyling job and her favorite foods. At one point, the friends she abandoned at the table stop by to say their drunken goodbyes. As she introduces them to Tom, he carefully pulls his hat down closer to his eyes and he rubs his hand over his jaw to obscure the more unique aspects of his facial structure.

"I swear I'll bring you back your phone tomorrow morning," a woman who just kissed her cheek says with a grin.

Charlie looks relieved. "Oh my god, thank you! I keep forgetting I left it at your place. I feel like I am missing a limb." They laugh together as they plan for the next day. In the throes of conversation, her elbow knocks her small purse off the bar top. The contents spill onto the floor and Jeremy's eyes immediately lock onto a purple cylinder that rolls from the sequined bag. Before she can reach for it, he leans down and starts scooping everything back inside.

"Thank you, Tom." She places a grateful hand on his shoulder as he zips the bag back up.

"Of course." He grins, sliding the purse back in front of her and inconspicuously slipping that purple cylinder into his pocket. He waits patiently, politely nodding at her departing friends as they trickle by. Soon it's just the two of them. They carry on for another hour, maintaining a friendly but flirty exchange as he learns more and more about her.

She never fully surrenders to him, but she's clearly interested. Anytime she starts to fall into a bedroom-eyed discourse with him, it's as if she gets whipped back into reality. She shakes it off and brings the conversation back to a place where she feels as if she has the power. It's interesting to him. That kind of self-control intrigues him more than if she just gave in to her desire like the others.

After a long time, he shifts in his seat, deciding he can work with it. "Listen, you like adventure. Let's go exploring," he finally says.

"Exploring? What time is it even?" She sips her third drink, patting her denim pockets for her phone, before remembering again that she doesn't have it.

"Who cares? I thought you liked spontaneity." He smiles, letting his eyes convey nothing.

She lifts an eyebrow, something she does often, he has noticed. "What did you have in mind, exactly?"

"Ever explored the abandoned fairgrounds? At night, it's a trip," he says.

Charlie thinks for a moment, flicking her eyes around the emptying bar. "I've actually never gone. It's just down the street, right?"

He nods. "We can walk there."

"Let's do it." She slides off her seat, grabbing her purse.

"Excellent." He throws some cash on the bar.

As they walk through the room toward the door, he lets her walk in front of him. When they reach the door, she turns to face him, grinning. "Just so you're aware, I have mace."

He recoils only slightly but then quickly allows a smile to take over. "Wow, that's so smart. I promise you won't use it tonight." He is telling her the truth.

CHAPTER 15

WREN WALKS INTO SALEM HOSPITAL and looks around the lobby. The lights sting her eyes after the creeping darkness of the car, and she doesn't initially see Corinne. She got the call upon landing that the victim had died and would be heading to the hospital morgue before being sent to the medical examiner's office in Boston later that night.

"Wren Muller, as I live and breathe," says a familiar voice behind her, and she spins to meet Corinne's grinning face.

"Hey, Corinne." Wren pulls her old friend into a hug.

It feels as if Corinne doesn't ever age. The only difference between college Corinne and cop Corinne is a pixie haircut that accentuates her sharp bone structure and big brown eyes. She always projects warmth, winning anyone over with a brash sense of humor and a willingness to say what most people won't dare to. She's a welcome sight in this unfamiliar territory.

"Where's that big handsome lug of yours?" Corinne asks. "He come too?"

"Oh, Richard's waiting in the car for me," Wren says with a smile. "He's traumatized from Boston parking laws."

"Smart man." Corinne winks. "But I better be seeing him later."

"That's a promise," says Wren.

"Let's head down to the morgue. I let them know you were coming." Corinne gestures to a security officer and begins to walk. Wren follows at a brisk pace, with the guard at their heels. "How was your flight?"

"Very relaxing actually." Wren dodges a nurse. "Sometimes it's nice to float above it all, ya know?"

Corinne nods. "I can imagine."

They head down a flight of stairs, and the guard swipes his card at a double door, leading to another set of stairs. When they reach the bottom, he swipes again, and the door beeps open.

As soon as she enters the morgue, Wren feels competent. She feels comfortable and strong. All the doubt and stress of the last few weeks fall away and she's ready.

"Victim is a twenty-one-year-old female named Andrea Meyers." Corinne opens the walk-in refrigerator door, brushing past a technician who gestures for them to continue through. Wren nods an acknowledgment to the tech and follows Corinne into the deep freeze, grabbing a pair of gloves from a box on the wall.

"The ME in Boston will obviously give us the details and determine the entirety of this, but I just thought, and they agreed, that it would be wise for you to take a look"—Corinne pauses, unzipping the bag—"since you know *him*." She says the last bit under her breath slightly, as if it's a dirty secret.

Wren looks at the victim, Andrea. She's like a doll. Her skin is porcelain, with beautiful blue veins peeking through like brush strokes.

"Zip her up," Wren says abruptly, turning to the tech.

The technician startles, looking to Corinne and the security guard in confusion. "Aren't you going to examine her?" he asks.

"I am, but I need better lighting than the morgue, if you have it. Isn't there an exam room down here?"

The technician zips the bag closed, and Wren watches Andrea's green eyes disappear. "Yeah, I can bring her in there for you." He quickly pushes the gurney out into the hallway. Wren and Corinne follow, passing under dozens of hanging lights that flicker and sway slightly as their feet hit the floor. Taking a left and another left, they are brought into a small but well-equipped examination room.

"Thank you, I appreciate it"—Wren bends slightly to squint at his name badge—"Stephen."

"No problem." He smiles and takes a seat on a stool nearby, ready to help if needed.

Wren cranes the overhead light closer to the bag and unzips it completely. She looks around and grabs a blue towel from nearby, placing it gently over Andrea's chest and groin area for privacy. Even the dead deserve dignity.

With the better light, Wren immediately sees the deep set of ligature marks around her neck. They are crisscrossed and stacked on top of one another, all in various stages of healing. It's clear Andrea went through something very few can even imagine.

She runs her finger over the deep grooves in Andrea's throat and she can almost feel the woman struggle to breathe.

"See these?" Wren points to the scratches that tick under the ligature markings.

Corinne leans over, moving the light above them even closer to get a better look. "Yeah, my God."

"Those are fingernail scratches. She was unbound for some of the strangling, and she fiercely tried to loosen whatever was being used to strangle her."

"And her nails scratched this deeply into her skin?" Corinne is stunned.

Wren nods, counting each fingernail crescent in her head. Every mark a devastating reminder of how desperate for life this young woman was. "Wouldn't you scratch like hell to stop someone from stealing your breath?"

Corinne nods, taking a deep breath in, then releasing it slowly. "It's always a shock to me how evil people are."

"If it's ever not a shock, you should put the cuffs on yourself," Wren teases.

"That's a promise, Doc." Corinne slowly walks around to the other side of the table, never taking her eyes off Andrea.

"The fact that she wasn't bound tells me a lot. Jeremy Rose doesn't like to be bested. He wouldn't have let her fight. He craves complete control."

Corinne quirks an eyebrow. "Interesting. You think this is someone known to her instead?"

Wren nods, unable to take her eyes away from those fingernail marks. "I do. She was comfortable with this person.

At least in the sense that they didn't feel the need to tie her hands."

"We have some of our guys reaching out to her close friends and family. We will hopefully get some names or descriptions of people she may have been seeing or hanging around often."

Wren nods again, half listening, distracted by how deep the lacerations are on her neck. She lifts Andrea's head, moving her black hair away from the nape of her neck. Just as she guessed, there is a deep, purple mark on the back of her neck. The mark is bruised and there are narrow cuts into the skin. Little hairs at the nape of her neck have been shortened and stick out like newborn baby hair.

"She was garroted," Wren says to the room without looking up.

Corinne lets out a breath. "No way," she says quietly, walking over to stand next to Wren.

"Unfortunately, yes," Wren responds, showing her the horrific markings. "See, the stamping is an obvious giveaway, but see how her hairs are all short here?" She points to them with her gloved finger. "That's from hair getting stuck in the garrote. As they tightened it, the hair ripped and broke off."

"What a sick fuck." Corinne rubs her own neck in an instinctual response.

"The garrote made it easier for the assailant to release the pressure and then turn it up again without ever losing the control. That's why these marks are crisscrossed and haphazard. He let her get to the brink of death before reviving her several times, I'd say. This is certainly a familiar kind of brutality, but I still don't think this was done by Jeremy Rose."

"Really? You don't see this kind of prolonged torture very often. It struck me as close to his methodology."

Wren shakes her head. She moves Andrea's hair once more, searching her skull for lacerations or contusions. What she finds is a dried trail of blood that has leaked from her ear. Upon first glance at Andrea's face, Wren had noted the bloody nose. Putting it together with the ear, the garrote finishes the puzzle. As she looks more closely at Andrea's face, her eyes weakly drooping now in the haze of death, Wren can see the heavy makeup that covers them.

"I won't do it, but my bet is if the ME washes her face, they will find a healing black eye under all that makeup," Wren says. She wishes she could hit the rewind button and force Andrea away from whoever did this to her. Andrea's probably leaving behind an army of people who feared this day would come.

"So, you really don't think this is your guy?" Corinne asks, a tinge of disappointment in her voice.

Wren shakes her head, cringing at that same unintentional phrasing Corinne used. She shifts, walking around the table to move Andrea's legs outward. She studies the limbs, picking up on slight bruising. "Has she had a rape kit done?"

"They suspect she was sexually assaulted," Corinne says quietly.

"It's not him," Wren says bluntly, zipping up the bag and motioning for the technician.

"Damn it, I'm sorry I brought you here, Wren."

Wren pulls off a glove, placing her bare hand on Corinne's shoulder and giving it a squeeze.

"Don't feel bad at all. Strangely, it felt good to flex this part of my brain. I'm just sorry it's at this young woman's expense." She looks down at the bag being taken away, feeling a bit electrified.

"Well, I'm glad I could . . . help?" Corinne can't help but chuckle uncomfortably, always finding solace in gallows humor.

Wren rolls her eyes but lets a smile form on her face. "Besides, I have to head to Tyringham. There's another lead. This time I really think it's him. Leroux is flying in to meet me."

Corinne turns around in the hallway, giving Wren a look of shock. "Tell me everything."

CHAPTER 16

JEREMY FOLLOWS BEHIND CHARLIE, keeping his eyes on her as they cross the dark parking lot toward the road. The dirt crunches under their feet and a lack of streetlights makes the oncoming headlights feel blinding. The lights slice through the heavy darkness, forcing them to shuffle closer to the line of trees next to the road. They are nearly invisible to drivers, which would be dangerous if he cared. But this isn't an accident. He planned it this way. It reminds him so clearly of another night, more than twenty years ago.

"The back entrance is just around the bend up there." Jeremy points ahead of them, noting Charlie's unease in this dark.

"You don't happen to have a flashlight, do you?" she asks, her eyes darting nervously.

He reaches into his coat pocket, producing a small Maglite. He holds it up with a smile, clicking it on and casting the beam in front of them.

She is visibly relieved, allowing her shoulders to relax a little and chuckling to herself. "I'm glad you came prepared."

He can't help but smile to himself as the break in traffic seems to bend to his needs. "I always come prepared," he says flatly.

She is about to answer when the Maglite connects hard with her nose. There is a sick crack as blood sprays on his hand. Before she can conceive of what happened to her, he grabs her by the arm and pushes her through the dark trees next to them. They enter the thick mass of forest, and he violently throws her to the ground.

Charlie's crying now, unable to stand. She spits blood onto the ground, holding her nose while trying to rise from her hands and knees. She can barely comprehend what has happened to her, what will happen to her.

"Stay away from me!" She chokes the words out, shakily digging in her purse that's still slung across her body. At the same time, she scoots herself away from him, dragging herself blindly across the carpet of dry leaves.

"What are you looking for, Charlie?" He grins, lowering himself to his hands and knees. He slowly crawls after her like a slinking cat. She furiously backs away, not daring to turn her back to him, then searches through her tiny bag and sobs. He slinks toward her, maintaining a maddening distance until she stops and realizes what she seeks isn't there.

He stands, excitedly hovering over her shadowy frame below him. "Oh, are you looking for this?" He slips her purple canister of mace from his pocket, directing the flashlight toward it and allowing the beam to display it in his hand. Without warning, he clicks the safety off and sprays it in her face.

The shot of chemicals hits her directly in the eyes and she falls backward as if it were a bullet. She desperately claws at her eyes, coughing violently. When everything registers, her scream gets caught in her throat. In an instant, he traps it there with his hand. He sits, pressing himself down on top of her and holding his right hand to her throat in a tight grip. She chokes, prickly tears streaming down her face.

"Charlie, you should always know where your mace is. That was stupid of you." He dangles the canister in front of her, then shoves it back into his pocket. "Now, you are going to walk with me, and you are going to be silent. If you try to scream, I will pull your kidney out through your fucking belly button, got it?" His grin is wide and teasing. This is the release he was waiting for. If he wanted to, he could continue gripping her neck, applying consistent and continuous pressure until the light in her eyes goes out. But he's looking for a lingering high, not momentary ecstasy.

She nods and he releases his grip. For a moment, she seems to give up. She just stares at the distorted image of him bent over her in the dark. When he pulls her to her feet, she blinks, dazed, and tries to control the fluids flowing from every hole in her face. Blood drips from her chin, having made a pathway over the small swells of her lips. With a growl, Jeremy drags her through the dark, using the flashlight and following the well-worn old trail that he and Philip created when they were kids.

Part of him is surprised the trail still exists. It's still a windy, exciting path leading to something mysterious and dark. It ι and looking straight ahead. The light from his flashlight ιnces ahead of them, illuminating a path to pain.

She shakes her head to indicate no.

He stops, shining the beam of light directly into her swollen, red eyes, blinding her temporarily. "You can see the evidence right there on East Mountain." He points into the darkness toward the giants in the distance. "You've driven by it for years of your life and had no idea where those scars in the land came from?" He shakes her when he says this, jerking her arm hard. She squeals, almost letting out a true scream but not daring to.

After staring at her through the blinding beam of light, he suddenly takes a sharp left, toward the decaying grandstand. He pulls her along with him, marching through unseen debris and rotting wood. As he walks, he speaks.

"I heard the trees were all twisted where the tornado touched them. For weeks afterward, it sounded like gunshots kept unexpectedly going off as they started to naturally untwist themselves."

Charlie sobs quietly, trying to use her dead weight to slow his forward momentum. He just jerks her into position each time.

"Can you imagine that?" He raises his eyebrows and shakes his head. "It must have been a nightmare. Something right out of a Guillermo del Toro film."

The light swings back and forth, illuminating bits and pieces of this place. As they enter the grandstand, various papers are strewn along the sides of the floor, folding chairs are haphazardly lying around, and graffiti has taken the place

used to be littered with soda and be\[...\]
walked it with a Ouija board tucked u\[...\]
forbidden but innocent. They felt as if the\[...\]
tal to an unseen realm where the ghosts of \[...\]
hats and shiny shoes bet on horse races and at\[...\]
nival delicacy came from the booths at the end\[...\]
stands. It was a trail to adventure.

Now it's his. It doesn't belong to innocence any\[...\] maybe it never really did. Now, it's his carefully chos\[...\] to hell.

"An F4 tornado ripped through this place in '95, ya k\[...\] Hell of a storm. People died. Lives were ruined. I rememb\[...\] being pissed my first trip up here got postponed," Jeremy say\[...\] as they enter the fairgrounds.

"What the fuck?" Charlie yells, trying to yank her arm from his grasp.

Jeremy stops, allowing his mouth to form a playful smirk. "Don't be too sanctimonious, Charlie, I was like ten years old."

She struggles to keep a whimper from escaping her throat, wiping her mouth with the back of her hand and pulling slightly on the grip he has on her other arm. "I was five." She says this quietly, wincing again as if he might hit her. The only thing she can think to do is keep him talking. She doesn't realize that Jeremy has seen this tactic before. It's abortive and irritating. He turns it against her, drawing out the conversational tone of their encounter. False hope is the ultimate executioner.

"No shit? Well, you must have at least heard the stories?" He starts walking again, haphazardly pulling her along with used to be littered with soda and beer cans, and they only walked it with a Ouija board tucked under one arm. It was forbidden but innocent. They felt as if they had created a portal to an unseen realm where the ghosts of fairgoers in derby hats and shiny shoes bet on horse races and ate whatever carnival delicacy came from the booths at the end of the grandstands. It was a trail to adventure.

Now it's his. It doesn't belong to innocence anymore, and maybe it never really did. Now, it's his carefully chosen road to hell.

"An F4 tornado ripped through this place in '95, ya know. Hell of a storm. People died. Lives were ruined. I remember being pissed my first trip up here got postponed," Jeremy says as they enter the fairgrounds.

"What the fuck?" Charlie yells, trying to yank her arm from his grasp.

Jeremy stops, allowing his mouth to form a playful smirk. "Don't be too sanctimonious, Charlie, I was like ten years old."

She struggles to keep a whimper from escaping her throat, wiping her mouth with the back of her hand and pulling slightly on the grip he has on her other arm. "I was five." She says this quietly, wincing again as if he might hit her. The only thing she can think to do is keep him talking. She doesn't realize that Jeremy has seen this tactic before. It's abortive and irritating. He turns it against her, drawing out the conversational tone of their encounter. False hope is the ultimate executioner.

"No shit? Well, you must have at least heard the stories?" He starts walking again, haphazardly pulling her along with him and looking straight ahead. The light from his flashlight bounces ahead of them, illuminating a path to pain.

She shakes her head to indicate no.

He stops, shining the beam of light directly into her swollen, red eyes, blinding her temporarily. "You can see the evidence right there on East Mountain." He points into the darkness toward the giants in the distance. "You've driven by it for years of your life and had no idea where those scars in the land came from?" He shakes her when he says this, jerking her arm hard. She squeals, almost letting out a true scream but not daring to.

After staring at her through the blinding beam of light, he suddenly takes a sharp left, toward the decaying grandstand. He pulls her along with him, marching through unseen debris and rotting wood. As he walks, he speaks.

"I heard the trees were all twisted where the tornado touched them. For weeks afterward, it sounded like gunshots kept unexpectedly going off as they started to naturally untwist themselves."

Charlie sobs quietly, trying to use her dead weight to slow his forward momentum. He just jerks her into position each time.

"Can you imagine that?" He raises his eyebrows and shakes his head. "It must have been a nightmare. Something right out of a Guillermo del Toro film."

The light swings back and forth, illuminating bits and pieces of this place. As they enter the grandstand, various papers are strewn along the sides of the floor, folding chairs are haphazardly lying around, and graffiti has taken the place of paint on the walls. She trips over a piece of plywood lying in their path, awkwardly careening to the floor and barely able to get her hand out to break her fall. She scrapes her arms against the wood, feeling splinters pierce her skin. She lets out a cry, but Jeremy hoists her back to her feet without breaking stride. He is focused on very particular bits of this ruin.

"This." He stops her suddenly in front of an old white door. He points the light at it, tightening his grip on her upper arm to keep her upright. She blinks a few times, processing that this white door has been turned into a canvas. The artist spray-painted the words, "If you could live forever, would you?" On top of the written question, there is a crude drawing of what looks like a demon. She pulls back slightly, only to find herself thrust forward in front of it.

"Interesting question, right?" Jeremy asks, pulling the knife out of his boot. She faces the door, staying perfectly still, aside from her trembling he can see even in the dark. "It feels like everyone thinks they would. Live forever, never die. It's all very *Lost Boys*, right?" He chuckles, flicking the end of her hair with the blade. He twists a curl around it, relishing the way it looks.

Her eyes are closed in fear. He pauses for a second to admire her profile. It's delicate, like a painting of a long-dead noblewoman. A bead of sweat rolls down her temple, but she tries to remain stoic as he hovers the knife near her neck, casually twisting more pieces of hair around it.

"Would you?" he asks suddenly, pulling the knife back and moving in front of her now. "Would you live forever?" he prods.

She opens her eyes slowly, measuring her breaths and swallowing hard. He sees her throat bob. "No," she says, softly.

He grins, moving fully into her space. His breath ghosts across her face as he speaks. "Why not?"

"I'm assuming that everyone else doesn't get to live forever in this scenario." The words come out broken and quiet, but there is still strength under them that she is trying to thrust to the surface. She locks her eyes with his finally, and although they show her fear, she is overcoming the paralysis of the previous moments.

He laughs, walking around her now. He surveys her, smelling her perfume and noticing the way she fights her body's basic instincts for fear and protection. She must be experiencing the chills, as the hairs on her arms stand up, with noticeable goose bumps spreading across them. When he crosses back in front of her, he takes a second to admire her red cheeks. They're flushed from her blood vessels dilating as a result of her fight-or-flight response. Her sympathetic nervous system gives her away. She tries to quiet its screaming betrayal, but it's like trying to hide an infant in a silent room. It cries loudly, and she's ill-equipped to stop it.

"Well, Charlie, you'll have to forgive me. This question was sprayed onto a decrepit door in the middle of a field. Without the original artist, we are just left to wonder about the specifics, aren't we? Unfortunately, my world-building skills weren't sharpened for this occasion. So, leaping from *your* baseless assumption, I am using context clues to assume you wouldn't choose to live forever without your loved ones living forever too?" He gets close to her face as he speaks, ending the question by almost touching her lips with his own. He's so close, he can smell the sharp odor of fresh blood that still trickles from her nose.

She doesn't move back, although every cell in her body implores her to do so. He sees her flinch with every word, fighting herself. Her fear is powerful in its own way. He can't help but devour it. He usually views it as a treat, but tonight it's the entire meal.

"Yes," she says, flatly.

"That's really sweet," he says, mimicking her emotionless tone. "So, you don't want to live forever. But do you want to live until . . . tomorrow?" He grabs her arm tightly, emphasizing his last words.

Charlie almost collapses and lets out a sob that has been bobbing in her throat the entire time. She lets it fall from her mouth but catches it quickly, pursing her lips to hold it in. She's still trying to fight her system. He pulls her body back to her feet by one arm. He can see the closeness bothers her, so he moves his face right back into hers.

"You should answer me. I don't like asking twice," he growls.

She nods, tears rimming her irritated eyes.

"Wonderful." He pulls his face back with a smile. "I have a fun activity, if you're interested." Dragging her along again, he makes his way to a dark corner of the enormous innards of the grandstand. Shining his flashlight at a pile of old papers, he reaches in and pulls out a gun. Charlie's eyes go wide as she struggles to distance herself from his grasp. He digs his fingers hard into her arm, whipping her back to him. "Relax, it's a paintball gun."

She looks confused. Her brow knits together and her eyes dart back and forth, trying to make out something, anything in the darkness that surrounds their beam of light.

"You're very quiet, suddenly," he says, reaching into the pile again. He brings out a pair of night-vision glasses and places them over his head with one hand. "I thought you were the adventurous type! Didn't you say some shit about wanting to bungee jump or something?" He isn't even looking at her, fiddling with the paint gun.

Suddenly, another wave of strength punches its way from beneath the thick layer of fear, and she sets her mouth in a severe line. "Skydiving," she says angrily. "I told you I wanted to go skydiving for my next birthday."

He looks up, catching her defiant and angry expression. Something about his sudden disinterest has touched a nerve. It has motivated her to stand tall. He lets a smile creep across his face. "Skydiving, sure. I was honestly checked out of the conversation by that point, so you'll have to excuse me." He holds the weapon out to her, tilting it to show a safety switch. "Do me a favor? I can't flick that switch while holding your arm. Turn the safety off for me?"

She stares into his eyes angrily and shakes her head. "No." She says it loudly, trying to take command of the situation.

He releases a laugh, then wrenches her toward him roughly. "Turn off the safety or I use the real gun that's been at my waist the entire night." He lets his face go blank, boring into her eyes, daring her to call his bluff.

She hesitates, searching his eyes for deception before reaching out with her free hand to turn the switch off, effectively turning his docile toy into a real weapon.

"Great, thanks for being such a team player. Let's go over the gameplay. First, I am going to let you go."

She's confused again.

"Once you take off, I am going to try to tag you with paintballs. If I tag you twice, I get to use the real gun for my next shot and your time in the game will be coming to a swift end. Following me so far?"

She shakes her head, continuously whispering "no" over and over again. She pleads with her eyes as tears begin to fall, burning raw skin.

He continues, undeterred. "I'll take the crying as tacit compliance so far. There is a rule, though. If you make a sound, I use the real gun and end the game without completing the gameplay." He touches his forehead to hers and she closes her eyes tightly, trying to block him out. "And don't run into the road, promise?"

She opens her eyes. They are uncomfortably close to his and it mutates the look of them. He could tell she was fixated on them in the bar, the way they swirled as if they were painted by an artist's brush. Now it's probably like looking at a storm up close. The blue seeming to be swallowed up in darkness. She nods, only now being reminded of the busy road that lies just out of reach.

Jeremy notes the sudden change in her face. He smiles, knowing that she took the bait. The very mention of a reachable road gives her hope. That's exactly what he was looking to do. He wants her to run for the perimeter, and she's easily led to her own demise.

"Are you ready to play, Charlie?" Without hesitation he pushes her to the ground, slipping the glasses over his eyes and grinning wildly.

She hits the floor hard, slamming her arm into the wood at a strange angle. She instinctively grabs at it for comfort. But he advances on her, looming over her like an impending storm. Charlie scrambles backward, through the crumpled papers, and desperately tries to create distance between them. Her breath is mixed with choked sobs. Her eyes burn and blur even in the darkness.

As she finally gets herself to her feet, she takes off running into the stairway. Jeremy watches as she blindly trips down the loose steps. She stops briefly, listening for his footsteps. He knows she can hear nothing. She begins to catch her breath, hiding herself behind an old concession booth. But he won't let her rest. Lifting his weapon, he shouts into the stillness, "Run, rabbit!"

CHAPTER 17

Wren takes a bite of her burger and allows an indescribable noise to escape her as she does. "This burger is my religion."

Richard laughs, taking a bite of his steak. "Yeah, this is amazing too. Must be that Salem witchcraft."

Wren pauses midbite and stares at her husband. He catches her eye and winks.

"Yeah, I know. Bad joke, but sometimes you have to just let it happen, you know?" He follows it up with a sip of his drink and a shrug.

She bursts out laughing. "I respect that you committed to it, but never again."

"Did Corinne recommend this place?" Richard asks, changing the subject.

"Yes, and now we are forever in her debt."

He smiles. "She's hot shit, huh? It was like watching a comic do a tight ten last night."

Wren chuckles, shaking her head. "She really is. She's good people."

"You seem lighter," Richard says after a moment of comfortable silence.

Wren pauses, taking in the fresh smell in the air. "The morgue helped. I felt necessary and in control. I felt competent."

"That's what I figured. You know we all just want you to—"

"Heal. I know," she interrupts. "I appreciate all that. But I think this is how I heal. By doing what I am good at."

Richard grins. "By eating burgers the size of your head? Got it."

They eat greedily, feeling the exhaustive hunger from their last twenty-four hours. After they pay the bill, they head out into the dark Salem night.

Wren can't help but feel at peace here. It reminds her of New Orleans in a way, with its rich and dark history, quirky style, and unique shops. It hits her in a different spot, but it makes her feel cozy all the same.

"I want to take a walk through the old burial ground." She pulls Richard's arm, steering him in the direction of the graveyard that lies in the heart of Salem's historic district.

"You never miss a cemetery, do you?" he asks, looking around at the interesting characters that pass by them.

"Of course not, and this one is really something. It's the oldest in Salem and close to the oldest in the whole country. I thought *we* had the oldest." She drags him through the gates and takes it in. Right away, she can feel the history and the weight of this place. The stones are ancient looking. Some of them are broken and toppled, and others bear a weathered look that signals an era long past.

She pauses in front of a grave that sits off to the left, crouching down and touching it, letting her fingers caress the letters carved into the stone. It's an important gravestone, encased in granite to protect the original stone.

> *Here lyes interd*
> *Ye body of Colo John*
> *Hathorne Esqr*
> *Aged 76 years*
> *Who died May ye 10th*
> *1717*

"They spelled *interred* wrong." Richard bends over, squinting to read the epitaph. "Also, *lies*."

Wren shakes her head at the dad joke. "This judge is infamous."

"That name sounds familiar," he says, looking around at the other stones.

"John Hathorne is Nathaniel Hawthorne's great-great-grandfather. He was one of the most cutthroat judges during the Salem witch trials."

Richard crouches to get a better look. "I wonder what Nathaniel thought of great, great gramps."

Wren chuckles, excited to share information with him. Richard is a fountain of random knowledge and always teaches her new things. Whenever she can do the same, about anything outside of forensics, she takes the opportunity.

"Actually, Nathaniel once said something about John here having the stain of witches' blood on him." She didn't know what a heavy feeling this place would have. The burial ground especially feels sacred, full of tragedy and anger. It's a little frightening, but it's fascinating as well.

"Wow, that's a pretty brutal roast." Richard shakes his head, running a hand back through his hair. He's tired and punchy, with glassy eyes that look as if they could close while he's standing up.

"Well, he never apologized for his role in the trials! He was one of the only holdouts who never repented for how batshit it all was."

She begins to walk farther into the burial grounds, and she thinks about Rebecca Nurse. She had read once that Judge Hathorne was ruthless with her in particular. When Rebecca went on trial, no one had admitted that the court intended to murder accused witches. Hathorne tried to bully a confession out of the sick and elderly woman by informing her right in court that if she denied the wild accusations of spectral witchcraft against her, she would be labeling her accusers as murderers. This is how Rebecca found out that they intended to hang her. This is how Salem village found out what was at stake. It wasn't a game, it was a cleansing. The fear that Rebecca likely felt in that moment must have been unbearable.

Soon, they come across a raised tomb in a quiet spot of the cemetery.

"This looks like it belongs in New Orleans," she says, walking closer to it to get a better look.

"Who gets this treatment here?" Richard asks.

THE BUTCHER GAME   163

Wren can't help but run her hand over it, studying the name engraved on it. "Bartholomew Gedney."

"Oh, what's that tone I detect? Who is this fella?" Richard can't help but laugh a bit.

"So, I guess he's not *the* villain of the entire story, but he was a judge for the court formed specifically for the witch trials. He allowed spectral evidence and he really leaned into the hysteria of it all." She looks up, seeing the amused look of Richard's face. "I have a personal vendetta against any judge from that whole situation."

"Good news is they are all dead, so you win, I guess." He chuckles, looking around at the other stones surrounding them.

She smiles, playfully hitting his arm. "Man, I knew I would like it here."

They continue through the haphazard rows of gravestones, and after reading a particularly old epitaph, Wren looks up and freezes at the sight of a familiar figure.

"Whoa, this one is even older than the trials." Richard bends down, looking closer at a stone.

Wren doesn't reply. She just stares at the man standing by the entrance of the cemetery. He's tall, sticking out a bit from the group of people who surround him. They appear to be on a guided tour, but he isn't a part of it. He casually lingers on the perimeter of the tourists around him, periodically obscured by someone walking by. Each time she sees his face reappear, he's looking at her. It's Jeremy's face. It's unmistakable.

He moves a piece of blond hair out of his face, leaning against the stone wall and staring at Wren with frigid eyes.

She feels paralyzed in place, swallowing so hard that it hurts. For a moment, she unintentionally holds her breath. He narrows his eyes, chewing on his lip before pushing off from the stone wall and walking toward her. He rubs his hands together, grinning cruelly as he makes his way in between the graves.

"Richard," she says, her voice almost a whisper.

"1673. They had no idea what was coming." Richard is still marveling at the ancient grave marker, crouched down.

She squeezes her eyes shut.

He wouldn't do this here. There's so many people. He wouldn't do this here.

When she opens them again, everything seems to have slowed down. The air feels heavy and silent. Everything around her blurs and her eyes feel like two-ton weights rolling around in her skull. Her gaze falls to him again and now he's right on her. His shoulder slams into hers, hard, and suddenly everything comes back into focus.

"Oh, excuse me! I'm sorry!" The man's green eyes are kind. He puts a hand up apologetically. He's a stranger, resembling Jeremy only slightly.

Wren hesitates for a moment, staring into his face and wondering how she ever thought she knew him. The stranger raises his eyebrows, waiting for vindication before he leaves.

"Are you okay?" he asks, concerned.

She nods. "Yes. Yes, I'm okay." She feigns a genuine smile, shaking her head and trying to understand her hallucination.

He smiles. "Good. Sorry again."

The man quickly walks behind her, immediately hugging someone and walking with them out onto the sidewalk. Suddenly it's clear to Wren that he was looking at someone he knew behind her the entire time.

"Did that guy apologize?" Richard stands, placing a hand on her back.

"Yeah," she says, blinking away the panic. "Neither of us were paying attention, I guess."

It felt as if a nightmare leaked into reality for a minute, and she feels a little dazed from the adrenaline, but she shakes it off.

As they exit the burial grounds, her phone dings. It's a text from Leroux.

> Just landed. Driving up. See you
> tomorrow. Let's get a bite to eat
> and go over this double homicide.
> I have a lot to share with you.

She sighs, showing the text to Richard, then replies.

> Sounds good. Have a safe drive.
> I'll scope out some dinner spots.

"Guess we better get going. How far left to go?" she asks.

Richard is already pulling up the GPS on his phone. "About two and a half hours."

She looks down at the time, seeing it's nearing closing time for most of the shops around them. "Can we stop in for a tarot reading before we leave? It feels wrong not to."

Richard rolls his eyes but grabs her hand and walks her toward the shops on Essex Street. "Let's go find one. Then we should hit the road. I want to get to the house and make sure it's as good as the photos online."

Wren nods and follows Richard, sad to already be leaving this perfect little haven.

After a few blocks, she pauses in front of a shop called Mystic. "This one," she says.

There are purple velvet curtains lining the windows, and the divine smell of scented candles wafts out into the street. They step inside and approach the woman behind the counter. She's sitting with a book, looking effortlessly cool and straight out of a witchy teen film, but something about her feels more authentic.

Her smile is genuine as she greets them. "Good evening. What can I do for you tonight?"

Wren's eyes scan the objects around her. Crystals, candles, and incense seem to ooze from every inch of the place. She finds it weirdly calming, when anywhere else it could feel overwhelming.

"Do you by chance have any readings available?" she asks with hope lining her voice. "It's okay if it's a quick one."

"Of course. Esme is available right now for a ten-minute reading before her next appointment, if you would like." The young woman motions toward the curtain-covered corner in the back of the room where Wren assumes they keep Esme. "Follow me."

Caught off guard, Wren stumbles over her words. "Oh! Um, great, yes."

"I'll, uh, wait outside," Richard says.

She follows the woman, who opens the curtain with a swish of her wrist. Sitting behind the fabric is a woman who looks to be two hundred years old. She is tiny and frail, with white hair piled up into a bun and eyes so blue they almost look translucent.

"Sit down, dear," Esme says sweetly, gesturing to the stool across from her. "Just a general reading?"

"Please," Wren responds, taking a seat.

Esme begins to shuffle, tossing the cards to and fro in her hands and loudly shifting their positions around over and over. They snap and slap against one another in a soothing way. Wren finds herself entranced by Esme's delicate hands, covered in rings.

When Esme is satisfied, she lays a card down in front of her. Without any hesitation, she puts her hand on the card and looks at Wren.

"You're ignoring the signs," she says flatly.

Wren is intrigued, feeling a familiar rise of anxiety in her chest. "Am I?"

"Stop ignoring the signs, or you will stop receiving them." Esme's voice is gentle but firm.

She pulls another card. It's the Ten of Swords, and she pats it with her finger. "You can't stop whatever is happening. It will only end in loss." She looks up. "Does this resonate at all?" she asks.

Wrens nods, feeling a bit speechless.

Esme carries on. She pulls another card and slides it below the two she previously pulled. It's the Tower. As soon as it hits the table, in the reversed position, she brings her hand to her face and her eyes to Wren.

"The Tower," she says sternly. "You can feel it coming. It's all around you, but you are trying to push it away. Remember, the foundation is crumbling. It was always weak. It has to fall in order for something better to take its place."

"It's telling you all of that?" Wren asks, leaning forward to look at the card herself. The Tower is facing her. Shiny gold leaf makes all the intricate details of the design pop. The tower itself looks so beautiful, but it's collapsing dramatically, with lightning crashing into it from all angles. People dive out the windows to safety. Flames burst out of the sides. The beauty is marred by destruction, and no one can stop it. They can only react.

"If this resonates, then listen to it. This is another warning. Heed it."

"Okay," Wren says, pushing her stool back and standing. "Thank you, Esme."

She pays in a daze and shuffles back outside to Richard. He notices her worried look immediately.

"Oh no, was it not a good one?" he asks.

"No, it was okay. But she told me not to ignore the signs. She said I can't fix everything." Wren's still stunned by the cards, not wanting to admit that they might match her own instincts, a gut feeling she has been ignoring.

Richard rolls his eyes, throwing an arm around her shoulders. "They want you to pay for a longer reading out of pure terror. It's a brilliant marketing tool. Trust me."

"Yeah, I guess that makes sense." She shakes her head, letting herself smile at her gullible moment of weakness. "You're right. Let's get going."

Wren's phone vibrates in her pocket. She sees Corinne's name flash across the screen.

"Hey, miss me already?" Wren says as she answers, trying to shake the message she just received.

"From the second you left." Corinne chuckles before changing to a more serious tone. "Listen, we talked to our victim Andrea's sister."

Wren nods, motioning to Richard to veer off to the side of the walkway. "I knew you wouldn't waste any time. Anything come from it?"

"Imagine if I called you to say there was nothing gained?"

Wren laughs. "Wouldn't be you."

"The sister says Andrea has a couple of ex-boyfriends that we should take a look at. We will be paying visits to Daniel Roy and Peter Gilmore tonight. Neither of them are making great strides in life at the moment. Lots of spots on both records for petty theft and minor assaults."

"Is there any history of violence on Andrea or stalking concerns?" Wren motions for Richard's phone and opens a text message to herself when he hands it over.

"She had a restraining order out against Peter. Apparently, he made a lot of threats, but as far as they knew, he never followed through on them."

"And Daniel?" Wren types the information into the text box, sending it over to her own phone in fragments for later.

"No incidents between Daniel and Andrea, but some resentment was expressed after their breakup. So, he's worth looking into, but I think Gilmore is at the top of the list."

"Well, I am curious to see how this shakes out."

"Oh, I'm not done yet," Corinne warns.

"There's more?"

"Andrea's sister told us that she believes our victim was currently seeing someone."

"The plot thickens. Here I was ready to tap Gilmore as our guy." Wren sits on a nearby stone wall.

"Well, the sister and some other family members were concerned. No one ever met the guy, but Andrea occasionally mentioned an older man named Phil."

"Let me guess." Wren sighs. "She was showing up with marks on her from time to time?"

"Unfortunately, yes. It looks like they tried to talk her into leaving the mystery guy in the dust, but she was very secretive about him."

Wren shakes her head, suddenly raising an eyebrow. "You said she referred to him as *Phil* to her family?"

"The sister thinks that was the name she gave."

"No last name or any other information?"

Corinne clicks her tongue. "Nothing. Seems like she had a pattern of dating bad men. So maybe she was embarrassed this one wasn't panning out well either. We will obviously do some digging and see if we can track him down too."

"Yeah, keep me posted if you are able to."

"Of course. Thanks for your help. You were right. In the end, it looks like an intimate-partner murder."

"I love being right, but not at times like this. Talk to you later, Corinne."

She hangs up, turning the information around in her head.

"Update on the case from last night?" Richard takes his phone back, putting it in his pocket.

Wren nods, standing. "Yeah. It's looking like a boyfriend from past or present. Not Jeremy."

"Well, then I guess it's good you cleared that possibility." He looks at her, recognizing something is on her mind. "She say anything else?"

"No, that's it. They will chase down those leads and she will let me know when they have more."

"Good. Let's get going then." He holds out his hand and she takes it.

Hand in hand, they walk down the street together, grabbing a coffee for the drive as they head back to the car. She's dreading the next leg of their journey. She can't help but wonder who Andrea's mystery man really is and whether he was the one who brutalized her. She shakes her head, trying to focus on what is in front of her, but as much as she tries to dismiss her lingering questions along with Esme's warning, they haunt her.

CHAPTER 18

CHARLIE TAKES OFF RUNNING, clapping her hand over her own mouth to stifle the sounds of terror that force their way out. Despite all her talk about being an independent and rebellious spirit, Jeremy appreciates that she's following the game rules.

Through his night-vison goggles, Jeremy watches her from the stairway and takes aim with the paintball gun. He follows her form as it tears across the open space between two old carnival booths. Just as she passes in front of a tree that looks as if it could reach out and grab her, he squeezes the trigger. A paintball hits her directly in the ribs. She squeals, unable to stop the sound from escaping. The sudden impact forces her to fall into the trunk of the tree, and she grabs her side, feeling it for injury. Her hand recoils and she lifts the wetness up to her face. Jeremy knows she's wondering whether it's blood or paint.

"Too quick. No fun. Keep playing," Jeremy shouts, sauntering down the steps.

Charlie shakes her head, clearing the confusion and terror and replacing them with as much adrenaline as she can muster. She takes off running, darting between decrepit buildings and old signs, hearing him walk in the distance. His shoes crunch through the gravel and dead leaves and he oscillates between silence and loud taunts when he's nearby. It's like an unfair game of Marco Polo.

"Don't give the farmer his fun, fun, fun!" he shouts in a singsong voice. He listens carefully for movement and then laughs to himself, startling her. His demeanor switches so fluidly between madness and ice-cold rage, it's unnerving to witness.

He can see her hiding between the timeworn slats of the concession stands. She's attempting to stay motionless, but her body shakes and she wrings her hands, trying to contemplate her next move. She keeps turning her eyes toward the road just out of her reach. He planted that seed in her head and now she's wondering whether she should make a run for it.

He meanders around her hiding spot, loudly continuing to sing "Run, Rabbit, Run" by Flanagan and Allen.

As he approaches, he can feel her fear. It reaches out from her hiding place and touches him. He welcomes its warmth, letting it coil around him like a snake. Her fear fills him like fuel. Everything begins to work more efficiently and it all comes into sharper focus. Just a sip, and he's charged to one hundred percent. Being the source of someone's paralyzing fear is a pleasure he has yet to replicate.

He stops moving, slowing his breath to an undetectable hush. Now he just quietly hums the song, slowly stepping down the dirt path in front of him. To his right he detects movement. Snapping his head to spot it, he can see her shape in the dark. She crawls across the opening between a concession stand and a ticket booth. She seems to be inching closer to the perimeter.

She may roll the fucking dice after all.

She stops, catching her breath. She is weighing her options, and something tells Jeremy she will be running for the road.

He shoots a paintball at the tree next to her and is rewarded with a soft, muffled whimper. Making his way around the side of the booth, he throws a few stones in the other direction to throw off her sense of where he actually is. Every once in a while, a rock will hit something hard or fall into a pile of dead leaves, making it seem as if he is off to her left.

He can see her now with his night vision, but she can't see him. She is looking to the left, where the sounds keep coming from. Again, he allows the ground to absorb his steps before taking the next one. He throws another stone and steps silently, letting her attention go to the louder noise first. Once he is within range, he aims and shoots.

A blue ball of paint explodes on her temple. If her fear was tangible before, her pain is now. The force of the paintball sends her careening backward, clutching her head in her hands. She screams, forgoing the rules of the game as she grasps her head, rolling onto her stomach and stumbling to her knees. She still grasps her temple, sobbing and spitting. The pain must be extraordinary, because she begins to gag and vomits in the dirt in front of her. He watches in disgust and fascination as she shakes and slumps back against the ticket booth's side. She breathes heavily, weeping in terror.

He stands, now about twenty feet away from her. His full height looms over her crumpled body in the dirt and she shudders with his sudden appearance.

"No!" she screams through sobs.

Jeremy tosses the paint gun to his side, letting it clatter to the ground with a startling crack. He reaches behind his body, producing the single-action handgun that sat snugly in the waistband at the small of his back. "I bought the big bag of paintballs, Charlie. What a waste." He pulls the hammer of the gun back, letting the clicking sound cut through the air harshly. "Make it up to me, huh?" She can see his teeth in the dark. They are like a Cheshire cat smile floating above her.

She shakes her head, beginning to do a clumsy backward crabwalk to get away from him. She doesn't want to lose sight of him by turning to run, and the gun has paralyzed her ability to stand up.

He holds the gun out in from of him, aiming it directly at her.

"Stand up for me, Charlie."

She stands slowly, softly crying, steadying herself on the side of the ticket booth. Blue paint stains her cheeks and drips down the side of her face and neck. It mixes with bright blood that trickles from the welt. She doesn't turn to run; she just stares at him in the dark. She closes her eyes, ready for him to end the game.

But Jeremy is irritated now. He thought she would be more of a challenge. He could just kill her and be done with it. She still serves her purpose, even if she disappoints him personally. He holds the gun out, watching her fail to save herself, and he decides to make her work.

He lowers the gun, tucks it into the back part of his waistband, and begins to walk toward her. This makes her move backward from him. He picks up a small stone that someone has laid on the sill of the ticket window and launches it at her. She attempts to block it, and it hits her in the arm.

"What the fuck!" she cries.

Well, that's better.

She looks shocked, completely thrown off, so he bends down to grab another stone. Charlie staggers backward and turns to run. He throws the rock anyway, hitting her between the shoulder blades. She winces, grabbing the spot where the stone hit, but she keeps running. He lets a laugh escape, and he holds his arms up in triumph as he jogs after her.

"Yes! It's an adventure, Charlie! Seize the fucking moment!" he yells.

She makes her way past another abandoned concession stand and he takes out his gun and aims it again. He shoots, purposely missing. The strange sound of the shot mimics the snap of a whip. Wood splinters next to her ear and she screams. It's clear she is running toward the road again, despite her promise.

Jeremy smirks to himself as he sees the hair-thin perimeter wire shining slightly through his night-vision goggles. He strung an entire spool of the stuff around the areas near the road. It is strong piano wire. He pulled it as tight as he could and now she's running right toward it. He hoped to see what kind of damage it inflicted on her ankle or shin and how long she could last afterward. It's always fun to experiment.

He follows quickly, taking aim and shooting her in the back of the thigh just as she is heading to the perimeter of the fairground. Charlie shrieks, grabbing her leg and half spinning around. This move causes her body to spin in a strange way right before she reaches the wire barrier. To Jeremy's delight, the back of her leg connects with the wire and the full weight of her body brings her forward. It doesn't make a sound, but blood immediately pours from the wound and she screams a shrill cry like an animal makes as it dies.

He runs to stand over her. She isn't concerned with his presence anymore, only with the pain. He realizes her Achilles tendon has been sliced in two by the wire; her tight, animalistic grip on the back of her calf confirms this. She is crying on the ground, trying to make sense of where her night out went wrong.

"Charlie, I thought that wire was going to just cut your shin." He looks at her limp foot, the blood pouring from the laceration in heaves. The more she cries, the heavier the flow. "This is so much better."

He's bewitched, watching her writhe and cry. He never imagined her body would twist in such a way to allow a total severance of her Achilles. "I am sure by now you have realized this is just a pellet gun, right? I was hunting you with toys."

He holds the revolver in front of her face with a grin. "Doesn't matter now, I suppose." He waves it toward her foot, emphasizing his point.

"Please," she says quietly.

He crouches, looking at her. Tears, mucus, and blood cover her face. They mix together in rivers, matting down her curls and distorting her features.

She's disgusting, he thinks to himself.

He looks from her to the wire and waits a beat before reaching out and grasping her hair between his fingers. He wrenches her head toward the wire, pulling up and hovering her over it with her neck exposed, like a reverse guillotine.

"Maybe you gave me an idea, Charlie. I didn't realize this wire was so strong." He says this through clenched teeth, growling it right into her ear. His breath tickles her in a nightmarish way and he pushes forward onto his knees, digging them into the rocky dirt. He holds her there as she gags and cries, pleading for him to stop, then pulls her to lie with her back to his chest. Sitting on the ground, with legs outstretched in front of him, his arm slinks over her neck. He puts her into a headlock, speaking right into her ear again while he reaches down to grab his knife.

"You were so charming at the bar tonight." He brings the knife up from his boot, petting her hair with that same hand and keeping her body locked against him with his left arm. Her choked voice is quieting as she tries weakly to struggle against his grip. He buries his face into her hair as she pulls away as best she can. "You deserve a personal touch," he whispers sweetly.

In one quick motion, he brings the knife down, jamming it into her stomach and ripping to the side. Her moan is pitiful, and he holds her tightly as the life pours from her abdomen. There in the dirt, he watches as she heaves and sucks in pointless air. Her eyes flick around helplessly, looking up to the endless expanse of brightly lit stars above them.

CHAPTER 19

AFTER STOPPING FOR GROCERIES, they arrived at the rental cottage exhausted and unsure of what they would find. She and Richard did a full check of the place, looking in every closet and under every bed. Wren knew no one would be there, but it was a routine she had fallen into. She desperately craved routine in unfamiliar places.

They fell into bed after stuffing the refrigerator full of necessities. Sleep didn't come for Wren. It didn't come at all.

Now, the morning reminds her how much sleep she has lost. She makes a coffee, warming up some oatmeal to eat outside. The fresh air feels rejuvenating, but only for a moment. It doesn't take long for her to remember that this isn't a vacation; it's the finale.

"Why don't we head into town and relax a bit before you meet with John?" Richard slides into the seat next to her, a piping-hot mug of coffee cradled in his hands.

She smiles, nodding. "That sounds good. I am eager to see

more of this place. I wonder if I will like it as much as I liked what little of Salem we experienced."

"Well, we might as well make the best of it. When do we ever get away together, right?"

"Let's not count this as a vacation," she says dryly.

Richard smirks, taking a sip. "Once it's over, we will start the clock. How about that?"

"*That* sounds better to me."

They park on a side street, and everything looks alive when Wren steps out of the car. It's not chaotic or loud, just alive. There are people everywhere, stopping in shops and eating ice cream on benches on the sidewalk. She wants to appreciate it, to admire it even. But she can't stop thinking about what lies beneath it all. She can't stop her mind from wandering to him. Afraid to see his face in a crowd again, she examines each stranger around her with trepidation.

Despite the thread of fear that runs through every step, she still feels comforted and even cozy. She quickly learns Great Barrington is not a comparison for Salem because they are two completely different beasts. Salem's mystical and historical atmosphere may have fed her in a more significant way, but she likes it here.

They walk down Railroad Street in Great Barrington, a couple towns over from where they began. She made herself sick in the car reading about hidden spots of the Berkshires, so she figured it shouldn't be for nothing. The town is like something out of a Hallmark movie. Twinkle lights are strung up everywhere you can see, and although it is still light out, she can imagine how magical it must look at night.

Wren notices that no one is in a rush, and no one seems riddled with anxiety. This is a place where people don't lock their cars; instead they leave the keys in the ignition. They get alarm systems so bears don't get too cozy on their property, not to keep human intruders from murdering their whole family for sport. It's different here, and it pisses her off that Jeremy came with a plan to decimate it.

They walk into a small cafe at the end of the block. It's very indie and cozy, with farm-fresh snacks and a variety of interesting brews. Wren waits in line, scanning the menu. The barista, a woman with long purple hair, starts chatting with a customer as she prepares a drink.

"It's horrifying. Did you hear any of the details?" she asks, prepping the milk frother.

The customer shakes her head, squeezing her eyes shut as she closes her purse. "I haven't heard anything other than what they released on the news. But that's enough for me. It's unbelievable."

The milk begins to steam, so they raise their voices to speak over it.

"How can anyone go there again? It's such a safe area! I mean, people bring their kids to see those ruins," the barista says.

"To think something like that happened even with the visitor center a stone's throw away. I swear I have been sick over it."

"I heard one of the victims has some kind of symbol carved into them somewhere," the barista says bluntly, pouring the milk into a mug.

The customer gasps, covering her mouth in horror. "No. What do you mean? What was it?"

The barista shakes her head, shrugging. "I'm not sure. They wouldn't say what it was, or where on the body. But that's some ritualistic shit, right?"

"It's gotta be."

Wren swallows hard.

"I keep looking around, thinking it could be anyone." She makes a show of glancing around under her lashes.

The customer shakes her head. "No way is this a local. It's someone passing through."

"You think?"

Wren tries not to stare while she eavesdrops, keeping her eyes from resting too long on anyone's face. The young cashier shakes her attention from the barista's conversation.

"What can I get for you?" he asks pleasantly.

Mind reeling, Wren places her order and tries to listen for more gossip, but the conversation has moved on. After grabbing her order, she joins Richard outside at their table. She puts down the coffees and places a spinach and cheese croissant in front of him.

"You wonderful creature," he says with a grin.

"Found out some more about this case," she says, sliding into her seat.

Richard takes a huge bite of croissant, looking around him. "How?"

Wren can't help but give a small laugh. "Inside the cafe, some people were talking about it. It's big news. They don't have a lot of vicious killers walking around this place."

"I imagine it's a shake-up. What did you hear?" he asks.

"There was apparently some kind of symbol that was left on one of the victim's bodies. In fact, I think they said it was carved into them."

Richard cringes, putting down the croissant. "Sounds like something he would do."

"Sure does. Of course, satanic panic is alive and well. The word *ritualistic* was tossed about." Wren rolls her eyes, knowing the media will likely run with that angle. They will fail to acknowledge that sometimes the devil is just a human who wants to inflict pain. He's not some entity to summon or some demon to combat. He's your neighbor. He's a teacher. He's a police officer. Humans are the real rulers of hell.

"I know how much you love that." Richard grins, looking around again. "When are you meeting John?"

Wren cups her coffee mug between her hands, breathing in the heat and spice that wafts up from it. "Hmm? Oh, around five. We are meeting right over there actually, so I'll just have him bring me back to the house after."

"Let's hit some bookstores after we finish our drinks. You know this place has some good, musty books."

She smiles, taking a sip of her coffee. "Sounds like a perfect plan."

She pushes the salad around her plate. It's a fishy dressing that she didn't order and wasn't expecting. Instead of sending it back, she took a couple unpleasant bites and then just accepted the mistake. It's something she would never find herself doing at work: silently accept a mistake. A misstep in the morgue doesn't do something as innocuous as taste like a salty, unwelcome anchovy. It leads to injustice, reopening of trauma long stifled, and bad people continuing to do bad things unchecked. She's hungry, so she bets all her chips on the main course being correct. Until then, she will just move the various green leaves around her plate. It's unlike her, but she decides that it must be a by-product of this healing journey that has taken her hostage.

"Want to dissect the elephant in the room now, or do you want to keep relocating your lettuce?" Leroux takes a drink of water, keeping his eyes on her plate.

Wren closes her eyes, putting her fork down and leaning forward onto her elbows. "I would have to eviscerate it first," she says quietly.

"What?" He looks confused.

"I was making a joke. Before dissection, I would . . . eviscerate." She waits for a response. When he returns her look with silence, she clicks her tongue and looks visibly annoyed. "Your cop is showing."

He puts his hand to his heart finally and breaks out into the grin he had suppressed. "You cut me deep, Muller." He pauses as he says the last word, waiting for his joke to land. Wren can't help but laugh, shaking her head.

"You're unbelievable," she says, lovingly.

"I may be, but that doesn't change the fact that we have to talk about these bodies." His lighthearted tone quickly turns serious as he shifts the mood in the direction of the unthinkable.

Wren was clear on the fact that this was intended to be the main event of the evening, but she was hoping to avoid it. She smiles, leaning back in her chair. "Do we?" she asks.

"We do. It's not looking at all like a copycat, Muller. This looks like it could be the real deal."

"I still feel like it's an auditory hallucination to hear anyone mention 'bodies,' as in, more than one." She rubs her temples, trying to ward off the headache that threatens to begin.

Leroux nods, pursing his lips. "Unfortunately, you are lucid and heard correctly. A man and a woman. They are out in Tyringham, and like I explained in my message, they fit his methods."

"Yeah, I overheard some townies talking about it earlier. He's hard to pin an MO on, John." She shakes her head, crossing her arms across her chest in a defiant position. She's not ready to accept this quite yet.

"Look at the third photo."

She ignores his request. "I mean, isn't that why I'm here in the first place? There was a case that *matched his methods* in Salem?" The restaurant suddenly feels small and suffocating. "And what happened? It was a red herring."

"Look at the third photo," Leroux says again.

"So, we're just going to chase every stupid fuck with a loose screw now?"

Leroux sighs, squeezing his eyes shut in frustration. "Wren."

"Maybe he *is* dead, John. Maybe we don't have to focus on this anymore, and this can just be a cozy getaway. Hasn't that thought even crossed your mind?" She stabs at the lettuce with her fork.

Leroux sits back in his chair, arms crossed over his chest. He gives her a silent look as if asking, *Are you finished?*

Wren drops her fork in exasperation, letting it clank to the plate.

She puts her hand out. "Give me the photos."

He sits forward, pushing the stack of photos across the table. His eyes tell her there is something she doesn't want to see there. It won't be gruesome, she's sure of that. He would never warn her about a body horror moment when she routinely has her arms elbow-deep in a thoracic cavity. This is something poignant that will turn her stomach like a migraine. She prepares herself for it, internally placing her armor on.

As she flips over the second photo to reveal the third, she isn't ready. She isn't safe from or prepared for what she sees. In glossy color, there is a close-up of the victim's wrist, bruised and bloody. There, sliced crudely into the skin, is the outline of a bracelet. Little notches in a row, followed by what is meant to be the bracelet's charm. The deep wound representing it is unmistakably in the shape of a heart.

Wren's mouth goes dry. She feels a rush of her nervous system igniting and places her hand over her mouth to trap a scream. Leroux senses the change in the atmosphere and quickly pulls the photo away. Before he can place it back into the pile, Wren reaches out and grabs his hand. He looks right into her eyes, communicating without saying anything. In response, she shakes her head, motioning for him to hand her the photo again. It's a silent discussion, one that can happen only between two connected minds. A fascinating side effect of the trauma and rage that bind them, they are forever tapped into each other's instincts. Leroux slides the photo across the table toward her again.

"I'm sorry, that wasn't what I expected," she says dryly.

He takes in a heavy breath, nodding slightly. "Yeah, not what I was expecting either. But it's gotta be him, right?"

Wren holds the photo up, macabrely admiring the way the subcutaneous fat makes the faux bracelet appear to have been dipped in gold. He cut almost to the bone on purpose, using the body's own anatomy to his aesthetic advantage. The heart is cut to reveal the raw dermis layer. Red, like a heart should be. It's all so artistic and repugnant. It's Jeremy. It's the perfect dichotomy of beauty and horror, just like him.

"There is no doubt this is him. The townies were kind of right," she whispers.

"What were they talking about?" he asks.

She shakes her head, not able to break her eyes away from the photo. "They mentioned a symbol was carved into one of the bodies. This must be what they were *incorrectly* referring to."

"Ah, let me guess . . . satanic?" he asks, leaning back in his chair.

She unexpectedly smirks, finally looking up at him. "Basically. It's being called a ritual sacrifice of some kind. Guess it's too hard to consider that sometimes people just like

THE BUTCHER GAME   189

to cut other people up." Her stomach turns and she pushes her food away.

"Look, I know this is a lot for you to take in. We always knew he could call out to you again, but it still isn't something you can really mentally prepare for."

"What do we do?" she asks, squeezing her eyes shut for a moment.

Leroux sighs, pulling the photos back finally and bringing a piece of food up to his mouth. "Well, I have been dealing with this Kingsborough Police Department all day and they are not very forthcoming. I had to call in a big favor just to get these photos. It will be an uphill battle to be kept in the loop, but we will beat them into submission."

"Why Kingsborough?" she asks, confused.

"Tyringham is such a small department, they have joined their resources together and Kingsborough seems to be the type to take over. Bunch of babies over there."

She chuckles, rubbing her hands over her face. "Isn't that always the way?"

"I'll keep at them, and in the meantime, lay as low as you can. I'll keep you updated with anything pertinent. You remain a vital part of this, and if those bozos have a problem with it, they can answer to me."

"Throw a crutch at them," she says, biting back a smile.

He scoffs, leaning forward on his elbows. "I'll have you know I left my crutch at home."

"Can we FaceTime Andrew, please?" she asks, taking a sip of her drink. She needs the distraction.

"He's at work, but we can try." Leroux takes out his phone, dialing Andrew's number.

After a few short rings, a very chaotic scene appears on the screen. It's the kitchen at Andrew's restaurant and he props the phone against something while he prepares a delicious plate. The noises are overstimulating, and people whoosh by him from every direction, but he remains cool as can be.

"John, you okay?" Andrew asks without even looking at the screen.

"I'm fine, I'm with Wren. She wanted to say hi."

He looks over now, a big grin crossing his face as he passes off a plate. "Wren! How are you, doll?"

She smiles. Something about Andrew's light always brings her back to a place of contentment. "Andrew! I miss you! I'm sorry we called you while you are chef-ing. I just had to see your face."

He looks back at the project in front of him again and wipes his brow with his sleeve. "Never apologize. My two favorite people can always annoy the shit out of me during my work hours."

"I heard you're getting some time off in a couple of weeks. Let's get lunch at that new place that just opened—"

"On Magazine Street?"

"Yes! The one with that chandelier!"

"We absolutely have to. I've heard their chef is almost as good as me, and honestly, it's been too long since we let someone else cook for us." Andrew smirks, passing off another plate before starting something else. His hands never stop. He glances to the phone every now and then, but he's a machine.

"I fully agree. All right, we will let you go before you need to be plugged in and charged for the night." Wren waves.

"Love you both! Be safe and take a picture with a moose or some shit for me!" He's already yelling to someone else before the call ends.

Leroux blushes a bit and ends the call, placing his phone face down on the table. "Are there even moose here?"

Wren shrugs as the server places their main courses in front of them. "Not sure, but if we see one, we know what to do."

"Remember that," Leroux says, placing his napkin back on his lap and looking right into Wren's eyes. "We know what to do."

CHAPTER 20

MOST PEOPLE DON'T TRULY SEE astonishment in their lives. It takes something truly special to trigger that kind of emotion on someone's face. Astonishment is more than awe, it's thicker than amazement, and it's more elusive than shock. It's something like pure, untouched bewilderment. Today, Philip Trudeau stands in the doorway of his home, wearing a flannel shirt with the arms rolled up and a look of astonishment on his face.

"Phil, I know you want to shut that door right now." Jeremy's eyes dart back and forth. He can't help but smile slightly, feeding on Philip's anxiety and also the sense of his own power, bubbling beneath the surface.

Philip shakes his head, silently protesting and leaning one arm against the doorframe. He runs the other hand over his face, bringing his eyebrows together into a tight knot. "What the fuck are you doing here, Jeremy?" When the words finally come, they are breathless. His voice sounds as if it might break, as if he is looking at a wraith standing before him.

Jeremy shifts his weight to the other foot, fighting the urge to break into a full smile. He forces his mouth into a tight line. "I need help, man. I need a friend." His eyes lock with Philip's.

"Jesus, Jeremy. What the fuck am I supposed to do? I can't believe you're standing on my—how did you know where I live?" Philip yells the last part of the sentence. His face registers about five emotions as he processes each bit of new information.

"That's not important, Phil. I just—"

Philip puts a hand up, stopping Jeremy before he can finish. "No. Get the fuck off my property. You're lucky I'm giving you the opportunity for a head start before I call the police. Leave." His jaw tightens as he moves to slam the door shut.

Jeremy catches it, wrenching it back open. Philip breathes heavily. His eyes are furious and terrified. Jeremy leans in closer. His voice is a harsh whisper.

"Make sure you start at the beginning. What was it? 2002?"

As soon as the words slither from Jeremy's lips, the color drains from Philip's face.

"I don't know what you're talking about."

Jeremy continues, in a punishingly quiet tone. "When you call the police, make sure you tell them there are two murderers on Wheaton Road right now."

Philip's eyes squeeze shut. He stands there in silence, absorbing the words like bullets. After what feels like an eternity, he flicks his eyes to meet Jeremy's once more. "Fuck you," he spits out.

Jeremy lets the smile come now, still leaning in too close. "Yeah. Fuck me. It doesn't change the fact that we should be thrown in neighboring prison cells, my friend."

"You can't tie me to shit." Philip's voice is unsure. It's timid and afraid. He could never win a hand of poker when they were kids.

Jeremy laughs, shaking his head as he pulls back a little. "Then take a risk, Phil. Take a risk. Let's roll the dice and get Officer Small Town in here to make the final decision." He stares into Philip's eyes.

"What do you want, Jeremy?"

"Relax, man, I just need a place to crash." Jeremy breaks his locked gaze for a second, stepping back out of Philip's space. "We used to be friends. Isn't there some kind of nostalgic connection still?" He smiles.

Philip runs a hand through his hair. "Get in," he says gruffly, stepping aside to allow entry.

Jeremy nods, walking through the door cautiously. He can feel the weight of his hunting knife strapped to his ankle. He's keenly aware of it. Philip isn't a killer by nature, but he could rid himself of a lot of problems by making Jeremy disappear. It's clear this fact isn't lost on either of them. Jeremy will constantly be testing both himself and Philip with this experiment. For his part, he will always have to be on guard, never assuming his former friend isn't ready to finally erase the past. Philip will have to fight against that urge. He will have to choose between a short-term suffering or adding additional burdens to his conscience.

The home is the perfect picture of a New England cottage. The walls, ceiling, and floor are covered in wood, with only area rugs to break it up. Jeremy walks through the living room, running a gloved hand along the blanket that covers the back of an old leather couch. There's a massive natural-rock fireplace adorned with hunting trophies. Philip is a hunter. His walls are a testament to his skill, with antlers and stuffed animal corpses covering nearly every surface.

He spots photos of Philip's son too. He's cute, probably six or seven years old and clearly an object of importance to his father. There are school pictures, Little League photos, and memories of the two of them in frames positioned all around the room. He notices a photo of Philip with a few friends on a hike. There are five men in the image, all wearing flannel and carrying backpacks. They smile from the summit of Mount Who-Gives-A-Shit, but Philip's smile looks hollow somehow, the warmth doesn't reach his eyes. Of more interest to Jeremy, however, are the divorce papers clearly scattered with chaotic intent across the counter. The red tabs point like taunting fingers to empty lines where someone still needs to sign. So, Philip is in the throes of a divorce. Even with that detail confirmed, this is going to have to be a purely psychological game to keep the control in place. He's learned that the real move is *acting* as if he has all the cards and truly making someone believe he holds them. If he can manage that much, then actually possessing them is not necessary. Philip will jump at the insinuation that his family is in possible peril, and he won't require much proof of it.

There are crosses on several of the cabin's walls; too many to ignore but not enough to qualify as alarming just yet. He doesn't spot a true crucifix among them, and that makes Jeremy wonder if he is practicing. Philip had grown up reluctantly going to church, but maybe he had developed a desire to believe in something later in life.

"This is an inordinate number of crosses. You a priest or something, Phil?" he asks, running his hand along a cross.

Philip seethes but says nothing.

Jeremy looks back, noticing that Philip hasn't moved. He stands by the door with his arms crossed, watching Jeremy with a very pure kind of anger.

"I don't want to be a part of whatever you've done and whatever you're planning on doing, Jeremy," Philip says.

Jeremy laughs softly, allowing his gaze to fall to the raggedy old blanket. "You've been a part of it since the beginning, Phil."

"Philip," he corrects him flatly.

Jeremy's eyes flick up to meet his and a smile spreads across his face. "Philip." He almost laughs out the word, mocking him.

Philip curls his lip in disgust, dropping his arms and crossing the room to where Jeremy stands behind the couch. Jeremy clenches his fist at his side, preparing for an attack. It doesn't come. Instead, Philip stops close enough to where their breaths intertwine. "You're a killer. You. Not me," he says through gritted teeth. The words are there, but the truth doesn't reach his eyes. Something isn't registering as true. There is something hidden in those words.

They stand almost exactly the same height, but that's where the similarities end. Philip's features are dark. His hair and eyes are deep brown and years in the sun have tanned his skin. He has more muscle. His arms and chest show strength. Upon first glance, they are not in the same fight class. It's almost as if they once were two halves of a whole, representing each other's opposite in every way. It used to be what drew them together, but now it's the biggest thing that binds them, repels them apart like the matching poles of a magnet.

Jeremy sucks a breath in through his nose. "Ethically, that may or may not be true. But legally, we are two of a kind. I think you know that."

Philip searches Jeremy's eyes. The facts are laid bare before him. Years of repression and guilt seem to trickle out from behind his eyes as he tries to argue. When he breaks away from their standoff, he leaves a heaviness in the air. "I wanted to get her help. She could have been helped, Jeremy. You ended both of our lives in an instant."

Jeremy scoffs. "My life began that night."

Philip faces the window, but he turns to look at Jeremy as he speaks. He walks a few steps closer to him, stopping a few strides away. "I meant my life and hers. Your life means nothing to me." His breaths come in heaves. "I watched her family on the news. I still see them at the store, Jeremy. They are part of my fucking congregation!"

Ah, this isn't just idolatry for idolatry's sake.

"You dare to stand in my home after what you did!"

"What *we* did!" Jeremy yells.

Philip opens his mouth to speak but nothing comes out. Instead, he bites at his lower lip as he used to do when they were kids. Anxiety pours out of him easily. He was never able to hide it. After a long silence, he speaks.

"We would have been able to get her help. We would have only gotten a slap on the wrist. You got to leave, Jeremy. You went back to your shithole town, while I had to stay here and watch the searches and the vigils. I had to swallow the truth and lie to everyone I ever cared about." His face twists into a confusing look as he relives that night.

Jeremy remembers that night too, though he rarely thinks about it.

"I saved your ass that night. It's because of me that you have a life. They weren't going to give you the benefit of the doubt, Phil. It doesn't matter who your dad is or that you have cops in your family. You would be a murderer."

"All you saved is your own skin."

Jeremy ignores his bluffing. "Phil, it's time I call in that favor."

"Favor? You think I owe you a favor?" Philip laughs freely now, sitting himself down in a beat-up blue chair. "Wow, you really are delusional."

Jeremy's blood stirs, but he wills himself not to get angry. He leans against the arm on the couch, not ready to commit to completely sitting quite yet. "Maybe *favor* isn't the word? Maybe there isn't even a word for it." He leans forward, daring Philip to do something. "I guess it's just that there is a body tied to you out there, a body that you have tried to forget all about. Her memory has faded from head-lines and town gossip, but it wouldn't be hard to start up the rumor mill."

"You're truly a piece of shit, huh?" Philip asks flatly.

Jeremy smiles. "Sure. But you're already a part of this, so you may as well hear me out. Besides, there is a financial gain to be had from this too."

Philip sits back now, gesturing for Jeremy to continue.

"Ten thousand. I'll give you half now and half later."

Philip scoffs. "You're a lying sack of shit."

Jeremy rolls his eyes, reaching into his back pocket and pro-ducing a dirty envelope. He slaps it down on the coffee table and points at it. "It's all in there. Go ahead, call my bluff."

Philip's eyes drop to the envelope, and he leans forward, peeking inside. He flicks his thumbs across the bills before dropping it back down and shrugging.

"Hey, if your priest job pays better, then I'll see myself out."

"Just keep talking while I'm allowing you."

"Listen, I know you have a family now, Phil." He nods at the photo of Philip's son on the mantle.

Philip's expression changes from amused to severe. His eyes go cold and his jaw ticks angrily. "You are treading on dan-gerous ground, asshole."

Jeremy grins, holding his hands up. "Relax, Phil. Nothing will happen to your family . . . probably."

In an instant he's up and Jeremy shifts behind the couch.

"I'll kill you myself!" he yells, pointing his finger in Jeremy's face.

Jeremy pulls back, putting space between them. "Yeah, but you should know that if something happens to me, a call is set to be placed."

"A call." Philip says it like an incredulous statement. He's red-faced and breathing heavily, with only a couch separating him from Jeremy. It's clear he is ready to pounce, just waiting for the right moment. He's been pretending that animal doesn't live inside of him, but it's moments like this when he struggles to tame it.

"A call to let the right people know what you have done. I go, you go, and who knows what happens to your family after that." Jeremy erases any trace of humor from his face. He locks eyes with Philip.

There is a beat of silence as the air hangs heavy between them. "What do you want?" Philip says.

CHAPTER 21

THE FIRST COUPLE NIGHTS in an unfamiliar place usually bring shit sleep along with them. Wren struggles to relax, fighting to find a comfortable spot in a comforter that isn't hers. This one is scratchy, with a pattern on it. It looks like a patch of wildflowers if they were painted by a nervous hand. The fabric is supposed to look like brush strokes, but it just looks like a mess to Wren.

She prefers a simple pattern, if any at all. She is one of those people who gets bored of any design after a while. In fact, it will end up causing some overstimulation if it sticks around long enough. When it comes to sleeping, her bedroom must be calm and uncomplicated, neutral. Her life, especially as of late, is chaotic and unpredictable enough.

She isn't going to get that kind of calm in this strange room. Richard's comforting form snores beside her, but as she throws off the comforter, she can't shake the feeling that she's under a persistent threat. Now that she's closing in on Jeremy's trail, working her way closer to his new hunting grounds, his presence looms over her at all times—especially at night. As soon as she found her grandmother's ring on his coffee table, the one that had sat by her bedside night after night, her cocoon of perceived safety was torn open. Nights are fitful now and full of nightmares that are too vivid.

As her eyes finally flutter closed and she curls into the sandpaper comforter, Wren begins to enter her nighttime prison. Her mind won't save her; it won't even try anymore. Night after night, she is dragged helplessly into a world of terror, where she can't escape until daylight.

Tonight, she finds herself in the forest again. She slogs through wet ground that grabs back at her feet like hands trying to keep her here forever. Again, she doesn't know where she is or where she is going. It's an endless dark that stretches in all directions and reaches to the corners of a world she can't conceive. She falls forward after trying to lift her foot from the muck. It grabs back at her, not allowing her to take a full stride. At the sudden halt, her hands slap down on smooth earth that feels like slime. Even though it's a dream, she feels the slap on her hands. The sting stays for a moment, reminding her that this night world is always full of pain.

Suddenly, it's autumn.

At least that's something different.

The leaves are vibrant and fluttering in the air all around her. They fall from twisted branches and crunch under her feet. Gone is the sludge that always exists in this place. But even with crispy fall leaves, the air is still humid and thick. It's as if her mind won't allow her a true reprieve. Immediately, it feels like a trap, but one she will walk into willingly just to get it over with.

She's suddenly comforted. The warmth isn't as suffocating as it was before. Now it's like a blanket, but for once, a blanket that isn't pulled too tight. She relishes this change, spinning around and catching a leaf in the air, then two and three more after that. She crushes them in her hand, letting the pieces fall into the breeze like spooky confetti. It's lovely here tonight. She knows it won't last, but it's been so long since she had a true dream, she's going to enjoy it as long as she can.

As she walks along, her foot squashes down on something that comes apart under her weight. For a moment she freezes, unable to bring herself to look at what is under her foot. Experience in this nightmare realm has told her that this could be something unimaginable. But she looks, because it feels like the only thing she can do. When she brings her eyes down, she immediately lets out a relieved puff of breath. A rotted pumpkin lays cracked open beneath her. It's disgusting, but almost comical in a way. She smiles to herself, thinking of carving pumpkins and eating roasted pumpkin seeds. Again, the warmth flows over her. As she trudges on, the trees start to get brighter, like a dimmer switch has been turned up.

Suddenly the reds and oranges and yellows jump out at her, making her eyes burn. For a moment, the colors seem to almost hurt her. She can feel the pain again, too vivid. Then, just as quickly, the trees around her begin to die. They shrivel and flex in on themselves in misery, but only the ones that directly surround her. The trees in the layer beyond her are still vibrant and shedding delicate leaves, but they don't touch her orbit. She's in a decaying prison of her mind's own design and it happened too fast for her to escape.

Then John Leroux's voice hits her like a block of ice. He sounds like a man being torn apart, screaming her name with pure pain.

"Wren!"

The sound comes from everywhere and nowhere all at once and it crashes into her. She gets the distinct feeling that he wants her to run from him, to save herself from whatever terror he's experiencing. Even in a dream, Leroux pleads with Wren to save herself.

She doesn't. Instead, she runs toward him, through the death and the rotting pumpkins that now cover the ground. Branches whip and scratch at her arms as she propels herself further into her nightmare. Just as she is about to reach him, another scene comes into view.

Before her stands a stag. He's fragile and beautiful, juxtaposed against the decay that surrounds it. He stands tall, staring at Wren with sad eyes. She feels drawn to him, forgetting Leroux's screams. She walks toward the deer, stretching out her hand. He flares his nostrils slightly, not moving. The dream takes hold of her, compelling her to move forward despite this show of fear.

As she takes a step closer, a snapping sound echoes through the forest. It's sharp, and she covers her ears, screwing her eyes shut instinctively. Another snap splits the world apart and she finally opens her eyes, trying desperately to find the source.

That's when she sees it.

The stag's legs begin to break. The front right and then the back left. Both snap at odd angles, causing the creature to tilt in a strange way. He never breaks eye contact and doesn't change his demeanor at all. He just stares stoically as his front left leg breaks and he falls over. Wren screams, clawing at her own face and then frantically trying to reach out to the broken animal.

She falls to her knees, feeling the wetness leak through her pants as she hits a rotten pumpkin below her. There is no sound, just the wind whipping through the trees every now and then. The deer moves his head to look at her, but not an ounce of pain or fear shows on his face. She reaches out, cradling the deer's head in her hands and he allows it.

A sob escapes Wren, and she leans forward, closing her eyes. She lets her cries come out in heaves as she holds the deer's head close to her. After a few moments, she gathers herself and sits up, looking down to see that she is cradling Richard's head in her hands. As soon as she locks eyes with him, he opens his mouth and gurgles. In an instant, blood flows from it like a waterfall.

She reels back, screaming and grasping his face, trying to find the source of his bleeding. She screams again, looking up into the sky as it disappears before her eyes. It's caving in, falling in giant pieces. They crash to the ground and splatter the rotten pumpkins. A piece plunges down, directly aiming for Wren and Richard.

Suddenly she is awake, sitting up in an unfamiliar bed. Cold sweat drips down the back of her neck. She breathes heavy and fast. Richard doesn't stir. He remains curled in the comforter, warm and solid.

It's early, but she rises anyway, knowing sleep is not going to return. She spends the rest of the morning watching the hummingbirds gather around a large bush out back. They flock to it, more than she has ever seen. In fact, these are the first hummingbirds she has *ever* seen.

Finally, as the sun rises, Richard comes to join her. They sit together in silence for a bit. Nature chatters around them, offering its unspoken opinion.

She sees another hummingbird, followed by its friend. They hover over the bushes, drinking greedily. Almost as fast as they appeared, they are both gone. They show up quickly, take without judgment, and move with unmatched speed and grace. Then, when they are done, they leave without ever having to explain why.

She wishes she were a hummingbird.

CHAPTER 22

S UMMERS IN THE BERKSHIRES were an escape, and Jeremy always took full advantage of the time away from his parents. He loved the comfort of the region. It felt insulated and afforded him a new kind of environment to explore. He and Philip would find themselves breaking into an old, abandoned barn at one a.m. simply because it was there. They would crack open some contraband beers and try to contact the dead with a Ouija board.

Philip was never worried about real bad guys on these adventures. He never considered what sitting ducks they truly could have been. They were just two tipsy teens in a dilapidated building after midnight dabbling in the occult. He had no reason to fear a physical threat. His community was safe. People left their doors unlocked and waved at their neighbors.

To tell the truth, Jeremy knew that Philip was more worried about what would happen to his soul if they kept messing around with a Ouija board. Growing up in a religious family from Louisiana usually came with a healthy fear of the afterlife—although not for Jeremy. Despite his mother's constant berating, Jeremy never felt as if he had a soul to risk.

It was July 6, 2002. Jeremy was seventeen, and Philip had just turned eighteen. They had spent the evening at a local bar using some pitiful-looking fake IDs. Luckily, the bartender didn't ask questions and the beers stayed flowing.

It probably helped that Philip's father, who'd been born and raised in the area, was a judge. Their family roots ran deep, and when they'd moved back from Louisiana, his dad was elected to serve as first justice of the Northern Berkshire District Court. This meant his only son got away with everything. In general, Philip was not a bad kid. He got up to the kind of trouble one would expect of someone living out in rural Massachusetts. He took his parents' speedboat out late at night on the lake, committed some trespassing violations, partook in underage beer drinking, and whipped his brand-new Jeep around with a certain air of invincibility. Jeremy envied that Philip was like an untouchable god.

But in an instant, that all changed.

It was New England warm. The kind of night that draws people out into the darkness. After they had stumbled out into the parking lot of the bar, Philip had tried unsuccessfully to toss his keys to Jeremy. His aim obscured by a few too many stale beers, they whistled past his head and almost hit a young woman saying goodbyes to her friends. Jeremy shook his head, jogging over to pluck them from the gravel.

As he looked up, she locked eyes with him and smiled, clearly amused at the near miss. She was shorter than he was and appeared to be in her twenties. Her brown hair was cut into a short bob, and she was wearing deep red lipstick. His mother always said that red lipstick was for whores, but he found himself drawn to it. He closed his hand around the keys and grinned back.

"I hope that wasn't a ploy to get my attention," the girl said as she tied her light blue sweater around her waist.

Jeremy immediately felt annoyed at the joke. "It wasn't. Don't flatter yourself," he said dryly, turning to walk back to Philip's Jeep. He could hear her scoff behind him.

"Fuck you," she said with a laugh.

He stopped in his tracks.

There was a moment where he considered saying something else, but instead he turned around to look at her. Her cheeks flushed and she hurried away, slinging her purse across her body and heading down the dark road alone. Something inside him pulled toward her. It was as if every inch of him were tied to her by invisible bonds, and he felt compelled to follow, but he stifled it—that insidious part of himself that always tried to break free. He could feel his jaw clench, hear his teeth grind against themselves like gravel under a tire. The feelings were familiar, and he had learned how to control them. So, he just watched her walk into the dark, unlit path ahead of her.

"Jer, stop trying to score and drive us home. I'm starving." Philip's voice cut through his thoughts. Jeremy gave one last look at the now-empty darkness of the road.

"You're an idiot. I am not driving, Phil." He tossed the keys back at him.

Philip caught them, looking at Jeremy with confusion. "Come on, man, I had more than you!" he protested.

Jeremy shook his head and got into the passenger seat. "Nope, nice try."

Philip staggered into the driver's seat, smelling like potato skins and too much cologne. He was exaggerating his inebriated state, but he wasn't exactly in a position to drive a Jeep down a dark, woodsy road either.

"You're an asshole." He fumbled with the keys, finally finding the ignition.

Jeremy looked out the window. "I know. Just go slow."

"Any other driving tips?" Philip asked as they pulled out of the parking lot.

Jeremy grinned, still staring out the window.

"How am I still so hungry? I swear . . ." As was common for Philip to do at this kind of late hour, he went into a string of random thoughts that he felt necessary to say out loud, and Jeremy tuned him out as he always did.

The dark was different here, inkier. He imagined it would feel like velvet if he reached out to touch it. He felt himself getting lost in the air spilling through his open window and closed his eyes for a second to try to force the remaining, unspent anger away. He didn't initially notice when the interior of the car went silent.

He had only a split second to see Philip's head nodding and then the human form lit up in front of the headlights. The ensuing sound was a sickly thud, following by the screech of tires. Philip yelled and grabbed the wheel. The car skidded to a stop facing the opposite way on the side of the road, dust swirling into the open window.

"What the fuck was that?! Did I hit a deer? What was that?!" Philip was frantic, looking over the steering wheel. He jerked open his door and looked out at the road.

Jeremy stayed silent. He knew it wasn't an animal they had hit. He saw the look in her eyes and the shape of her arms raised in a fruitless bid to shield her body. He gazed out through the window in front of him, searching for her but seeing nothing but darkness, illuminated in the eerie light cast by their vehicle. Slowly he stood, walking around his door and examining the dent in the hood. Jeremy touched it and pulled back to see blood smeared across his fingers.

"Jesus, it demolished my fucking Jeep!" Philip ran both his hands through his dark, wavy hair, a look of frustration casting over his face.

Jeremy walked forward, looking side to side as he did. He should have felt scared. He should have felt as if his whole life were over. He should have felt the guilt that most anyone would feel knowing they hit a person with their vehicle. He felt none of those things. He was excited. His hands trembled with anticipation and his eyes darted to the ground, scanning for the prize. He had to see it up close. He had to confirm that he hadn't hallucinated her.

"Jer! Do you see it?" Philip yelled, staying a good distance from where Jeremy had wandered.

That's when Jeremy heard her. Soft, breathless cries came from an area just off the main drag. He walked to his left, and there she was. The first thing he saw was her light blue sweater, spread out on the road a stone's throw from her body.

It was knocked right off her waist. He made his way toward her. She was on her back and trying to grab her right leg, which was clearly broken. Her eyes were wild and there was blood pouring from a head wound. It dripped down the right side of her face and matted her dark hair down, turning her short brown bob into a red one.

"Help me! My leg is broken, help me!" she started yelling through sobs, clutching at the mangled limb. Her pleading eyes shot to Jeremy and locked on him for a moment until recognition flashed. "You. You hit me! You hit me with your car!" She was hysterical, but also beginning to fade in and out of consciousness.

He stood over her for a moment, taking in the whole picture before him. She tried to scoot away, to force some space between them, but it was useless in her condition. So she started swatting at the air to keep him away. He kneeled next to her, never breaking her gaze. "Wrong," he answered dryly, reaching into his pocket and slipping his pocketknife out into his palm. She was unconscious now, her bleeding head resting on some undergrowth.

"Oh my God." Philip came up behind him. He started at the scene in horror. "What have I done? Is she dead? Oh my God, Jeremy! How did this happen?! We have to call 911!" He paced frantically, pulling out his flip phone and staring at it as if he had forgotten how to press buttons.

Jeremy stood up, grabbing Philip's arm tightly and forcing him to stop. "You fell asleep, Phil. She's alive, but she's got a pretty severe head injury, judging by the blood."

"Her leg is so bad, dude." Philip's eyes flicked to the mangled limb. Tears were already spilling down his face silently.

Exasperated, Jeremy tried to refocus his attention. "It's broken. It's useless to her now. But Phil, this is vehicular homicide if she dies. If she lives, you are fucked too. You're drunk."

Philip's eyes squeezed shut. "Oh my God! What did we do, man! You were supposed to drive!" He pushed Jeremy away, grabbing his own head with both hands like a vice. "Should we leave her and call anonymously? Can we do that, even?" He was pleading for a solution to come.

Jeremy shook his head. "No. That's way too risky. They'll trace it back to you." He kneeled next to the young woman's body again, reaching over her to open the brown purse that had been slung across her. He pulled out a license, holding it up. Morgan Davies, twenty-one years old. Her hair was longer in her photo, but it was definitely her. The smile was the same amused grin she had shot him back in the parking lot.

"We have to get rid of this, Phil," Jeremy said quietly, still looking down at the license in his fingers.

Philip stopped his frantic pacing, looking over at him incredulously. "What? How? What do you mean?"

Jeremy stood, motioning to him. "Help me pull her into the woods."

Philip stood frozen, mouth open but nothing coming.

"Do you want to go to law school or not?" Jeremy asked flatly. "This isn't a completely abandoned road. Someone is bound to come by any second and see us."

After a moment of paralysis, Philip nodded. "Okay. Tell me what to do."

Jeremy nodded too. He ran back to the car and turned it off, switching off the headlights. Hopefully it was well-enough hidden on the shoulder. He hurried back to Philip and the woman, a plan forming in his head.

"Grab her arms and pull. I'll try to keep her leg up, so it doesn't rip apart on the ground."

"Jesus, Jeremy." Philip's face twisted in disgust.

"Just do it."

Philip fumbled around her upper torso. When he finally found a grip that worked, he lifted her slightly and started to pull her into the darkness.

Jeremy slid his arms under her good leg, letting the broken one hang as he lifted her. They stumbled through brush until they were deep enough in the woods to be hidden by the still-thick trees. In the daytime, they would be standing among a sea of shades of green. But tonight, it's just that inky black that now feels heavier than before.

"Here. Drop her." They both let go. She flopped to the leaf-covered ground with a thud. "Do you have a light?"

Philip dug in his pocket, producing his cell phone and flicking on the flashlight. The white light cast a sick spotlight onto Morgan's battered frame.

"Hold it still." Jeremy instructed, squatting down and producing the pocketknife, which he slung open with a flick of his wrist.

"Wait, what are you going to do?" Philip asked, letting the light dip a bit.

Jeremy sighed, looking up at his friend. He snatched the phone from his grasp and leaned it on a rock. "I am securing your future."

Philip understood almost immediately. "Jeremy, you can't. Dude, I know you think you are helping me, but we can get out of this. My dad will get me out of this." His breathing kicked up. "We can call 911 and she will be okay! We can explain what happened! She was on a dark road. Anyone could have hit her!"

"But *you* hit her, Phil! You did!" Jeremy yelled, standing to face him directly. "Your dad can't get you out of this. It will ruin you, and it will ruin him. You will lose everything, and for what? An accident. This bitch was in the middle of a dark road. She was asking to be hit."

He let his eyes drop to Morgan, feeling rage and disgust rise in his throat like bile. "She's not worth you and your family's future."

There was a long beat of silence as Philip's mind battled to pick a side. Finally, Philip shook his head. "I don't want to know what you are going to do. We didn't have this conversation." His eyes were filled with tears, but the emotion had left. He stared through the beam of light before turning around to walk a few steps away.

Jeremy bent down again, looming over her face. He studied the way the blood had begun to dry in spots and watched as fresh blood still oozed from the laceration near her temple. He held the knife close to her neck, touching it to her skin and then pressing only slightly, just to make her bleed. As he did this, Morgan's eyes flicked open. They moved wildly, trying to understand what was happening. She reached up, grabbing Jeremy's hair in her fist and crying out in a choked scream.

Instinctively, he wrapped his hand around her neck and slammed her head back against the ground as she continued to grab at his face and hair. Her head hit the ground with a hard crack.

"Stop, stop!" Philip was back at their side, panicked and conflicted.

Jeremy didn't stop. He dug his knee into her side, forcing her hands away from his face. Taking his hand from her neck, he tangled it into her hair, pulling her throat into an exposed position and choking off her screams. He leaned in close, meeting her wild eyes with his own, and he whispered in her ear, "How's this ploy to get your attention?" Then he dragged his knife hard across her neck, putting the force of his entire body down on it as he hit bone. He felt that her sputtered chokes went silent immediately, as blood and air left her body in tandem.

Philip was yelling now. But even though Jeremy could see his mouth open and his hands reach up to claw at his own face, he heard nothing. It was as if he were in a womb, silent and warm.

Jeremy watched the blood snake its way past Morgan's outstretched arm, soaking into the ground. He picked up a fallen leaf that had been perfectly painted by summer. Now, it had flecks of red spattered across it. He thought it looked like a piece of art.

Philip heaved. He gagged and braced himself against a tree trunk, tears streaming down his face. As he did, his wallet slid from his back pocket and onto the leaves.

"When you're done, we have to get rid of this." Jeremy wasn't even looking at him. He kept his eyes locked on the red-speckled leaf in his palm.

Philip wiped his mouth with the back of his hand. "Listen to yourself!" he spat out. "No fucking way! Fuck you, man!" His breaths were loud and panicked.

Jeremy sighed, bringing his eyes to Philip's face. "I understand you are upset. But we should save the discussion for later. Grab her legs."

He shook his head and stared at her on the ground. "No."

"Phil, you know as well as I do that you are officially complicit. You aren't going to walk away from this unless we hide her where she won't be found. Put aside whatever it is you're trying to prove and save yourself." Jeremy picked up Morgan's shoulders, waiting for help.

Philip's eyes widened as he stalked toward Jeremy. "Save myself?! You son of a bitch, I had no part of this! I wanted to get her help and you . . ." His voice cracked and trailed off. He had come to a stop right in front of Jeremy, who was standing now. Philip's eyes dropped to the battered body between them and the words died in his throat. For a moment, there was something like silence as they stood almost nose to nose with a murder victim between them. The leaves rustled in the trees and crickets chirped softly.

Finally, Jeremy spoke. "Grab her legs."

This time, Philip surrendered to Jeremy. He lifted her legs and Jeremy noticed his wallet on the ground below them. Reaching down to grab it, he pulled out his high school identification, sliding it into Morgan's pocket before holding the wallet out to Philip. "You dropped this."

Together they walked quietly into the deep vastness of the forest. They barely spoke aside from Jeremy directing them farther and farther away from the road. He was more familiar with these woods than Philip since he hiked the trails while Phil was at work. Philip was a rich kid, but his parents forced him to take on two or three shifts a week at Dunkin' Donuts. Although Phil felt supremely above it, the perks were an assemblage of stale donuts when he came home and some requisite time alone for Jeremy.

Jeremy had become an experienced outdoorsman by his early teens and had easily adapted from the swampy bayou to the unfamiliar spookiness of Massachusetts woodlands. There are always commonalities in nature, but it was those stark differences between the two areas that really intrigued him.

In particular, the Beartown State Forest challenged him in a different way than the gnarled Louisiana landscape. Beartown had a crisp, almost frozen quality about it. Especially if it was early in the morning, it felt as if everything stood still. Suddenly, he would feel as if he had entered a realm he wasn't supposed to know about, as if the veil between the past and present had thinned enough for him to slip through it. He had felt this most profoundly when he stumbled on an abandoned hearth off one of the beaten trails. It stood there tall and perfectly preserved, as if a homestead still bustled around it. He had half excepted some smoke to billow out from the decrepit chimney. The hearth was filled with loose dirt and leaves, undisturbed for what appeared to be years. He wondered what kind of darkness could be hidden there, securely.

That was where they took her. They buried her in the hearth, under the dirt and dry leaves. Phil had even found a few large stones and silently added them on top of her grave. Jeremy remembered watching him take in the burial site. He stood there for a few minutes of quiet reflection, before they left her there to decay, all alone, with Philip's high school ID in her pocket.

Their friendship was never the same after that. She always seemed to be there, between them. Even now, as Jeremy stands in Philip's home, it's as if she's in the room, haunting everything.

CHAPTER 23

WHEN LEROUX CALLS in the late morning, he informs Wren that the police department's stonewalling act is still going full force. They fight him at every turn, questioning why he is even up here to begin with. He's pulling in favors just to get any kind of questions answered or progress made.

"They don't look further than their own noses, Muller. It's unbelievable." Leroux's voice has hit his anger level. Whenever he gets really mad, his accent gets thicker. Pure Louisiana pours from him now.

"Unfortunately, they are under no obligation to include us in any part of the investigation," Wren says.

"I don't give a shit. They want to catch him and get the glory? Then they should utilize people who have the fucking experience. These dipshits don't have one clever thought among them. If they did, then it died scared and alone. Not a friend for miles."

Wren laughs, shaking her head. "Honestly, I can't say I disagree."

"We'll talk more in person." The line is dead before she can say goodbye.

Wren suspects Leroux is right about the local police. Small, local departments always think they know best. The lack of communication and unwillingness to cooperate is always incredibly frustrating. Even when they're dealing with a case that's out of their league, instead of accepting help and external resources, they pull rank and build dams against the flow of communication. It's why some of the biggest cases in history have gone cold. No one wants to put aside their egos and work together for a common cause.

When Leroux shows up at the rental house, Richard is sipping coffee and reading a book on the front porch. To Wren, her husband looks so peaceful, but it's a false sense of calm.

"I heard you don't know what you're talking about, John," Richard jokes as Leroux walks up the front path.

Leroux laughs, flipping him off as he gingerly hops up the porch steps. "Yeah, yeah. I guess almost a decade of experience working major cases in a city with a massive crime rate doesn't qualify me to help with the Hallmark-movie-of-the-week crowd."

"Leave it to the professionals, would ya?" Richard teases.

Leroux pats Richard's shoulder. "That's what I tried to tell your wife," he says with a smile.

"Come out back, I need to pretend we're relaxing here." Wren waves him through the front door then out to the backyard.

"This place isn't too bad." Leroux follows her onto the open back patio. Wren takes in the lush, green surroundings that are just starting to be touched by autumn and Leroux plops into a patio chair.

"Yeah, it's more comfortable than I anticipated," she says.

"So, I tried to get you in for the autopsies. Department won't even ask the ME," Leroux says disdainfully, lighting a cigarette.

"That's fine for now. Unfortunately, there will likely be more. I've been reading reports—trying to see if there's anything we missed. Maybe he left a trail up the East Coast."

"Could be. There is a woman that's been missing for a day or so. Friends said they saw her with a man."

"Well, that's something," Wren says.

"I did also manage to get out of them that there's someone local who the police have worked with in the past to solve cases. They're connecting with him for this. Right now, there seems to be a steady stream of useless information coming in about those two bodies. Of course, no one is particularly forthcoming to me." He rolls his eyes, taking a long drag of his cigarette.

Wren quirks her brow. "They have some kind of informant?"

"They aren't exactly sharing what they have. I think it feels like some idiot trying to get out of trouble. From the sounds of it, they don't have anything solid. No one up here is close enough to Rose to give us anything worth chasing."

"He's got old ties here though," Wren says.

"Yeah, but that doesn't mean they're willing to get wrapped up in this."

She chews at her lip. "But you pushed again about Philip Trudeau?"

He nods. "Of course I did. They blew me off."

She raises a brow. "How so?"

"They said they cleared him, and that was all they were willing to spill. Trudeau has a lot of cops in his family and his dad was a local judge for years. Philip's got a job as a pastor at some tiny, terrifying church."

"I did a little online sleuthing and noticed that too. He seems pretty intense."

"Who knows. He seemed to drop Rose like a bad habit when they were kids."

"Yeah, I guess that would be a pretty big risk to take on Jeremy's part. Philip's basically a stranger to him now."

Leroux nods. "Unfortunately for us, Rose isn't a bumbling fool. His brain may be repulsive, but it was in fairly decent working order last time we saw him."

Wren shudders, shaking her head to clear away the memory. "So, we just have to keep beating on the cops for the next bit of information? Why did we even come up?"

He sighs, leaning back in the chair. "I know it's incredibly frustrating, but we need to be here. Like I said, they aren't going to be able to handle this if it is him. He's going to send that department into bedlam."

"He chose the perfect idyllic place to poison." She looks out into the dense forest that surrounds them and can't help but feel sorry for it. Wickedness has made its way up here and nothing will ever be the same.

"Well, let's head over to the precinct tonight. We can meet with Lieutenant Brixton and see if he's willing to discuss the lack of teamwork."

"It *would* be nice to have an ally in there."

Leroux scoffs. "Don't hold your breath on that one."

"Well, who knows, maybe Jeremy left after this double event. Maybe he's already out of the state." She scratches at the wicker of her chair.

"He's not the type to leave a hunting ground so quickly. He knows he can do some real damage here. And he doesn't know we've followed him."

"I hope so. I haven't exactly tried to keep myself a secret . . . maybe I should have." Wren peers out into the trees, suddenly fearful.

"I'm not going to let anything happen to you, Wren. And we're not going to use you as bait." Leroux gives her a hard look. "You've kept a low profile."

Wren feels sweat prick her palms. She won't let Jeremy violate her space again. "I'll tell Richard to move inside."

"Either way, I bet this isn't the last we'll hear from him in Great Barrington. You and I both know it's only a matter of time before he makes another attempt at communication."

"Sometimes I think I should stop listening," she says.

CHAPTER 24

H E CAN HEAR THE PARTY from the lake.
He had found himself appreciating real silence for
the first time in a long time. But now, music, laughter, and
voices carry into his moment of silent reflection. The sounds
skip across the lake like polished stones, distractingly landing
right in his lap. It's frustrating and disruptive. He can feel
his anger building to a boil and he doesn't try to control it.
Instead, he lets it come. He invites it. He lets it seep into his
cells and take up space in his veins. His fingers play with a
splintered piece of wood on his borrowed chair's armrest and
he closes his eyes. He tilts his head back and listens, letting the
sounds feed his indignation and fuel his compulsion.

Standing now, he opens his eyes, scanning the dark lake for
signs of life. Across the water, all is quiet and dark. Houses
are sleeping or vacant. But the sounds come from his left, out
of place and unwelcome in this site of solitude. The water is
still and unbothered, but Jeremy knows this unwelcome folly
threatens it.

Drinking in the crisp air, he stalks his way toward the trees to his left. As he allows his eyes to adjust, he reaches down to touch the handle of his knife secured in his boot. Following the sounds as they get louder, he begins to feel heat in his head. The blood burns beneath his cheeks as he walks purposefully and swiftly through unbeaten forest, forging his own path where one never existed. Singularly focused now, he lets the sharp pines reach out and scratch him. They guide him with pain to his destination and he is grateful. Their touch feels like nails on his skin. Grazing him, preparing him for release.

After only moments, through thick brush, lights begin to come into view. The sounds get louder and a glass shatters close by. As the dense trees open, they reveal a massive house, nestled closer to the lake than his own temporary residence. This home is alive. At least a hundred bodies gather there, holding drinks and performing the mating rituals expected of them. Every light is on and groups congregate in clumps outside and inside the home. There are lawn games and beer pong in full swing, and all around them the speakers wail with Top 40 nonsense.

A quick sweep of the demographic tells him everything. No one looks like they could point to Australia on a map. This is a party thrown at Mom and Dad's lake house and they are openly trashing the place. Glasses shatter, drinks spill, and people barely out of their teens fall over themselves with complete disregard. It's Sodom and Gomorrah, but it's the store-brand version.

Jeremy slips his glasses on, running a hand through his hair and emerging from the tree line quietly. Not one head turns to question the stranger who oozed from the forest. He moves into the perimeter with ease, but he remains alone, hovering on the edge of the outside crowd and observing their behavior.

He was right to be angry. The volume of the music is such that every person is yelling to another just to be heard. It's maddening and pathetic. Every single thought that he involuntarily hears screamed into another person's face is excruciating. With such overstimulation, he finds it hard to focus his attention. His eyes dart from face to face, waiting to feel that familiar compulsion, that delicious convergence of chemicals that tells him that it's time. Usually, this is a narrower arena, but tonight he's a shark in a sea of red.

Then he finds it.

He locks his eyes onto her, but she doesn't notice him yet. She's probably around twenty-five but there's a naivete there that defies what her birth certificate likely says. There's just something about her eyes that shows age but none of the wisdom that should come with it. She has the kind of blond hair that always looks dirty, slicked back into an intentionally messy bun. She's unremarkable, really. But there's one thing that makes her stand out. She's boorishly stuffing her face. In a sea of Solo cups, pizza, and cigarettes, she has a paper plate with a small portion of sandwich on it. In the small circle she stands in, she garishly talks and laughs with at least three other partygoers as she takes bite after bite. She holds the plate high to catch crumbs and speaks with her mouth full, giving her friends and now Jeremy a front-row seat to the process of mastication.

He watches her closely as she abruptly places the plate on a chair behind her, leaving the half-eaten remnants for someone to sit on.

"Gotta pee. I'll be back." She puts both her hands up in declaration to her group. They chuckle in response. She's dramatic. He hates dramatic people. The need for constant attention and validation is a truly foul trait that too many uninteresting people have.

"Charming," he hears one of the young women in the group say quietly as the blond wanders away from the house.

He observes her staggering slightly toward the tree line, instead of the house. She's going to pee in the woods. Confused, he moves to the trees, casually stuffing his hands into his pockets. He moves quietly, following the sounds of cracking twigs and rustling leaves. She helps him find her by singing to herself. When she comes into view, he sees her leaning against a tree and squatting. After a moment, he steps on a twig loudly, causing her to jump, quickly pulling her pants up with a look of urgency on her face. He may have accidentally sobered her up with fear.

"Oh, I am so sorry!" He holds his hands up, turning his head to the side. "I was coming out here to piss, I didn't realize the forest would be occupied."

At first, she seems angry, until he comes into full view. Now she seems to blush and lets out a laugh. "Jesus, you scared the absolute shit out of me!"

He smiles but keeps his head turned to the side. "I could tell."

"You can look, I'm decent."

When he finally turns to face her, she remains unimpressive, even with moonlight streaming through the trees. "You know, I heard there is a bathroom inside the house," he says teasingly.

She cocks her head to one side. "I could say the same to you, buddy."

He chuckles. "Touché." As he speaks to her, he pretends to pee behind a nearby tree.

Jeremy can tell she's inspecting him. She unties and fluffs her hair with her fingers in an obvious show of interest, silently choosing to stay in the woods with him instead of leaving. He feigns zipping up his pants and walks toward her, keeping that crooked smirk on his face.

She can't help but return his grin. "I just didn't feel like going inside. The air is nice tonight, and this bathroom never has a line." Her eyes don't move from his.

"Except tonight," he responds coyly.

She bites her lip. "Well, touché back, I guess." She's coherent, able to make flirty small talk but still slurring her words slightly. Her eyes are half-lidded and her makeup is a bit smudged. It's like the perfect storm.

"I'm Brett," he lies.

"Jenna," she says, boldly stepping into his space.

"Well, Jenna, want to take a walk? I need some time away from the noise." He doesn't waste a second. She's going to accept his offer without much effort on his part.

"Absolutely, Brett." She is practically drooling at this point, forcing her arm through his, even though he didn't offer it up to her. They begin to walk arm in arm farther into the dense forest. There is a trail that looks overgrown but provides just enough of a guide to make her feel as if she's still safe. "So, how do you know Jeff?" she asks.

He waits barely a beat, assuming Jeff's parents are the one whose vacation home is currently being destroyed. "Oh, Jeff and I used to be roommates," he answers with conviction.

She grips his arm with her other hand, being the actress he predicted she would be. "Oh my god!" she squeals. "I think I remember him mentioning you! You guys lived in Cambridge with Dave, right?"

He stops a laugh from escaping his lips. He has never known a Dave in his life. "Yeah, Dave is such a dick."

She snorts out a real laugh now, bumping her hip into his slightly. "Shut up, he's at the party!"

He's amazed by how she is spoon-feeding him this conversation. "Oh, really? I haven't seen him. He still owes me money for the couch."

She's getting more and more touchy as they move down the trail. Her hip keeps brushing against his and her fingers graze his arm every now and then. "Do you still live in Cambridge?"

"No, I actually have a place nearby. Right up ahead actually." He motions where the trail turns slightly into a small sandbank. It's not even where he had been staying, but he passed it on the way to the party and made a note of the dinghy left next to the water.

"Are you taking me to your house, Brett?" She slithers the words out, trying to catch his gaze with her tired eyes. If he were a sandwich, she would have eaten him. He always chooses correctly.

"Not yet. First, I'm taking you on a romantic boat ride. The full moon on the lake is incredible." He pulls her to the right and into the outlet where the small, sandy beach appears.

Initially, she is elated, almost tripping over herself. "Ooh, did I stumble upon a prince in the woods tonight?"

He chuckles, approaching the dinghy and beginning to push it toward the water. "More like a pirate," he says.

She staggers forward, then pauses. "Wait, isn't this like . . . the biggest no-no? There must be something that says not to get on a boat with strangers." Even through the booze, she knows this is inherently a dangerous idea. Everything that has ever been said, written, or thought tells her not to get on a boat with a strange man.

He had been expecting this reaction and he's not worried. "Well, the good news is that I am not a stranger. I am Jeff and Dave's former roommate. When I shake down Dave later for the couch money, you can verify my charming nature." He smirks, knowingly turning her into putty in his hands.

It works. She giggles, letting her eyes drop to her feet and tucking a tendril of hair behind her ear. "Well, when you put it that way, it sounds like we are friends."

He holds a hand out to her, which she takes eagerly. Stepping into the boat, she takes a seat next to him as he loops the kill switch cord around his wrist. It was pure luck and circumstance that this boat wasn't secured. He had banked on it being unprotected and he was right. The Berkshires certainly isn't a crime-riddled area. The reality is people leave doors unlocked and boat motors unsecured because it just isn't an issue for them up here. He would have been shocked to see that one of these lake houses didn't trust their neighbors with something as banal as a dinghy.

"Ready to set sail, friend?" He places the gear into the neutral position, readying the motor to be engaged.

She leans forward, close enough for her breath to mix with his own. "Let's go."

He clears his throat uncomfortably, taking hold of the starter cord. "You should move over a little. I don't want to accidentally hurt you when I pull the cord." It is the truth. He doesn't want to *accidentally* hurt her.

She moves over a little bit, letting her head drop back to look up at the stars above them. He gets the motor roaring with a couple pulls and pushes the gear shift lightly into the forward position. He keeps it as quiet as he can as they slowly pull into Lake Garfield. He guides them toward the southern edge of the lake, where there is a good mile of unoccupied shore. At first, they drive in silence. The lake is like glass that they slowly shatter together.

CHAPTER 25

"**H**EY, JUNIOR! COME ON IN!"

Upon entering the Kingsborough Police Department, the tone is set. A young officer with the name tag BRADLEY sits back in his chair, grinning at his own wit. The officers around him snicker at the implication that Leroux's position is purely nepotistic. Cops definitely talk, and the fact that Leroux's father worked the Butcher case before has become a source of contention among this local department.

"And you brought Angela Lansbury with you, how nice."

Wren stops beside Leroux, looking behind her and then back to Bradley. "Wait, am I Angela Lansbury in this scenario?"

He scoffs, turning his chair to face away from her.

She can't help but smile genuinely. "Not only is that reference incredibly dated, but it doesn't even apply. Have you ever watched *Murder, She Wrote*?"

Bradley stays quiet and refuses to look at her, using his disrespect as his answer.

233

An officer next to him shakes his head, seemingly agreeing with Wren. "Yeah, that sucked, Bradley."

Bradley spins to face his peer. "Fuck you."

"Great to meet you all. Is the adult in charge of you around?" Leroux rolls his eyes, scanning the room.

"Share the sandbox, kids," Lieutenant Brixton's voice booms, catching Wren off guard. He saunters out of his office imposingly, locking his big eyes on Bradley before shifting his gaze to Wren and Leroux. "Dr. Muller, Detective Leroux, take a seat in my office, won't you?"

They cross the room, sliding past a few nasty looks. It feels tenser than it should in this precinct. By now, Wren's a pro when it comes to dealing with the varying levels of ego in her line of work, but something about this situation feels darker somehow. She can't help but scan the room, trying to see if anything can explain the feeling of dread that besieges this building. This is a young crop of police officers and detectives, and she notes that maybe it's just bold inexperience that radiates so repellently.

They take seats across from Lieutenant Brixton. With the door closed, the feeling Wren was struggling with seems to dissipate.

"Dr. Muller, it's great to finally meet you." Brixton extends his hand across the table, allowing Wren to shake it.

"Pleasure to meet you as well, Lieutenant."

"I apologize for Bradley. Eventually he will learn he's not funny."

Wren smiles. "It's a hard lesson to learn."

"Send us a picture of the moment he learns it." Leroux leans back in his seat, projecting his obvious frustration.

Brixton faintly chuckles. "Will do." He taps his finger on a file in front of him, sliding a photo out that reveals one angle of the double-homicide scene. "Listen, I know you have some insight into who may have done this. We realize this isn't a run-of-the-mill homicide."

"What's with you guys? Jeremy Rose committed this act. You know the Butcher case as well as anyone." Leroux scoffs at Brixton's noncommittal tone.

"I do. And the only reason you are sitting here right now is because I respect the hell out of your father and his dedication to the Butcher case. That respect extends to you, but it isn't bulletproof. Don't for a second assume there is an infinite flow of communication here if you start trying to throw your weight around."

"I appreciate the acknowledgment that you need our insight. Maybe you can share that with the rest of your department. But the reality is, no one else is intricately carving a replica of Dr. Muller's bracelet on a murder victim."

Wren is a bit taken back by the formal way Leroux mentions her to Brixton. She clears her throat, nodding. "I have to agree with Detective Leroux here. The bracelet was not specifically mentioned in media reports. They said it was a piece of jewelry, so this would be an incredible coincidence if it wasn't someone with intimate knowledge of the original series of crimes."

"Irregardless." Brixton puts his hand up, interrupting her.

That's barely a word.

"We are going to investigate this without a preconceived narrative. Of course we are going to keep Rose at the top of the list of suspects, but that doesn't mean we are going to blindly follow that singular lead."

Leroux shakes his head. "Look, we aren't trying to insert ourselves into the entire investigation—"

"Wouldn't matter if you were. You aren't part of this department," Brixton says, interrupting Leroux's thought before he can finish it.

Wren looks over to see Leroux taking a deep, obvious breath through his nose. It's the telltale sign that he is about to explode, but he's desperately trying to keep it together.

Wren finishes the idea she knows Leroux was trying to convey. "Look, you want our experience and insight? All we are asking for is the smallest amount of respect and transparency."

Brixton nods, leaning forward and tapping his finger on the file again. "Listen, I respect you both. I want to catch this asshole just as much as you do. We all know what you went through down there." He pauses, looking at Wren meaning- fully before continuing. "I'll try to keep everyone on the same page, but they're going to feel territorial."

"Thank you, Lieutenant." Wren forces a smile.

Brixton nods again. "As you both know, it's a process. We have to be deliberate about this investigation, or we are going to end up chasing nonsense in an attempt to close it out."

Leroux clears his throat. "Maybe you guys need to double back on some avenues up here. Tap into Philip Trudeau again.

They spent a ton of time together up here as kids; he has to have some kind of wisdom to share."

"I told you we cleared Trudeau." Brixton's tone shifts noticeably. The change registers to both Wren and Leroux at once.

"I don't think Detective Leroux is suggesting you interrogate Trudeau again. Maybe we can just chat with him for some local knowledge. He may know some places Jeremy liked to frequent or—"

"Dr. Muller," Brixton says abruptly.

This man can't let anyone speak a full sentence. It's maddening.

"We don't make it a habit to harass people around here. What you two need to remember is this isn't Louisiana."

Leroux scoffs. "Harass people? Gathering information is part of your job, Lieutenant. It's not harassment."

"Detective Leroux, we cleared Trudeau. We're going to spend our time looking for new evidence instead of fishing the same old pond," Brixton says, standing to indicate the end of the meeting.

"So, that's it?" Leroux asks.

"That's it."

"I don't know what's happening, but it feels like this is going to be a real struggle to get them to narrow their focus." Wren pushes open the front door of the precinct and walks out onto the sidewalk. The air is warm and a cool breeze snakes past her.

"I'll tell you what's happening. We're getting iced out." Leroux lights a cigarette immediately, making Wren cringe.

"We knew this was going to be tough."

He slides into the driver's seat of his rental car and sighs. "They are moving too slow." He pulls out onto the street, sticking his cigarette out the window. "No one has a sense of urgency here. And they think the South moves slowly."

Wren chuckles, rubbing her hands over her face. "Yeah, that's what gets me too. They are clearly in over their heads and they aren't willing to admit it."

"Instead, they will fumble this case while we are standing right here."

"Did you find out about the injuries on the male victim in the double event?"

Leroux takes a long drag, blowing the smoke out the side of his mouth. It swirls out the window behind them. "Yeah, he had a crossbow bolt in his ankle, a laceration across his cheek, and he was nearly decapitated. It was vicious."

"A crossbow bolt?" Wren rolls her eyes. "Man, he needs to play a new song."

"You're telling me."

"Do you think we could track down Trudeau ourselves? Maybe pay him a visit and get some information? They just seem so dead set on keeping him out of this. It feels off to me."

Leroux nods, turning down a side street. "Something stinks about it to me too. We can't formally interview him, but there's nothing stopping us from having a chat with the guy."

"Do you remember the name of his church?"

"Covenant of something. Covenant of the Lamb maybe? Or something to do with righteousness?"

"That's incredibly unhelpful, but let me see if I can find something similar nearby that rings a bell." Wren shakes her head, entering as many key words as she can into the GPS, trying to wrack her brain for the name. Several churches come up on the screen and Leroux glances at them at a stop sign. He recognizes it at the same time as Wren.

"Covenant of Grace Church. See? I was close."

"It's a few miles away; let's head that way now."

They drive in silence, each trying to plot out the next move. Trudeau might have some information they could use, but he might just be the dead end he was when this all started. It's hard not having authority up here. It's not something either of them are used to.

Shortly after they roll past businesses and houses, bustling with people and activity, the buildings become scarcer and nature becomes dominant. Run-down farms and crooked trees poke out from the roadside. The vibes become less Hallmark movie and more Stephen King.

"There it is." Wren points to their left. Covenant of Grace Church looks just like it did during her online search. It is a small gray dwelling. The outside is weatherworn and there is a spindly steeple stabbing at the sky that looks as if it were drawn in creeping ink. They pull up in front, both staring up at it with unease.

"Let's go." Leroux opens the car door, stepping out into the gravel.

Wren follows, a bit flustered. "What are we going to do?"

"We are just going to chat."

As they walk up the front steps, the double doors loom over them. Intricately carved wood has seen age but still maintains its beauty. She can't help but be in awe of the deep, sculpted carvings and details that seem out of place next to the austerity of the church itself. Wren runs her fingers over the elaborately designed cross in the middle of the doors, before Leroux pushes them open. The sound cuts through the unnatural silence that blankets this place. The doors creak and crack, echoing loudly around the church.

Inside, a group of about twelve people looks up, alarmed. They hold Bibles in front of them casually, appearing to be involved in some kind of group discussion. A man who looks to be in his late thirties stands up and nods to them.

"Hello. Are you here for Bible study?" he asks. His voice is friendly, but there is an edge to it that Wren wonders if Leroux can detect too.

"Are you Philip Trudeau?" Leroux asks, walking down the aisle toward the altar area where the group is gathered.

"Yes, what can I do for you?"

Wren notices his posture change. He stiffens; the muscles in his jaw clench a bit. Leroux sees it too. He smirks slightly. The man loves a nervous interview subject.

Leroux holds out a hand and shakes Philip's. "I'm Detective Leroux, we spoke on the phone a little while back."

"Oh, wow, Detective Leroux. It's great to meet you in person, I guess." Philip puts his Bible down, rubbing his jaw with one hand.

"This is Dr. Wren Muller."

Wren holds out her hand as well, but Philip hesitates. It's only for a second, but she clocks it. His eyes widen slightly, then the smile crosses his lips, genuinely. It's a strange reaction, but it doesn't look as though Leroux caught it.

"Nice to meet you, Dr. Muller." He grasps her hand tightly and she returns a strong grip of her own.

"Please, call me Wren," she says, searching his eyes for anything revealing. Self-righteousness is like a haunted stain. You can paint over it to make it look presentable, but it will always bleed through. Philip tries to hide it, but his stain of moral superiority is front and center to Wren.

"All right then." After a beat, he breaks eye contact and pulls his hand back. The rest of the group stares, whispering to one another softly. "You'll have to excuse us; we were in the middle of our weekly Bible study." He gestures around.

"Hey, we were the ones who barged in here. We apologize for interrupting." Wren smiles, making eye contact with some of the group members. They mostly smile back, nodding. Some of them look suspiciously at her, seemingly irritated at the intrusion.

"Is there something I can do for you folks? All the way up here from Louisiana. Can't imagine you just came to join the group." Philip chuckles, but it's fake.

Leroux narrows his eyes slightly. Wren's relieved to see it's not just her evening of internet sleuthing informing her opinion of the pastor.

"Is there a room we can go to talk for a moment? I promise we won't take up a lot of your time." Leroux grins at him, challenging him to say no in front of his flock.

"Of course, Officer." Philip gestures for them to follow.

"Detective, actually," Leroux corrects him.

"Of course. Detective." Philip nods, something icy emanating from his eyes before he shakes it off, a seemingly warm smile projecting now. "Continue the discussion, everyone. I'll be back in a minute. Stephanie, I liked your interpretation. Don't lose momentum on it." He places a hand on Stephanie's shoulder, giving it a subtle squeeze.

Stephanie smiles, visibly blushing.

"Follow me." He leads them to a room behind the sanctuary. It's one of two offices, littered with papers but orderly in its own way. Photos of a young boy are framed on the desk, along with a family photo, wife and all. Wren arches an eyebrow, wondering what story his congregation got about his divorce. When a marriage ends badly, there is usually a little creative storytelling involved. It's like an unintended crash course in public relations, where controlling the narrative becomes paramount.

Judging by Stephanie's flushed face when Philip left, it feels safe to say that he likely has a lot of them wrapped around his finger. Wren wonders if Kathryn's side of the story is getting erased, hidden behind a man whose congregation will always find credence in his word above all. One day she's the beloved pastor's wife, the next she's silenced into posting thinly veiled adultery allegations on social media.

"Please, sit." Philip's voice startles her away from her thoughts.

They take their seats across from him as he settles into the authority position. He steeples his hands and leans back a bit, showing them that they are in his house now.

"Listen, Mr. Trudeau—" Leroux begins.

"Everyone around here just calls me Pastor Philip," Philip interrupts, a small smirk playing at the edges of his mouth.

Leroux smiles, sensing Philip's tenuous grip on his own power. "You're not my pastor," he says dryly.

Philip nods. "Fair enough."

"Look, this isn't an interrogation or an interview."

"Oh, I know that. You don't have jurisdiction up here," Philip answers, using Leroux's own logic against him.

Leroux pauses. His smile fades and Wren sees him purse his lips together subtly. Sensing a blowup, she places a hand on his arm. He looks at her, breaking the tether of anger that seems to connect him to Philip.

"Pastor, I'm sure you have heard that Jeremy Rose may be in Massachusetts," she says, maintaining a strong but friendly tone.

"I have," Philip responds.

"Well, since you and Jeremy spent a lot of time together when you were young, we were hoping you could maybe give us some ideas about where he might go."

"Why would I have that insight, Doctor?" Philip doesn't maintain the same friendly tone in his response to her. Something in his voice is on defense.

Wren creases her brows together. "Well, I think my previous statement answers that question, don't you?"

A grin spreads across his face. "I mean, when we were kids, we spent nights hanging out in my parent's basement, being reckless teenagers, and sneaking up into the old watchtower at the abandoned fairgrounds. Is that really going to help you?"

"How reckless did you get, Philip?" Leroux leans back in his chair, starting to challenge him a bit.

Philip smiles, shaking his head. "Nothing that would interest you, Detective. Regrettable acts of immaturity like using Ouija boards and sneaking some cheap beers. Now I try to make it one of my missions to stop kids from unknowingly messing around in occult practices."

"You're right, none of that interests me," Leroux says, gruffly.

"Any information is helpful, Pastor. Remember, you are under no obligation to tell us anything," Wren says firmly, trying to keep the flow of conversation from tipping too far off a ledge.

"This is just an informal chat between new pals," Leroux chimes in.

Philip sighs. "Look, I should get back to the group. I'm sorry I can't be more help to you." He stands, rubbing his hands on his jeans before walking toward the door.

"You haven't heard from him, right?" Leroux asks, grinning at his small act of provocation.

Philip stops, turning around. "No. I haven't spoken to Jeremy Rose since we were eighteen years old. I told the police, the ones who have jurisdiction here, that as well." He turns sharply and opens the door, standing and waiting for them to exit.

Leroux stands to leave, stopping close to him. "Just a chat between new pals, Phil. No need to get defensive." He smiles, stepping into the hallway.

Wren sighs, stepping away from her chair and accidentally brushing a few papers off the desk. She bends down, scooping them up and placing them back where they originated.

Before taking her eyes away, something flashes at her, the word *Salem* on a receipt for gas. It's the second paper in the stack and it only slightly pokes out. Everything inside begs her to take it, but she can't. She reaches out to move it closer into view, but she startles and jumps back at the sound of Philip's voice.

"Dr. Muller?" he asks, watching her. "It's time for our informal conversation to end. I'm working."

She takes one more passing glance at the word *Salem* before exiting after Leroux.

Settling into the car, Leroux is on fire. He huffs, slamming the door behind him.

"What a power-hungry little shithead," he says, seething.

"John, you can't say that! He's a pastor."

He scoffs, looking at Wren incredulously. "You think I give a shit? He could be a canonized saint and I would still call him a shithead. Since when do you care?"

"I don't really," she says, clicking her seat belt into place. "It just feels weird, I guess. Maybe that religious upbringing never fully left my DNA."

"Should have had it surgically removed like I did," he says dryly.

Wren steers them back to the purpose of the visit. "So, you think he is worth keeping an eye on?" she asks, turning over the interaction in her mind, wondering why it all felt so tense.

"I think he is worth keeping in our orbit. Something just feels off to me about him. My hands are tied here though. I can't push this or it's my ass on the line."

Wren nods. "Yeah, I noticed something interesting before we left."

"What did you see?" Leroux almost jumps at the notion.

"It wasn't anything crazy, but I saw a receipt from a gas station in Salem, Massachusetts."

He pauses, trying to make the connection.

"The case I consulted on before I came here was in Salem, remember?"

"Oh yeah, I guess that's interesting then." He's not convinced.

"Corinne said the victim was possibly seeing a man she called Phil." Wren moves her hands as if she's trying to pull the reaction from him.

"All right, well, that's more interesting. Did you see the date he was there?"

"No, I didn't want him to see me snooping."

"Smart. But, aside from the nickname, all you really have is him going to Salem at some point. Remember, it's fall in New England. Doesn't everyone flock there during this time of year?"

"I guess. But how many pastors are partaking in the Salem Halloween shenanigans?"

He laughs, looking back at the closed front door of the church. "True."

"I know it's a long shot, but I just have a weird feeling about him." Wren leans back in her seat, looking out the window as Leroux pulls away.

"I do too, but we have to keep our noses clean. The last thing I want is to get iced out completely."

Wren nods, chewing on her lip. "I suppose you're right."

"Why don't you talk to Corinne and see if they have moved that case forward at all?"

"That's exactly what I'll do."

CHAPTER 26

"**S**o I'm assuming you're single." Jenna breaks the silence to say something stupid.

Jeremy stifles an audible sigh, pulling the shift to just above a putter. He turns to face her. "What makes you say that?" he responds, deciding to play along until he reaches the isolated part of the lake.

She feigns a shocked expression, scooting closer to him again. "Well, I guess it isn't smart to assume, huh?" Her eagerness to kiss him is going to get her thrown in the water.

"Maybe you were right," he begins, directing them to the right a bit as they enter the more isolated piece of shoreline. "Perhaps I *am* a stranger. Maybe I lied." He's smirking, keeping her docile.

She's not catching on, pushing forward to try to close the space between them instead. "I don't think you're a stranger, Brett," she whispers, dropping her eyes to his mouth.

He smiles with teeth now, not moving away and letting the space linger there for a second. "My name's not Brett," he hisses.

Her eyes quickly flick up to his. In them he sees the flash of panic, but she doesn't move away initially. Her sense of self-preservation is muted by alcohol-soaked hormones. "Shut up," she says louder than her previous whisper.

"My name is Jeremy," he says dryly.

She pulls away. Her face twists into confusion. "Wait, what? Why would you lie about your name?"

He lets his head fall back to see the stars that dot the open sky above them. He can't help but let another chuckle tumble out. "Because I could, Jenna. I lied because I *could* lie to you."

She's incredulous. Her eyes flitter back and forth, and her breath begins to hitch. "What does that even mean?"

"It means you were right to question getting on a boat with a stranger. Do you always make stupid choices?" He gives her a genuinely questioning look.

"Take me back to the party." Anger flashes across her face. It's mixed with fear, a fear he is about to pull to center stage.

"No, I think we'll stay out here and enjoy our romantic moonlit boat ride a bit longer." As he speaks, he pulls the knife from his boot. He holds it in front of him and leans forward to her. "Jesus, you were ready to come home with me. Can you imagine?" He laughs.

She recoils slightly, as much as the small boat will allow her to put space between them. She scans the open water around her, likely looking for a house. She finds none. They are in the mile-long stretch of uninhabited shoreline. "I'll scream," she threatens, her voice shaking.

He shrugs. "I'll cut your throat before it matters."

The answer shakes her into a sob. She eyes the blade and knits her brows together. "What do you want?" she asks desperately.

"I want to get you wet," he whispers, biting at his lip.

She doesn't answer. Her eyes go wide, and she licks her lips. Her mouth is probably dry. He can almost feel her fear now. It's become something he feels like he can reach out and stroke. Every horrible outcome is flashing through her mind, sobering her up completely.

"I mean I want you to take a swim, Jenna. Jesus, did you just get out of prison or something? I'm not going to fuck you."

"I am not getting in the lake." She shakes her head in terror, glimpsing at the black water that surrounds them.

"I mean, that's totally up to you. But I feel like I should tell you that staying in this boat with me is a really bad choice. And haven't you kind of filled your bad-choice punch card already tonight?" He grins again, removing the useless glasses from his face and stuffing them in his pocket.

She shakes her head, weeping softly and leaning far away from the knife. "Please, just take me back to the party. I don't even remember your real name. I won't tell anyone."

"Oh, I know you won't tell anyone," he says, checking his watch.

"I swear . . ." she whispers again.

He glimpses back up to her. "Let's give you thirty seconds, huh?"

"Thirty seconds for what?" she asks, looking more and more like cornered prey.

He holds his wrist up to show his watch to her. "Thirty seconds to make your decision. Jump in and give swimming to shore a go or stay with me in this boat and roll the dice."

She is frozen. Her eyes look at the water and back to him several times, but no words follow.

"Twenty seconds. You were much happier before. Where did that smile go? Maybe I can make you one." As he says this, he traces a smile in the air with the blade.

She shakes her head, seemingly trying to will him away. She looks to the shoreline to her right, appearing to judge the distance from the boat. They are almost dead center in a very wide section of the lake. He made sure of that.

"Ten seconds. You can swim, right? It's no fun if you just sink like a stone."

She takes a couple moments to look at the shoreline again and another to look back at him and the knife. She hesitates for only a second before wordlessly launching herself over the side of the dinghy. The water is freezing. It must feel like a thousand knives at once. She comes to the surface sputtering but quickly begins swimming toward her salvation. Jeremy smiles, pushing the boat into just above a crawl and following right behind her. She tries to scream as she furiously propels herself forward in the dark, freezing lake.

"Ready to race, Jenna?" he yells as he positions the boat directly behind her. "Keep your head in the game, I don't want the boat propeller to have all the fun!" He revs harder, jolting the boat forward to touch her slightly.

She wails and chokes on water but continues pushing forward. He watches her as she fights, but exhaustion begins to slow her strokes as they try to push her to reach for land. Each time he revs forward to touch her or gain on her in the boat, she changes course slightly to try to put distance between them. This unintentional serpentine is siphoning her energy at an alarming rate. But he doesn't let up. If she even pauses for a second, he makes her pay for it.

She gags on dirty lake water and her head dips more than once under the surface. He doesn't want her to drown, but he wants her to feel like he wants that. Just when he thinks she might give up, he lets off the motor, dropping back a bit and allowing her space to gain some headway. The water should be shallowing now. Soon her tired legs will hit the slimy bottom. Rocks will punch at her feet to inform her she is close to land. She'll feel such relief. But that's because she doesn't know what comes next.

He slows the boat to a slither and watches as she finally hits that shelf where she can touch the bottom. She reaches forward, grabbing hold of a tall plant sticking up from the water and pulling herself to stand in the chest-deep water. Her breaths come out in heaves and she spits between cries. After a couple steps, she falls to her hands and knees, crawling to the shore. For just a second, she collapses on the sand and rocks, trying to control her breathing and shivering visibly.

He revs forward, sending the boat careening toward the shallows and pulling the safety cord to cut the engine just as it bumps against the shelf. As soon as she sees the boat again, she staggers up to her feet and takes off running into the tree line. He follows at a jog, hearing her crashing feet and choked yells in front of him. She makes no attempt to stay quiet or hide; instead she leaves a conspicuous bread crumb trail by which to follow her.

Jeremy knows these woods. She doesn't. Jeremy is dry. She is soaked to the bone in freezing lake water, including her boots, which audibly squish and no doubt weigh her down considerably. He stays quiet, following her at a leisurely pace but never losing track of her movements. His eyes have adjusted to this thick layer of darkness. They were born to adjust to it. She likely sees nothing but black around her, unable to make out any forms in her blind panic. Abruptly, her chaotic movements stop and he hears some soft rustling of leaves and a twig snap.

"Oh, thank God. I swear if you just kept running like a damn fool, I would have really lost my temper." He laughs heartily, letting his voice hit every corner of the forest around them. Once he gathers himself, he just listens. He hears crickets lazily chirping, waiting for the first frost so they can die. An owl haunts this place with a deep call.

Under it all, he hears her breathing. She whimpers with most of her breaths and can't seem to still her heart rate, which only makes the puffs come out faster and louder. He softens his own steps as he makes his way toward her sounds. "Sounds like you hid on me. Careful, if I see the whites of your eyes out here, they will be the first thing I remove."

She stifles another cry, and he spots her. Through the rich darkness he can see her crouched behind a tree up ahead, off to the left of his path. He changes course, silently placing his boot down and letting the dry earth absorb some of the sound. He keeps his weight on his back foot and smoothly probes the ground in front of him with his other foot. He clears places to step as he goes, blending in with the way the breeze moves the leaves around them and sometimes waiting for a well-placed owl sound to step loudly.

All the while, he never takes his eyes off her. He watches as she rushes to another nearby tree, trying to move farther and farther away from where she believes he is. He keeps expecting to see her sprint away, but she never does. It's a true sign of weakness that she refuses to execute the one maneuver that would, at the very least, give her a fighting chance.

She moves to a third location behind a large rock next to a tree. It's good coverage, if she weren't so loud. He can see that she thinks he is coming from the other side of the rock. She peeks around the side of it, staring out into the nothingness and seeing just as much. As he walks up from behind her, he senses that she may feel his presence.

She whips her head around and tries desperately to force her panicked eyes to adjust to the things they don't want to see. He stops dead in his tracks, almost an arm's reach away from her as she leans forward, still crouched.

Slowly, he crouches down too. Fascinated, he watches her hand grasp the emptiness. She knows something is there. Her basic human instincts must be firing enough to tell her there is something to fear out there in her orbit. But she doesn't run, only frantically tries to push the feeling back. Exhaustion keeps confusing her instincts. The lake has frozen the voice in her that implores her to listen to her senses.

After some time, he holds his knife out in front of him to give her something to touch. She takes a swipe into the air again and this time she catches her palm on the sharp edge of the blade. Even as she pulls it back, the knife slices deeper. A scream barely forms in her throat before he grabs her. One hand grasps her neck and stands them both up. The whites in her eyes are like two lights as they bore into his own with silent terror.

He walks her back and slams her hard against the rock where she found her final sanctuary. Her hands claw at his arm and try to pry his hand loose from her throat as only a choked, sputtering sound escapes. He holds the knife close to one of her wide eyes and he grits his teeth.

"I should blind you and leave you here." He spits out the words as if they are poison. They remain like that for a moment before he releases her throat and twists her striped sweater in his fist to hold her in place.

"You can still let me go, I won't tell anyone!" She is breathing hard, trying to steady her panic and make some kind of connection with him. "There are houses out here, you can't do this, Brett." She's frantic, desperately trying to reason with a fictional character.

"My name isn't Brett, Jenna! This is why you made these choices! You can't even remember my real name. You can't even absorb the easiest piece of information that I fed you." He shakes his head in disgust.

"See?" she pleads. "I can't turn you in! I don't even remember your name and I can't see your face!" Her voice comes out in a whine. "Just let me run away!"

"You didn't even try, Jenna!" he yells, suddenly bringing his face closer to hers. "You made every wrong choice that brought you here, you know that, right? *You* did this." He hovers the blade over her eye before plunging it into her stomach. Her eyes go wide, but no words come. He quickly drags the knife to the side and drops her to the ground.

She crumples into a ball and writhes, making the sounds a disemboweled person *should* make. He crouches over her as she reaches up to grab his jacket. Moving just out of her reach, he simply watches. He watches the life slowly pour out of her gut. Even in the darkness he can see the pain and regret dancing across her face.

When the sounds begin to cease and the blood has saturated the earth around his feet, he stands. The lights aren't quite out yet. Her eyes still flicker with life.

As he drags her through the forest, he feels calm. The crickets seem more lively, as if they aren't ready to succumb to an impending frost.

He's not ready to succumb either.

CHAPTER 27

S HE WAS FOUND by three teenage boys.

The youngest one is only fourteen years old. He and his two friends, who are fifteen and sixteen, had taken out one of their parents' boats for a joy ride early this morning, around four a.m. They had rocketed through a no-wake zone at a high-enough clip to cause some real wake behind them. Fearful that they would rouse the interest of the harbormaster, they slowed themselves way down to a putter as they neared the center of Lake Garfield.

As they essentially floated into the center of the lake on their own illicit wake, they spotted a small dinghy. It was motionless and seemingly without a captain. Something felt off to the boys immediately. They were three lifelong lake kids and an unmanned boat was always cause for concern.

They inched their own boat closer to the dinghy, planning to tow it back to the shore with them. It wasn't an entirely selfless act. They were hoping a good deed would soften the blow, should they be caught taking the boat out alone. As they neared the dinghy, the fourteen-year-old was the first one to see the contents. It wasn't until they had bumped up against the side of it that they finally saw inside.

Covering the bottom of the dinghy was a slick layer of some dark substance. It was smeared and pooled in certain areas, appearing like wet rust to some of the boys. As they wondered aloud to one another about the origin of this substance in an abandoned boat, the fourteen-year-old's eyes caught a dark lump in one of the pooled spots. As young boys are almost programmed to do upon discovery of an unknown object, they used a fishing rod to poke the item, rolling it over to get a better look at it.

After discerning what it was, they immediately called the harbormaster, who called the police. Interestingly, investigators were already on their way to the scene. They had received an anonymous tip that there was a body at the lake. Wren received a call from Leroux as the sun came up. Now they are standing on the shore of Lake Garfield, surrounded by lake houses and law enforcement.

"What did the caller say, exactly?" Wren walks toward the shore, trying to keep up with the gaggle of officers.

"No details," a middle-aged officer with blond hair answers her with irritation. Animosity prickles in the air. Leroux had warned her yesterday that the Kingsborough force would be difficult to deal with—and that is already proving true.

Wren rolls her eyes. "See, this is when a complete sentence would be great. Do you mean that you won't give *me* any details or that the caller didn't give *you* any details?"

"That depends. Who the hell are you?" The officer stops, looking Wren up and down with disdain.

"I'm Wren Muller, I'm the—"

He interrupts her, starting to walk again. "Yeah, I know who you are."

"Then why did you ask me?" She has crossed over into the world of truly annoyed now.

He finally gifts her a quick glance, still not bringing any sense of kindness to his facial expression. "The caller was pretty vague, only saying there was a body at the lake and then cutting the line."

"I am guessing a trace wasn't helpful?" Wren asks, deciding to ignore his strange behavior.

He shakes his head in response, quickening his pace away from her.

As they near the scene, Wren can already hear another power struggle gearing up.

"It's him." Leroux rubs his chin, taking in the grisly contents of the boat.

"Why don't you slow your roll, True Detective." An officer by the name of Michaels holds his hand up, as if to stop him in his tracks.

Leroux rolls his eyes, chuckling lightly. "Slowing your roll is exactly what got you here, isn't it?"

"Got me where, exactly?" Officer Michaels steps closer to Leroux, quirking his brow. He looms a bit, trying to intimidate with his height.

Leroux smirks, meeting his eyes. "Got you holding your dick with three bodies piled up."

Officer Michaels sucks in a breath. "I don't see a body here, Detective. Do you?"

Letting his smile widen, Leroux glances at the boat. "You're telling me the Kingsborough Police are executing a search-and-rescue mission for someone whose heart is currently outside of their body and lying in front of us in a blood-soaked dinghy?"

"Why are you even here? Did your dad get you this assignment too?" Officer Michaels asks, mockingly.

Leroux narrows his eyes, letting the smile drop from his face. "Listen, man, if your department needs an anatomy book, just say it."

Officer Michaels scoffs and walks back toward the group of law enforcement to their right.

Leroux follows, not ready to let it go. "No, really," he shouts loud enough for the rest of them to notice, "the NOPD would be happy to donate one if it means giving you rubes a basic understanding of why the human body can't function without a heart."

Officer Michaels whips around, red-faced. "Keep your hands out of our crime scene. Take your place with the bystanders, where you belong."

"It's him," Leroux repeats.

"As shocking as it may seem to you, murders do happen out here that aren't committed by Jeremy Rose."

Wren stands off to the side, watching this exchange in quiet amusement. Seeing the power struggle between police departments has always fascinated her. It's a job that should require teamwork, a removal of ego and impartial interpretation of the evidence. Yet, almost every time she's seen two different departments come together for a case, a playground pissing match seems to occur.

She heads over to the dinghy, taking a closer look at the heart lying on the bottom of the boat. It's been somewhat crudely torn from its owner, that much is clear to her. Part of the aorta that is still attached has been ripped, as if the killer used a few quick cuts of a blade, while pulling the organ out forcibly. But Wren also notices that there was some precision and skill involved. Whoever did this was able to remove the heart without damaging the heart itself. The arteries are worse for wear, but that clearly wasn't a concern.

She notes that the color of the blood indicates the organ hasn't been here for very long. She guesses only a matter of hours has separated this heart from its owner.

"Hey! We got a body!" A young officer rounds the corner of the shoreline, his youthful face etched with terror.

The group of officers leaps into action. A few race after him, and Wren and Leroux quickly follow.

"I fucking hate these pricks," he says.

"Remember, let's just try to play nice," Wren answers, craning her head to see beyond the cluster of officers up ahead.

"Did you talk to Corinne last night?" he asks.

"I did." She nods. "I guess they are really thinking one of her ex-boyfriends is the guy. He lied about his alibi, and he's got a pretty horrific history of abuse."

He shakes his head. "What an animal."

"Calling him an animal is kind. Corinne got updates from the ME saying there was a hole burned into her tongue;

straight through it. Apparently, it appeared to have been done with some kind of hot iron or rod. The poor girl was tortured to death."

"Jesus, they sure they can nail this guy?" Leroux looks genuinely horrified.

Wren shrugs. "They are pretty confident."

"Interesting. Glad they can close that one, I guess."

"Yeah, me too." Something inside her doesn't believe it, but she doesn't have a lot of time to focus on that, because as they near a thicket of trees, she comes into view.

The victim is sitting up, and upon first glance, she seems to be resting. Her legs are crossed in front of her, and her back rests against a massive, ancient tree. At first, Wren is hesitant because her head isn't slumped forward, but instead is looking straight ahead at her from what looks like a strong and supportive neck. As they walk closer, she notices the rope tied around the trunk of the tree. It's pulled taut around her face and head, looping right through her mouth and gagging her. It keeps her head steadily up against the tree, making her appear to be sitting up fully with a ghoulish grin pulled across her face.

More details start to come into focus as Wren moves closer. The woman's stomach is torn open, with a truly massive amount of blood staining her undershirt and pants. Upon first sight, Wren had thought her thin camisole was red, but as she gets closer she can see that it was once a totally different color, probably white. Her chest is cracked open and, although she hasn't examined her completely, Wren is willing to bet this woman is missing a vital organ.

On the left, the young cop who found the victim is retching in the bushes. Several other officers pace around the area, while a few investigators begin the process of securing the scene. The nervous energy is palpable, but everyone is doing their best to stay professional given the circumstances.

"You guys see this kind of thing often?" Leroux looks smug. He glances around at the tense scene and pops a piece of gum into his mouth, pointedly.

Wren shakes her head, trying to stay focused on the body in front of her. This department hadn't exactly rolled out the red carpet for them, but the folks in charge had at least allowed them to tag along. The move was met with a lot of resistance from most of the department. Some of the older officers are familiar with Leroux's father, and like Officer Michaels, they have never been shy about expressing their feelings. Those are the guys who believe it is nepotism that got Leroux his detective badge in the first place. As frustrating as it is to see a schoolyard mentality in such a somber setting, Wren worries that one wrong move and their all-access pass will be revoked out of spite. If they want to be part of these scenes, they will have to bite back some comments and just work together.

No one acknowledges Leroux's rhetorical question. They move together quickly, executing some kind of solemn choreography that none of them seem to be quite familiar with. As shocking as this scene is for this small department, it is clear to Wren that what they lack in experience, they make up for with care and thoroughness. They may be out of their depth, but they aren't ready to admit it quite yet. She can't help but relate to that feeling.

A young detective approaches Wren and Leroux. He's clean-cut, with his hair shaved close to his head. He rubs the back of his neck anxiously but still manages to exude some authority. "Well, Dr. Muller, we have an ME from Westfield headed this way, but it looks like you came prepared." He gestures to the black leather bag Wren clutches in her hand. "Would you mind taking a look and getting some initial reads?" He speaks in a hushed tone.

"Of course, Detective." She crouches down, quickly opening the bag and peeling off a pair of gloves from a wadded-up clump. She pulls one onto her left hand and readies the other when the detective crouches down next to her, startling her.

"James Warren." He holds his hand out. "Sorry, I meant to lead with that." He smiles awkwardly, still crouched next to her in the mud.

She smiles back, snapping on the right glove after shaking his hand. "Nice to meet you, Detective Warren." She stands, making her way toward the body.

"Wren, right?" he asks, following her immediately.

She glances back at him, feeling irritated. She always tries to get into a specific headspace before listening to a body, and Detective Warren seems determined to interrupt her process.

"Mmhmm," she says shortly, hoping he takes the hint. Approaching the victim, she squats to observe the rope pulled tightly across the head and mouth. Immediately, her own heart sinks when she notices the dried blood on the rope pulled across the bottom lip. Whoever did this had pulled the rope so tightly that it cut into the victim's skin. The presence of flowing blood indicates she was alive when this happened.

This has Jeremy written all over it.

She thinks about the cognitive dissonance it takes to pull a rope that tightly against a screaming woman's head, to feel it rip into the flesh of her face and still wrench it tighter. This specific brutality screams for her to recognize it. This kind of prolonged pain is caused by a true monster, one who stalks and plays with its prey.

But it's the removal of this victim's heart that speaks to her the clearest. A real-life version of her charm bracelet, which he has harvested as her gift.

Detective Warren interrupts her thoughts. "I know Detective Abberline over there thinks this is your guy, but I don't see any of his hallmarks." Warren looks at the hole in the victim's chest. His brows knit together as his eyes scan the torn skin and muscle.

Wren's focus is shattered. She looks up at him before standing to her full height. "Detective Abberline?" she asks.

Warren smirks, checking his phone quickly before gesturing to Leroux. "The lead detective working the Jack the Ripper case. The detective who connected all the murders? He's a spitting image of your pal over there."

"I know who Frederick Abberline is. It was just a poorly constructed joke, in my opinion." She suddenly feels entirely too protective of John Leroux.

"It was meant to be a compliment." Warren puts his hands up, still grinning at her. "Abberline is a legendary detective!"

She glares at Warren. "You followed the reference up by saying Detective Leroux is mistaken for connecting clearly linked murders together. You don't see how that's a bad joke?"

Warren chuckles. "Hey, your guy Leroux is tenacious like Abberline, that's all I was saying." The smug look on his face says otherwise.

She can't stop her face from showing her distaste. "All the interdepartmental chaos in the Ripper case, and you couldn't pull a better reference than Johnny Depp's character in *From Hell*?" She clicks her tongue. "Yikes."

"Wow, you know your stuff, huh?" He's teetering dangerously close to flirting next to a murder victim and it makes Wren's stomach churn.

She holds a gloved hand up to push back his physical proximity. "Detective Warren—" But he quickly interrupts her.

"Feel free to call me James," he says smoothly.

"Detective Warren," she repeats, "I need some space to work here. Would you mind keeping my perimeter secure? We don't want any connections being missed because of sloppy procedures." She gives him her best "bless your heart" smile.

His grin drops and he puts his hands up again, walking backward. "Got it, Doc. I'll let you force those connections in peace." He winks and spins around.

Wren's blood feels as if it's about to boil. "Funny your name is Warren. Isn't Sir Charles Warren famous for resigning in presumed shame before ever solving the Whitechapel murders?"

The detective stops in his tracks. He turns around with an amused look on his face. It's a menacing amusement, but it's there. "Your point?"

Wren shrugs, bending back down to the victim, finally wiping the smirk off her face. "It's just a better joke is all."

CHAPTER 28

"I DIDN'T AGREE TO ALL OF THIS." Philip holds his head in his hands, leaning against the small kitchen counter. He runs his hands under the faucet again, turning the knobs to be hot enough to steam. Jeremy notices that he doesn't even flinch as it pelts his skin. Red blotches form almost immediately as he scrubs his raw skin again and again, but it never comes clean.

Jeremy takes a sip from his water glass, his filthy glasses next to him on the table. "Technically you did."

Philip turns off the water to face Jeremy, his eyes glassy. "I said you could stay here, and I wouldn't call the cops. I didn't agree to drive down to the lake and help you stage a dead body!" He's yelling now, drying his hands furiously with a dish towel.

"You are being paid, remember."

Philip scoffs, throwing the towel on the counter and boring a look of pure loathing into Jeremy.

267

"Besides, you barely touched her." Jeremy keeps his tone unbothered.

"'Barely touched her'?" Philip charges forward, looming over Jeremy. "I can still feel the blood on my hands! I can feel the heat from it, and the smell of metal and meat! You butch-ered that girl, and you made me a part of it. Again!" He spits out each word, completely lost in his panic.

Something strange about Philip's reaction strikes Jeremy. It seems genuine enough, but there is something studied about his actions, as if he's in a play. Maybe Philip doesn't under-stand his own feelings about what he has been a part of—but his outrage feels forced somehow.

Jeremy lifts one brow, standing to his full height. "Let's not rewrite history now, Phil. *You* were driving, not me. I didn't make you a part of anything; you put us in a position where *I* had to clean up the mess."

"You know what? Someday you will be dragged out of whatever shit-covered hole you came from and have to reckon with everything you are. Someday you will be judged."

Jeremy laughs, following Philip as he walks into the living room. "Phil, make this easier on yourself. I'll be gone soon. You will never see me again. Just make another call."

Philip scoffs and sits down in his worn blue chair. "I am not bringing the police to my doorstep."

"You weren't traced when you called the tip line about our party girl, were you? No. Just call from the pay phone on Derby Road again." Jeremy lets his annoyance seep into his voice. He peeks out the window through the blinds.

His nerves have felt disruptive lately. It's not that he is afraid; it's a feeling of being overwhelmed. He has too many plates spinning and it'd be too easy for one of them to shatter. If there was a triage system with these plates, where one was less important than the others, that wouldn't be so bad. Unfortunately for him, they are all of similar value. He can't let even one slip.

It's the kind of pressure he felt in school. Again, it wasn't being afraid or feeling as if he couldn't handle it—it was just the pressure of making sure he doesn't disappoint himself. He never worried about impressing anyone else. No one else's opinion ever mattered to him. Only his own was worth anything.

Philip leans forward, tenting his fingers and tapping his foot. His nervousness is palpable. It feels as if he needs a mask to keep it from entering his pores and infecting his own body with weakness. Something is strange with him today, but Jeremy doesn't care enough to ask.

"I've done more than enough for you, Jeremy." He says it weakly now. He's weak.

"That was different, Phil. This is the important one. This is how we set everything into motion. This is how you keep your family safe."

Philip doesn't reply; he just stares at the crackling fire in the fireplace.

"All of our problems will be taken care of with one phone call," Jeremy continues.

"Our problems? These problems are yours and yours alone. I agreed to do this to get you out of my life for good. Don't confuse this." Philip gives him a look of disdain, running his hand through his hair anxiously.

"Like I said, I'll disappear. You can go back to playing family man in this house alone."

As soon as the words escape Jeremy's mouth, Philip is up and walking toward him. He points his finger in Jeremy's face, his own turning a deep shade of maroon.

"Keep my family out of this. Stop mentioning them. Stop using them. Get them out of your fucking vocabulary, you hear me?"

Jeremy smiles, leaning back against the window. "Sure, Phil. Chill out. You're going to end up giving yourself a stroke, and then we're really shit out of luck."

"What am I saying when I call?" Phil asks dryly without looking at him.

"We talked about this. Tell them the old fairgrounds is somewhere they need to sniff around. You don't need to give a ton of information. Just lead them there." Jeremy grins.

"I'm done with the phone calls after this. Done," Philip growls.

"For a man of the lord, you sure are angry." Jeremy watches the muscle in Philip's jaw twitch. Philip stares back as if he will lose it at any moment. Jeremy relents. "But, that's fair. Make the call."

Philip grunts and sinks back into his blue chair. "I'll think about it."

Jeremy sighs, rubbing his temples. "Phil, just cut the shit and do it. We both know you don't have a choice."

"No, *you* don't have a choice. You think you hold all the power here, but you are a golden fucking goose around this place. I could bring them your head on a platter, and I would be a hero."

"Except, you are forgetting that whole thing you just told me not to mention. Anything happens to me, it's like a silent alarm to make you a newly grieving parent." Jeremy looks at the photo of his son pointedly, driving home his point.

Philip bristles at the threat. Jeremy detects something else in his expression, but it's hard to pin down what it is. He's trying so hard to play the tough guy, but he's never been the tough guy. Jeremy can't imagine he suddenly found enough strength to fill that role as an adult.

He thinks back to when they were teenagers, maybe sixteen years old. It was before any of this truly bound them together. At that time they were bonded because they wanted to be.

It felt like fall, the weather not unlike today's. It was crisp but still warm enough to feel comfortable in most clothing. They had planned to do something risky, something reckless. Philip's friend Mike had come up with the idea to sneak up to Bash Bish Falls in the middle of the night. He wanted to get close to the falls, where no one was supposed to go. The stairs leading down to the falls were blocked off with caution tape. A move to keep idiots from trespassing too close.

There were local legends about the place. One that endured and had even made its way onto the sign leading into the falls was that a Mohican woman was sent over the falls to her death as punishment for adultery. People claim she haunts the area today, and no one could blame her if it were true. Either way, the place had some serious spooky credibility to it.

Philip offered to be the driver. He really didn't have a choice, because Jeremy was carless when he visited and Mike was a deadbeat. They planned to bring the Ouija board to the rocks at the base of the falls, and on the drive out, they talked about the questions they would ask this ghost woman about her untimely death.

Philip talked the biggest game. He acted as if he couldn't wait to get out there. He even planned a few crude comments to stir up some ghoulish anger. But something changed as they pulled into the parking lot and started walking down the long, mountainous trail leading to the falls.

The path was pitch-black, with animals rustling and all manner of unidentifiable sounds around them and thousands of bugs pelting their skin. The trees bent and cracked, moaning in the wind. The river rushed below with a perilous drop and no guardrail.

They walked along, their flashlight beams bouncing across the rocky pathway. Every now and then they stumbled over something, barely catching themselves before falling face-first into more rocks. Above them the trees came together to form a canopy, blocking out any light the moon tried to sneak through. It was terrifying for anyone, but Philip was almost in tears.

He trembled and whimpered, trying to turn back to the car several times before Mike and Jeremy finally shamed him into staying, as teenage boys often do.

"Phil, you fucking baby," Mike said, jumping up on a rock and letting his flashlight beam bounce down to the river below. "If Sarah ever saw you pissing yourself in the dark like this—"

"Shut the fuck up, Mike!" Philip yelled, shoving him off the rock. Mike stumbled, almost tumbling down the hill and into the water but stopping himself on a nearby tree.

"What the hell? You almost pushed me down there, you asshole!"

Mike lunged forward, attempting to grab Philip's shoulders, but Jeremy stepped in. He pushed him lightly back with a hand to his chest, flashing the light in his eyes.

"Stop the foreplay, you two. We are almost at the falls." Jeremy pushed Philip forward, staying behind him to make sure he walked.

When they finally reached the place where they could hear the thunder of the falls, Philip was in a full-blown panic. It was clear on his face that he regretted every decision that led him to this place.

Mike stepped over the caution tape first, making his way slowly down the unstable steps that descended steeply to the churning waters below. Jeremy watched Philip's fear, clearly visible in the beam of Jeremy's flashlight, which Philip neither moved nor flinched away from despite its pointing right at him. He was truly paralyzed with fear, something Jeremy hadn't yet seen before. It was fascinating. Philip's hands trembled, his face was pale, and his lips were dry. He had a faraway look in his eyes as he stared down the steep staircase into complete darkness.

"Your turn, Phil," Jeremy snapped, taking Philip out of his trance.

Philip cleared his throat and walked forward, grasping the rickety railing tightly with white knuckles. He carefully made his way down, making sure to plant each foot securely on the next step. His hand never left the railing.

That is, until he heard it.

Below them came a bellow unlike anything any of them had heard before. It was a cry of overacted pain, twisted and deep with theatrical desperation. Following it was a voice that was raspy and angry. "Philip, how dare you!" it screeched.

Jeremy stifled a laugh, impressed by Mike's commitment, but Philip had already taken flight. He ran back up the broken staircase and started dashing down the pitch-black trail toward the car. Mike's laughter echoed off the rocks in the cavernous area below the falls.

"Oh shit, did he take off?" he asked, beginning to climb back up himself.

Jeremy nodded, still stifling true laughter. "Yeah, we should go after hi—"

He was cut short by an ear-piercing scream. Philip's yell was loud and real. They followed down the trail as fast as they could and found him grunting and moaning in pain, sprawled out in the middle of the path. He had tripped over a fallen branch onto a group of sharp rocks. Jeremy flicked the light onto Philip's shin and immediately saw the carnage. A rock had ripped his skin wide open. Dirt and gravel were mixed with shredded flesh and muscle. It was a horrific injury that would certainly require stitches. Jeremy couldn't take his eyes away from it.

He and Mike had to drag Philip back to the car. Philip received forty-six stitches and still bears the scar. Tough-guy Philip. He never lived that night down. Mike never let him forget it, and Jeremy wouldn't either.

Now that same scared boy sits in front of Jeremy, talking a big game and acting as if he's ready to look into the eyes of a nightmare. Philip will make the call, just like he did before.

"Let's go make the call, Phil," Jeremy says, grabbing a book off the shelf and flipping through it.

Philip hesitates before standing and walking toward the front door. "I'm only doing this so you will get the fuck out of here."

Jeremy closes the book with a slap, standing and giving Philip a thumbs-up. "Pay phone on Derby Street," he replies, and follows Philip out the door.

CHAPTER 29

"I THINK THEY'RE THE SAME FLOWERS." Officer Michaels stands over the scatter of dead blossoms that litter the stairs.

"The same flowers as what?" Leroux leans over, steadying himself against a decrepit railing. Wren winces, waiting for the wood to break, but it never does. They're all gathered in the grandstand of an old fairgrounds, which sits at the outskirts of Great Barrington. The structure has seen better days. Wren stands a few stairs above Leroux, gazing down at the wilted blooms under their feet. Something about them feels familiar, but they're too decayed for her to place them.

"Someone scattered bouquets of white flowers all along Railroad Street. These look almost the same." Officer Michaels plucks one off the ground and rubs it between his fingers.

"You guys love to talk in riddles." Leroux sighs, pinching the bridge of his nose. "When did someone decorate Railroad Street?"

Officer Michaels gives a wry smile and a couple officers walk away.

"Friday," he says curtly.

"Did this strike anyone as unusual? Was anyone concerned about this?" Wren can't help but chime in. She gives Michaels a look of confusion. He can't miss it, even with the dimming light closing in on them.

"Are we here to talk about floral arrangements or are we here to check on a tip?" An officer with a mustache steps forward. He has a notable gap between his two front teeth, and it makes him whistle a bit when he hits particular sounds.

"Floral arrangements right now," Wren says bluntly, irritated by the lack of communication, even though Brixton promised to let Leroux and Wren in on everything regarding the investigation, understanding the value they add. But to her, it feels as if the on-the-ground officers want them to fail. Egos are a formidable opponent. When the world finally takes its curtain call, egos will be one of the last things left, along with the cockroaches and whatever they use to make spray cheese.

"We noted the incident on Railroad Street," another, kinder-looking man, Officer Blaine, answers, "but our detective said it could have been some influencer for social media, or like some fancy proposal. Totally innocuous." Blaine looks like he's the youngest on the force, with dark hair and striking green eyes.

"What kind of flowers were they? I can't quite tell what these are." Leroux picks up a stem. Brown petals fall into his hand. "I could swear they're Southern magnolias, but those aren't local to these parts."

Wren snaps her head to attention and shakes it. She tries to clear the answer from her mind, hoping it will disappear and give her a more preferable one. She is looking for a Magic 8 Ball experience. She's looking for anything other than what she just heard. She grabs Leroux's arm, causing him to stumble as the other officers continue up the stairs.

"Jesus, Muller, you trying to kill me?" He steadies himself against the crumbling railing again.

"That's my wedding flower, John." She doesn't look down, but Leroux does. He lets his eyes flick over the cascade of dead blooms below them, then back to Wren.

"Well . . . I would say we're on the right track, then," he says quietly.

"Why are my wedding flowers here?" she asks.

Leroux shakes his head. "No reason to go there right now. Let's keep ourselves alert. We can go over this later."

He brings her back down to reality quickly, not bothering with any kind of emotional coddling. She knows he is right. This scene is strange and precarious. It doesn't make sense or do them any good to focus on Jeremy's motivations or games. Something is here, and if it's dangerous, they need to be prepared for it.

She nods, continuing to walk up the steps to enter the grandstand.

"This feels like a place he would take someone. It's got that same heavy, paralyzing atmosphere. He would thrive in a place like this," she says with a shudder.

"This close to everything?" Leroux asks.

"He always rigs the game in his favor. He would account for it."

She breathes in the stale, dusty air that swirls around this place. It's getting darker. The sun still sits on its perch above the horizon, but it's getting ready to leave soon. The sky warns of impending darkness, but they push forward through the crumbling structure of a long-forgotten fair.

As they make their way through the grandstand, a smell begins to creep through the area. It's like old food and vomit were put into a blender. There are sweet notes that would make anyone's stomach lurch. Officers Blaine and Michaels comment on it. The two of them walk over to an open gap in the wood beams, seeking fresher air. But Wren follows it. She's trained to walk toward that smell.

It gets stronger as she enters the second floor of the grandstand. It's a large room full of debris and graffiti. Dust billows up around her legs as she shuffles through the broken doorway. Leroux follows, along with Blaine, Michaels, and a few other officers. They all recoil at the sudden waft of death.

Wren walks farther into the room, and the smell punches up from a back corner. Officer Blaine tries his best to keep his face neutral; the corners of his mouth twitch and it's clear he is holding his breath. Michaels throws his palm up to cover his nose and mouth, speaking in a muffled horror. "Holy shit, I don't think that's an animal." He turns his body away from the corner, shaking his head.

Wren approaches a pile of leaves. It's not just leaves though; there are formerly white magnolias littered on top. Most are shriveled like their companions outside on the steps, but some of them are fresh.

"He came back here," she says dryly. Wren gets closer. Her eyes seek out a form under the pile.

"Someone should bag some of this stuff," Leroux says. Wren can tell he's trying his hardest not to sound pushy, but it comes out authoritative anyway.

"Oh wow, thank goodness you're here," Michaels replies, gesturing for an underling to collect the flowers.

As they work to move the pile aside, the smell changes, getting more intense. It starts to hit a much sweeter and a considerably sicker note, slamming into the back of everyone's throats, causing a chorus of coughs to break out. It doesn't take long for a lock of hair to become visible and then an arm. The woman hidden under the leaves has been through hell. It's the only way Wren can describe what she is seeing.

The victim's hair was once light brown or possibly blond. Now it is stained red, brown, and black. Her face is covered in blood, dirt, bruises, and blue paint. There is a massive welt on her temple that is fresh and angry looking.

A look farther down her body shows a horrific tale of torture. There is a second welt on the back of her left thigh, and another over her ribs, with more blue paint splattered across her torn shirt.

Wren immediately recognizes the handiwork in the wound that crosses the stomach. It's a stab wound that has been dragged across her abdomen, exposing her vital organs. A part of her intestines pokes through the laceration, which looks like busted stitching on a stuffed animal.

"Jesus," Michaels says under his breath.

Blaine looks horrified, but he keeps his composure. Several officers search the rest of the space, while others secure the scene and call for the local ME and other specialists.

"It looks like his work, although I don't get why he hid her like this." Leroux peers over Wren's shoulder as she clears debris away from the woman's battered body.

"All of Rose's scenes have been in the open, yeah?" Blaine leans in, his arms crossed over his body.

Wren and Leroux twist to face him. Something about this department referring to him as "Rose" has been rubbing her the wrong way. It feels too delicate and too beautiful to be his name.

Wren nods, biting at her lip. "You aren't wrong, Officer Blaine."

"Yeah, he's a theatrical fuck, and he loves to have his victims stumbled upon out in the open," Leroux answers quickly.

"It would have been hard to find her without that tip. We may not have . . ." Michaels trails off, clearly wondering why this woman was kept hidden for so long.

Detective Warren appears, walking into the area like an unwanted pox. Wren immediately returns to observing the victim, using her gloved hand to touch the woman's left eye. It looks swollen, half-closed, by something other than the cruelty of decomposition.

"Smells like a credible tip, huh?" Warren says, snapping on gloves and moving closer to the body. As he nears the victim, he holds his arm over his mouth and nose, visibly cringing. "Wow, how long has she been here?" he asks, craning his neck.

"Not sure yet, but definitely a couple of days," Wren says without looking up at him. She's focused on digging in her bag for tweezers. She produces them and gently opens the woman's eyelid. As she suspected, there is something hidden inside the inner corner. It's white and spherical, covered in ocular fluids. She pulls it out and holds it up in front of her face.

"Shit, what is that?" Warren is appalled and steps back.

Blaine and Leroux move in to get a better look. Officer Michaels has all but left the room, standing and shaking his head in the doorway.

Wren studies the object closely, flashing her light on it and noticing that it has creases. "Paper. It's a tiny bit of balled-up paper," she says. "Can I have an evidence bag?" She holds her free hand out, waiting for someone to pass it to her.

Blaine is the first to move, grabbing one from another officer and handing it to Wren. She shifts to sit crossed-legged, smoothing it out on her lap and then placing the paper ball on top of it. Slowly, she pulls at the creases with her tweezers. The wet outer layer peels back like a heart's pericardium. It reveals a dryer inner layer that begins to open under her careful dissection. Once the ball is uncrumpled, she can see writing. Her eyes alight on the first word, *Richard*.

Her breath hitches and her heart begins to beat rapidly.

"Does it say something?" Warren comes closer, leaning over to see the note.

She scans the page that was stuffed into the dead girl's eye. She can decipher only Richard's name. The rest is scribbled nonsense. But that's all it takes to elicit panic.

Warren reaches out, moving the note toward him and trying to make sense of it.

"Richard," he says, reading the word aloud. The name sounds clumsy from his mouth. "Does that say, 'grape'?" He points at a word that doesn't look like *grape* at all.

Wren leaves the note where it is on the plastic bag. She grabs for her back pocket, sliding her phone out and calling her husband.

No answer.

She calls again, and again. No one answers.

Maybe he's in the shower or something. She thinks to herself, shaking any other possibilities from her mind. She texts him, knowing he will always answer a text.

Hey, are you at home?

She waits. Excruciating seconds go by, feelings like years. She stares at the screen, willing Richard to reply.

"What's with her?" Warren motions for an officer to bag the note.

Leroux sits down next to Wren, placing a hand on her arm, startling her. She jumps slightly, looking at him, then back at the note.

"What's wrong?" he asks, genuine concern marking his face.

"The note said Richard's name . . . the note in her eye. It said Richard's name and he's not answering." Her voice shakes.

Leroux sucks in a breath, rubbing his face. "He's fucking with you, Muller. This is a bluff."

He sounds so confident, as though he knows. For a moment, Wren nods and feels her anxiety recede. This is what he does. He tries to hit her where it hurts, and this is an elaborate and cruel bluff. It's perfectly Jeremy.

But the sick feeling of panic returns as the minutes tick by with no response from Richard.

Then a reply comes through.

| Wren, he found me.

CHAPTER 30

JEREMY AND PHILIP STAND TOGETHER in the tree line, peering through the dense thicket. Together, they watch movement through the large bay windows of the rental home. The design of the house offers unfiltered views of the interior, leaving unsuspecting renters under the scrutiny of voyeuristic eyes.

Too many windows, he thinks.

He's already breached their home back in Louisiana, and he relishes that memory. Jeremy closes his eyes, remembering the feeling of slinking up their creaky stairs and into their bedroom. They never knew he was there. He remembers the cascade of her hair spread over her pillow like red lace. And now he remembers Richard and his inability to secure their home. There is no doubt he has failed to secure this temporary one too.

"I double-checked it myself. He's in there." Philip tugs his baseball hat down, closer to his eyes. He's anxious and angry, being sure to keep himself hidden behind a large tree trunk at the edge of the property. He flinches as a figure crosses in front of the windows, passing between rooms and flicking on lights as they go.

"Your guy better not have lied." Jeremy's eyes follow the shadow from room to room. He's transfixed, not bothering to bring his gaze to Philip at all.

"My friend can be trusted. I told you, he knows the guy who rents this house. They are staying here," Philip says.

Jeremy spares him a glance. He's twitchy, barely keeping still. It's loathsome working alongside another person. It's necessary for the situation he has found himself in, but he won't be doing it again. Having to explain shit to someone all the time makes his blood boil.

Jeremy nods. "Need I remind you, if I go, you go." He doesn't go into details, but he strongly implies the potential of real danger. Everything is at risk for Philip now.

Philip takes a harsh, loud breath through his nose, not hiding his irritation. His face is red with rage and his hand pumps into a fist at his side. Jeremy fights back a grin. He knows that Philip is thinking of the words he didn't say. He's thinking of the threat that's loomed over him since Jeremy showed up at his door. He's thinking of his family. He's grieving the fact that there is no way out of this.

If Philip rolls the dice and kills him, he's calling Jeremy's bluff at the expense of everything. Jeremy knows Philip is physically capable of killing him—his body is classically strong, much stronger than his own, in theory. If he wanted to, Philip could choke him to death in his sleep, but he won't.

It's that little voice in the back of his mind, the one that Jeremy planted there, that tells him he would be setting his entire life ablaze. There's no way out.

Jeremy doesn't sleep much lately anyway. He can't seem to quiet his mind. Recently, his thoughts have been strange and disjointed at night. It's as if when he's at his most vulnerable his brain lets loose all the chaos he keeps inside. During waking hours, it stays at the fringes, allowing him to plan and react with removed purpose. But over time, it builds up, filling like a dam. In the middle of the night, disorder and doubt flow in like a series of spillways. He thinks of failure then.

It's always when he tries to sleep that he's reminded of what's still out there. Her continued existence is a reminder of his fallibility, of deficiency. The dark hollows under his eyes have become slightly more pronounced because of this, giving him a more menacing look. He feels ghoulish, his appearance finally matching the horrors that fuel his insides.

Now, looking at Philip's reluctant compliance, he can't help but smirk. Jeremy is powerful. Even out of his element, out of his comfortable womb of hedonistic exploration, Jeremy is divinely sovereign. The feeling of power in this situation is different though. It's unlike what he feels when he watches someone's life flicker to a close in front of him. It's more human, closer to that of a man who lords over a subordinate.

"Let's get this over with. Am I still selling him solar panels?" Philip steps forward.

"Just keep him at the door," Jeremy replies. He starts walking toward the house, not giving Philip any further instructions. Honestly, Jeremy doesn't need much, he just needs a diversion. Once he is behind Richard, the man will fall like an empire.

As Jeremy creeps around the back of the home, he is struck by the sheer number of entrance points.

I bet he *picked this place.*

There is no way Wren would have put herself in a place with this many windows. Emily wouldn't have, and he can't imagine that's changed about her. She was always cognizant of that kind of thing, watching too many crime shows and becoming paranoid as a result. She always claimed it was a productive paranoia, something more like a healthy readiness. He disagreed. Funny how all that could have helped her now.

The back door screen is locked. Jeremy slips on latex gloves then uses his knife to slice open the screen. This entrance leads right into the kitchen, and Richard has left the main door wide open to let in the crisp evening air.

This is almost too easy, he thinks. Backing away from the patio door, he peeks through a first-floor window into the front sitting room. He can hear Philip's knock on the porch screen and sees Richard cross the room to answer it. When Richard is out of sight, Jeremy steps through the long slice he has made in the screen.

Once inside, he feels a surge of energy. It's intoxicating, making his skin tingle and his insides buzz. He can hear Philip introduce himself with a fake name and begin his pitch. As he waits for the right moment, he takes stock of his surroundings. There is a takeout container in the trash and leftovers heating up in the microwave, providing more sound coverage.

He walks softly across the kitchen floor, noting the glass of whiskey that sits half-drunk on the counter.

An anxiety vice, he thinks to himself.

Jeremy knows he's the source of the anxiety, of disruption in their lives. He thinks about Wren and Detective John Leroux at his fairground crime scene, while Wren's husband drinks alone in their vacation home to calm his nerves. It gives him a jolt of pride.

He's in danger, he telepathically messages to Wren. Somewhere inside her, a warning signal is going off that something is wrong, that Richard needs her. Or maybe their connection isn't like his and Emily's. Maybe the spousal tether isn't as strong or lengthy as the one that binds her and Jeremy together.

As he turns the corner into the sitting room, he sees Richard's back, leaning casually against the opened door. Philip stands on the front porch, his hat pulled low and his eyes trying desperately to stay focused on Richard's face. He flicks them briefly to Jeremy.

Fucking idiot.

He can hear him going on and on about solar panels, as Richard tries to explain that this isn't his house.

"I understand this isn't your house, sir, but can you give me the information of the homeowner? I can come back at a later time." Philip's voice sounds strangely strong and casual. It surprises Jeremy.

"I think I have a card with his name on it. Stay here; I'll grab it for you." Jeremy watches Richard walk over to the other side of the sitting room. He shuffles through a pile of paperwork, finally producing a business card with the home-owner's name and cell phone number on it. He looks it over for a second before handing it to Philip. "That should be his info, right there."

As soon as he plants himself back in front of Philip, Jeremy slinks behind him. He pauses for only a second as Philip takes the card and holds it up.

Jeremy can smell Richard's cologne. It's clean and fresh, as he expected. He breathes in, holding it, letting himself fully experience this moment.

"Thanks, man, I really appreciate it. Have a good day, now." He nods and Richard moves to shut the door. Just as he starts to close it, Philip plants his hand across the entryway to stop it from swinging shut. "One more thing!" he says.

Richard is clearly confused, but before he can interrupt, Jeremy taps his shoulder from behind. Richard snaps around to face him with a look of sheer terror on his face. He was alone in his home, no one should be tapping him from behind.

"What the fuck?" he yells, jumping back into the doorway.

Jeremy smirks, allowing Richard to see his full crooked smile before unloading Charlie's mace into his face.

Richard yells, clawing at his eyes and moving to swing at Jeremy. He avoids the first punch, but the second punch con-nects with his eye. Jeremy blinks, crouching momentarily to collect himself. Philip slams the door shut and moves in to grab Richard from behind.

Richard's like a wild animal, fighting to break Philip's hold around his arms, but Philip has him clasped close to his body. Richard is strong like Philip. With a growl, he pushes himself backward, slamming Philip into the wall behind him. Philip's grip loosens, allowing Richard to slip out. He swings around and tightly grabs Philip's neck. Philip struggles, gritting his teeth and trying to pry his hands from his throat.

Jeremy is up now, readying the succinylcholine injection, as Philip kicks at Richard's legs, weakening one of them and sending them both crashing to the floor. They grapple with each other on the rug. Richard escapes Philip's grasp once more, rushing at Jeremy and tackling him.

The syringe is knocked from his hand and falls onto the couch, bouncing once and rolling under a pillow. Jeremy hits the ground hard, knocking into the coffee table and sending a large glass candle shattering to the floor. He recovers quickly, immediately head-butting Richard onto his side. At once, Jeremy is on top of him, sliding the knife from his boot. Richard blinks, dazed and in pain.

"I didn't want to do it this way, Richard!" Jeremy screams in his face, spitting as he does. He flips the knife expertly in his hand, but before he can move to use it, Richard swipes a piece of broken glass from the shattered candle and slices at Jeremy's face. It cuts a deep wound into his left eyebrow, opening the skin and starting a steady flow of blood into his eye.

For a moment, Jeremy's stunned. He grabs his head, allowing Richard a moment to throw him off and stand, wobbling, above him. Jeremy scrambles to his feet, stepping backward and holding the knife casually at his side. Blood pours down his cheek.

"You fucking loser," Richard heaves. He spits the words out as if they're venom. Jeremy can tell he's been waiting a long time to say them.

They stare at each other through wounded eyes. Richard's weep with the effects of mace and sweat; Jeremy's are bruised and bloody from Richard's hands. It's quiet for a moment, no one daring to move. Then Jeremy slowly lets his mouth form into another smile. His teeth are bloody, and there is a delicious taste of metal in his mouth, his own metal. Richard lunges at him, but it's too late.

Philip stabs the syringe into Richard's neck at his hairline, plunging the succinylcholine directly into his bloodstream. It wasn't the plan, but neither of them had planned on Richard being a fighter.

Quickly, Richard flips around to face Philip. He staggers a bit, the effects of the paralytic almost immediately taking effect. Philip steps back, stone-faced and breathing heavily. Jeremy is impressed by his calmness.

Jeremy saunters over to Richard, wiping blood from his mouth with the back of his hand. He presses his forehead right against Richard's.

"I don't ever lose," he growls. "Emily running a lot of marathons lately?" He smiles again, pushing Richard down to slump into the couch.

Richard's eyes dart back and forth, trying to understand what is happening to his body.

"What is this?" he asks, probably not truly wanting the answer.

Jeremy ignores his question. "She walk with a little limp?" He leans against the arm of the couch, lightly touching the wound at his eyebrow before returning his attention to Richard's tortured face. "Does it bother you that I gave it to her? Did you always feel me there, between you?" His smile is infinite now. He stifles a laugh.

Richard grits his teeth, trying to move but finding his body is useless. His left arm can still twitch, but the right is dead weight. His legs can't hold him up and the muscles he would use to stand are gone.

"You pathetic . . ." He begins to push himself forward but can't fight against the paralysis overtaking him. His breath comes out in quick bursts, hyperventilation setting in.

"Wren still runs," he says with a wheeze. "You don't matter." The last words rasp out, but they register. They hang in the air, taunting Jeremy. Richard's cell phone rings in his pocket.

He fights for every breath and every word. His eyes aren't even blinking, since those muscles don't work. The panic sets in, but there is also an irritating lightness in his expression. Jeremy angrily grabs his face in his hands, wanting to shatter the calmness of death.

"You regret coming to that door now, huh? Good Southern boy would never leave someone on the front porch." Jeremy lets his natural Louisiana drawl thicken.

The phone rings again.

Richard is succumbing to the apnea. His facial muscles are paralyzed, although he fights to work them. His breathing is labored as his glottis and intercostal muscles fall under the petrifying bewitchment of the drugs. He can't reach for anything, and he can't make it stop. It's happening too fast.

One more time the phone cycles through several rings and then a notification sounds. Jeremy pulls the phone from Richard's pocket and looks at the text on the screen. It's from Wren, but the screen is locked so he can't read it. He looks over at Richard, who sits wide-eyed and at the brink of suffocation. Jeremy flips the phone to face him. With a click, his face unlocks the screen and opens the text window.

> Hey, are you at home?

Jeremy can't help but smile to himself. He sits down on the couch next to Richard and begins typing a response. He deletes a few attempts and retypes, considering how he should play this. After several moments he sends a reply.

> Wren, he found me.

"What are you doing?" Philip finally asks. He's been standing motionless in the center of the room, staring at Richard, watching him die.

"Don't worry about it. They'll walk right into the trap."

Another message comes in.

> Where are u? Are u ok??

He sends a response and laughs, throwing the phone onto Richard's lap. Richard is quiet and still. His breathing has ceased.

The plan is in motion.

CHAPTER 31

T HE WORDS BLUR TOGETHER, forming a splotch of black on the screen. Leroux reads the text and curses.

Her head is dizzy and light. It feels as if it may fall right off her shoulders and onto the dirty floor. Her trembling fingers somehow type a reply.

> Where are u? Are u ok??

> I don't know. I woke up in the woods.
> I think my leg is brokwen. There's an
> old fireplace, like an old foundation.
> He called it Morgan's grave. I saw
> a street sign that said Chapel.

> Where is he? Are you alone?

She waits. Again, she waits for agonizing minutes and still nothing comes. It's as if the world fades away. Her body reacts immediately, sending every signal imaginable to every signal receptor. It's chaos inside her, with horrific images flashing through her mind on a torturous loop. Wren blinks rapidly, trying to clear them out, but it doesn't work. They slide by without reprieve, replaying her worst nightmares while she is awake.

"He's got Richard, John." Wren's breaths are so close together she feels as if she is dying. She wobbles to her feet, then bends forward, her head pressed between her legs. One long, spastic breath keeps coming but never fully satisfies her lungs. Her heart pounds so hard in her chest that she thinks it may stop altogether. It's a stress and a fear response that is so great, so powerful, it threatens to drive her mad. Her stomach lurches and her head spins.

"Wren, we are going to find him," Leroux says with conviction. "We are going to find him, and we are going to arrest this fucker." Leroux is holding her up now. As he leans on his bad leg, barely able to keep himself in a standing position, he holds all Wren's weight up against him.

She nods, unable to do anything else. She keeps nodding and doesn't stop for what seems like hours. When she finally blinks and confirms she isn't dreaming, tears begin to prick her eyes.

"Someone want to fill me in here? What the hell is going on?" Warren demands.

"What are we going to do?" she asks, pleading with Leroux to fix it.

"We are going to focus. We can't fall apart." He looks into her eyes, sternly forcing her back into a clinical role. She's always welcomed a reason to close off, to become removed.

She likes when things are stripped bare of extraneous sentiment. It's always been easy for her to distance herself, yet now it feels impossible. But if mothers find the strength to move cars off their children, then Wren can find that same strength to save Richard.

As Wren sits in the Kingsborough Police Department, she feels as if every part of her is bleeding.

Her energy is slowly but consistently being syphoned out of her. It hurts, as if long gauze packing was gradually being removed from her body after a surgery. Someone keeps pulling, and it feels uncomfortable and painful, but they won't stop. It's torturous.

A sob is constantly lodged in her throat. She tries to swallow it down, but it won't budge. It remains there, teasing her with its ability to take her breath away. Sometimes words try to escape, but they trip and come out broken.

Her hands shake; a tremor jolts her sometimes. Every now and then, a particularly aggressive shudder prompts one of those empty sobs to escape, and she chokes it away, stifling it.

This time she catches the sound, putting her hand over her mouth and digging her nails into her own cheek. Anything to dull the feeling of helplessness.

Everything inside her is trying to regain control. There is a battle, an entire war waging within her. She finds herself no match for the onslaught of horrific thoughts. She blinks, clearing them out of her mind whenever they try to force their way to the forefront.

The entire situation is strange. As soon as she relayed the information about the text messages to investigators, it set off alarm bells in nearly everyone's heads. After getting back to an area where they could connect to the internet, investigators used the device-finding app on Wren's phone to locate Richard's cell, and the results just confused everyone more. It located Richard's phone at the rental home where they had been staying since they arrived.

Wren was ready to go to the rental, but investigators questioned why Richard would say he was in the woods, if he was at their house. They also questioned why he wouldn't call the police if he had use of his cell phone. She didn't care. She just wanted to get him, to make sure he was safe.

"He doesn't use punctuation in his text messages," she told them earnestly.

"Why does that matter?" Warren had questioned.

Wren could feel that hopelessly frustrated feeling when you know you're right, but the words to explain why won't come. She felt as if she were trapped, trying to pull the explanation out of her mind piece by piece. She wanted to pluck it out and show everyone why it made sense. "Listen to me. Richard never uses punctuation. He is the king of relaying countless confusing text messages completely lacking any kind of grasp on the English language."

Warren and the other officers stood staring at her, waiting for the part that mattered to them.

"Those texts weren't Richard. They were sent by someone who communicates differently than he does, and if he was in true danger, he would never take the precious seconds to use full punctuation."

Warren rubbed a hand over his chin, seeming to listen to her. "So, you think it's Rose who sent those texts? I am starting to think the woods deflect is a possible trap."

"It's something Jeremy would do. We need to get to where the phone is. I need to get to Richard."

"We'll look into this. Sit tight." Without waiting for a reply, he turned and left her standing with tear-stained cheeks.

Now she sits, waiting for something, anything, to tell her they've located Richard.

While they formulate this mysterious plan of action, some of the officers seclude Leroux and Wren in a room with a guard. It's an unused interrogation room, complete with a barren table in the center.

"I need to get to Richard. We have to go!" she says loudly to no one in particular.

Leroux cringes, pacing in front of her.

"Trust me, Muller, I'm ready to launch to the moon right now, too, but we can't send you straight to him like a flank steak. He's setting something up, and you aren't going to be collateral damage." Leroux keeps pacing, biting at his thumbnail.

"But Richard can be collateral?" Wren rises from her chair. "We can't just stay in this police station and wait for someone else to rescue him!" She's pacing too, but more chaotically, looking like a caged lion.

Leroux sighs, pinching the bridge of his nose. "They are checking it all out, Muller. We just have to trust them."

"Oh *now* we are trusting them? I didn't take you for a coward." She stands to face him and spits the words out like a hex.

Leroux's pacing stops. He turns to look at her with fire in his eyes. "Coward? Are you fucking kidding me?" He walks toward her angrily, using his full height to try to gain control again.

"Well? What do you call this? What do you call sitting by and allowing other people to give us the thumbs-up to find my fucking husband!"

"I call it smart, Muller! I call it levelheaded! You may be feeling reckless, and I get it. But I care about Richard's safety too, and I sure as hell care about whether *you* meet your maker today!" Leroux is yelling now, and it's heartbreaking to watch the fear and sadness in his face.

She lets a slow breath heave out of her lungs, looking down at her feet and then back up to Leroux's face. "I'm sorry."

"You don't have to be," he says, pulling her in for a quick, but effective hug—the most Leroux can tolerate.

The door opens abruptly and a detective walks in. He places a file on the table next to them. "Hey, everyone, I'm Detective Holmes."

"Where is Richard?" Wren asks.

"We have a team departing for your rental home shortly. We still need to send a team to the woods, to rule it out completely, based on the details contained in the messages. And there are a couple other potential locations we want to keep in mind as well, based on information from our source."

Wren is incredulous, plopping back down in a chair. "Jeremy would never work with someone; he never has before. He won't be in the woods. He doesn't make the same mistakes very often."

Detective Holmes seems put off by her response. "Then we will confirm that for ourselves by sending a team out there. But the reality is that Rose apparently has someone in his orbit who is willing to turn on him, and we have reason to believe he trusts this person."

Wren scoffs. "I don't buy it."

"Well, it's a good thing I'm not selling it then. This is the plan. You are free to come with me and listen to the details of what's going to happen." Detective Holmes exits quickly, leaving a feeling of anxiety in the room.

Leroux looks at Wren, nodding in the direction of the door. Wren knows that if they don't want to get sidelined, they've got to follow. Together, they make their way into another, bigger room, with more windows. Lieutenant Brixton stands tall in front of a sea of officers. It's clear he commands respect from his team.

Brixton clears his throat to get everyone's attention. The room quiets. "According to our guy, Rose is going to be at the address you've all been given," Brixton explains. "You all know your role and you know the plan. We want to get Rose out alive, if at all possible."

"Couldn't this just be a trap?" Leroux asks loudly.

Everyone in the room turns to look at him. Officers scoff and mutter under their breath.

"We *did* consider that, Detective Leroux," Lieutenant Brixton says. "We don't take unnecessary risks without a fully fleshed-out plan."

Leroux gnaws at his lip and nods. "Good enough."

"Where is my husband?" Wren almost yells the question, her voice breaking in sorrow.

Brixton seems to soften, at least for a moment. "Dr. Muller, we are doing everything we can to find your husband. I can assure you that we are in full control here."

Wren's feeling of complete and utter helplessness is something no one should ever feel. Not like this. All she can do is nod, feeling both shattered and numb. As the officers disperse, it hits Wren that this is just like when Jeremy escaped from his own hell house in Louisiana. The meeting in the police station ahead of the ambush in the woods. Is he truly out there, waiting to be captured? It's surreal déjà vu.

A storm of emotions bubbles up to the surface as she fights with her own mind to focus on one thing: how it's different. This time, she doesn't care as much about seeing Jeremy taken down. She only cares that it is done at all and done fully. Her single focus is Richard and his safety.

"He loves a trap," Wren says quietly to Leroux.

He nods but then locks eyes with her. "We have fought for them to do the right thing every step of the way. I have to believe they're doing their jobs here. We can't risk derailing this plan with Richard's safety at stake."

She fights against a shudder. It wracks her body as the reality of the situation hits her again in a deeply torturous wave.

She grabs Leroux's hand and holds it tight.

Officers filter out of the room, heading in every direction. It's chaos, with a plan thrown together in what seems like seconds.

"What is happening? Where do I go?" Wren fights a fresh onslaught of panic.

An officer with the name tag GRAHAM approaches them. She looks to be around Wren's age and her blond hair is tightly pulled into a low bun.

"Dr. Muller?" she asks in a sweet voice.

"Yes, but you can just call me Wren." She holds out a trembling palm for a handshake.

"Great. Wren, you're going to be riding with me to your rental home. I'm Officer Graham, you can absolutely call me Ruby, and I'll explain everything that's happening while we're on the way. I promise."

Wren hesitates, searching Officer Graham's eyes for deception. She finds none. "Okay. I'm definitely going to need that explanation, but okay."

Ruby nods, placing a soft hand onto Wren's upper back, and hands her a Kevlar vest. "I never promise something I don't intend on delivering. Let's go, we want to head out immediately."

Leroux nods. "It ends today, Muller."

The car speeds down the streets of western Massachusetts, turning the landscape into a blur of brown and noise. Gone is the pre-autumnal magic. Now, in its place, are dread and dead leaves. Ruby goes over the plan with Wren as they head out to the far side of the lake. The logistics seem risky, but she can only stand by and trust that they will all execute their jobs well. She is going with a team back to the rental house, back to where Richard has to be. No one seems to know if Jeremy will be there, and if they do know, they are keeping that information from her.

But Wren feels a familiar sense of doom as they drive onto an unpaved dirt path. The police car bumps and rocks on the uneven terrain and they're surrounded by a line of dense trees. She is suddenly right back in the car on the way to Jeremy's home that day in Louisiana. She's sitting in that same chasm of anticipation, trying to predict an outcome in a nightmare world that's bled into reality.

Her head aches, and sharp twangs hit her eyes from within. She rubs her temples and forehead trying to ease the pain, but it's nearly constant. Although it makes it worse, she can't stop staring at her phone, hoping for another text from Richard. When the screen remains blank, her body sends through an immediate signal of stress. A wave of nausea hits, coating her in a cold sweat. She adjusts the Kevlar vest, feeling strangled.

It's so hot in here.

The heat envelops her like an unwelcome blanket. It bears down on her and feels heavier with each shaky breath she takes. Her mouth salivates and she's sure she's about to be sick.

She clears her throat suddenly, hoping to stop what feels inevitable. She opens the window, sticking her head out slightly and greedily gulping in the fresh, cold air. She stays that way for a minute, letting it calm her nauseated stomach and the feeling that was rising inside her. Finally, Wren can see the landscape as more than a depressing blob of brown. Now she starts to see color and life. Slowly, her nightmare world dissipates.

"Ya know, this is all a little déjà vu for me," Wren says, sticking her hand out of the window and moving it with the wind as she did when she was a child. It's a comforting gesture.

Ruby glances her way. "Oh, yeah. I can only imagine." Her voice is kind. Wren can tell that she's struggling with the best way to approach this situation and Wren appreciates her effort.

"I hope this one has a better finale." Wren chuckles a bit, trying to lighten the tension enough for them both to breathe.

Ruby grins. "I told you, I always deliver on a promise, and I can promise everyone is going to give their absolute best. We're going to take Rose in and we're doing our utmost to bring your husband home safely."

"I appreciate you not promising it will all be okay." Wren smirks, turning to look at Ruby. "I like people who refuse to bullshit."

"You won't find any kind of shit here," Ruby answers.

They pull around the corner and the cozy rental cabin comes into view, down a long driveway. A familiar scene begins to unfold, with police surrounding the place, but an eerie silence has taken over. Everyone moves fluidly, careful not to alert anyone who could be in the house.

Ruby pulls her car a safe distance from the home. She makes sure to go slowly to keep the tires from crunching loudly on the gravel. The plan is to approach Wren's rental home, the woods, and a third site—provided by the informant—simultaneously. If they can triangulate on all three locations, then Jeremy won't have time to escape, and hopefully Richard will be found. They park, and Ruby turns on a monitor. The video is bouncy and chaotic, but Wren realizes they are watching the live feed from an officer's body cam as he approaches the front door of the cabin. This camera is pointed at Detective Warren. Her breath hitches in her throat as he moves closer to the entrance.

They watch as Warren slowly climbs the steps to the front door. His breath is measured but sounds heavy with dread. It comes out in loud puffs that can be heard readily. He rests his hand on his weapon, likely feeling the waves of energy flow into his fingers, but he remains as casual as possible about his posture.

He roughly slams his fist against the door three times in quick succession. It's a jarring sound that cuts through the air, causing birds to startle and desperately fly away from a nearby tree. After the rush of flapping wings and primal screeches, movement can be heard from inside the house. In response, Warren angles his body in a way that will allow him to protect his vital organs.

He announces himself, letting his words hang there for a bit before repeating himself once more.

"Kingsborough Police, open the door!" Warren yells, stepping aside to allow a forcible entry, if necessary.

There's a beat. Everything feels as if it falls into slow motion. The clouds don't float by on the wind anymore, the trees stop dancing in the slight breeze, and leaves don't fall. It all stops, holding a collective breath for whatever comes next.

Then the door begins to open.

CHAPTER 32

THE THREE KNOCKS ARE FORCEFUL, coming in quick succession and sounding authoritative. Jeremy hears them from the basement, and he cranes his neck to listen.

"Kingsborough Police, open the door!" he hears a muffled yell.

Immediately an excited feeling overtakes his system. It's strange. He didn't expect this, but he had worried it might happen many times before. But he survived his last close call with some quick thinking. This time won't be any different.

Briefly, he wonders how they traced him to this place or if they even know that he's here. They were supposed to run to the hearth, the fireplace deep in the woods where their long-buried secret lies.

Morgan Davies was supposed to be found today. Philip had always treated Morgan as Jeremy's victim. He cut ties and found Jesus, brazenly lying to his loyal following, telling them he is righteous while fucking whatever young sheep he lured into his holy house. This was supposed to hurt him too. Killing someone doesn't always mean a heart has to stop beating. Killing comes in many forms.

Are they looking for Philip? Did they trace a call somehow?

A million different scenarios run through Jeremy's mind as he sprints for his bag slung next to where he has been sleeping. He fumbles through the contents, hunting for the gun he had stolen off Tom's body. *Where is it?* He dumps everything onto the floor and turns the bag inside out. It's gone. His gun is gone.

Philip.

Even in his mind, he sneers at the name. It all begins to come into focus now, the trap he allowed himself to fall into so comfortably. This isn't who he is. This isn't who he should ever have been. It suddenly occurs to him that he had stupidly left his bag unattended while they were in the woods outside the rental house. It was for only a few moments, but Jeremy was so focused on what he was about to do, the feelings he was about to feel, that he had been careless. He thought he had the upper hand with Philip—that he commanded obedience and control. But he was wrong to trust that piece of shit. The tenuous thread that bound them together is unraveling before his eyes.

Jeremy silently curses himself before he scans the room. He has to hide. He has to get the fuck away from this mess. It's time for battle and his sole defense is his knife, which will only suffice in close proximity.

On his first night in the basement, he'd scouted for a decent hiding spot, just in case. The only thing suitable was a tiny closet with an unfinished crawl space. He runs for it now, closing the closet door behind him and squeezing himself into the dirt hole—not even cement or wood—just dirt. It's only big enough for him to sit with his legs tight to his chest, and there's only a single way in and out. It's not ideal, but it will buy him time to assess the situation.

He hears the front door open and then the pounding of feet overhead. He knows it's only a matter of minutes before he has to make a decision. But even as everything closes in, time seems to almost slow to a stop. Everything warps and becomes quiet. It's as if he huddled himself under a heavy blanket. He lets his head fall back to lean against the wall. Dirt falls onto his shoulders. He feels it fall into his shirt, and the sensation somehow feels more pronounced than it should. Everything feels more pronounced as the world closes in on him.

He shuts his eyes, thinking. Surely, there are officers in the woods now too. They wouldn't ignore those instructions completely. Have they brought Richard out from the woods yet? Have they paraded his body past her? He imagines Wren's face, distorted into a look of horror. It would be like the look she gave him back in the bayou. Pure pain. The purest pain he can imagine. The vision satiates him for a moment. It's an oasis in a crumbling desert.

They probably didn't allow her to go.

Did that drive her mad? She's always in control, and here she is being told what to do, where she can't go. She can't play hero anymore. The stakes are too real and she's not prepared to face them.

Taking that person from her, leaving her alone to face what she has seen . . . that is how he kills her.

But at this moment, it's killing *him*. Being shepherded into a hole in the wall is not his idea of an ending. Suddenly, he regrets so much. He always told himself to never live with regrets, to always figure out a reason something happens. Regrets are pointless because they can't be fixed. They are the past. But now? Now the regrets come quick and hard.

Why did he think he could share this experience with Philip, with anyone? Humans are fallible, but he shouldn't be. His brain shuffles through the various points of weakness in this plan. He knew they were there, but he always expected to weather them. They were never enough to stop him from moving forward. Her death was far too important to him. He was ready to fight for it.

Something drips on his head. It's a hard drip that makes its way down his forehead. He puts his finger on it and switches on the small flashlight that's always strapped to his belt loop. He looks up. The mystery liquid is amber-colored and sticky, but it doesn't have a smell. Another drip, then another. A light rain of sticky shit begins to slowly soak him and there's nowhere to go. This unknown liquid begins a relentless assault, and the irony isn't lost to him.

As he studies the substance falling on him, a spider crawls across his foot. He kicks at it. It stumbles, stunned for a minute, before righting itself and powering toward him again. For a second, he watches it as it crawls near his foot again. It doesn't even hesitate before it crawls across it. He kicks it and the process continues.

No self-preservation instincts.

Upon its final journey, Jeremy takes his fist and slams it down on top of it, crushing the creature in an instant.

The liquid continues to drip. It falls onto his eyelashes now. He switches off his flashlight.

The muffled footsteps grow louder. They're getting close to the basement door. Jeremy sucks in a breath as the lock is blasted open roughly and the sound of boots comes pounding down the stairs.

They enter the room, bringing with them a strong presence. His senses are filled with the sounds of items being torn into and tossed aside. They are trying to show their authority, trying to intimidate him into surrender. He would smile if he weren't so angry at himself for being here.

The calamity drives closer to the closet door, barreling forward, and for once, he's powerless to stop it. He grasps his knife and his eyes flick around the dark space, hoping for some opening or a defense hidden in the dirt. There's nothing. There's nothing for him to do but give up or fight. He slides the knife into his left sleeve.

The closet door swings wide with a slow creak, and he feels a surge of power travel through his body. The closeness of the noise is overwhelming, but it ignites him. The click of a weapon stings his ears.

"Jeremy Rose." A loud, gravelly voice cuts through the darkness, pronouncing his name like an insult. "We have you surrounded."

He waits, breathing heavily, but still measured and controlled. He considers ignoring the officer and forcing them to pull him out—putting the people's tax dollars to work. But in the seconds he has to think, it doesn't feel right to be dragged out of this little box, covered in sticky shit.

He crawls toward the opening, keeping a smile on his face.

"Keep your hands where we can see them!" an officer yells, as two others close in on both sides, guns pointed at his head.

He slithers out, holding his hands up and never removing his smile. With his hands up, he makes a quick move to grab the knife from his left sleeve. He slides it out, nicking his own wrist in the process. In an instant, he swings the knife in front of him, slashing at the officers. The knife connects with one of their arms, causing minimal damage. That is all he had, and that is all it takes.

Before he can even consider making another move, Jeremy feels the pressure of a knee against his back. He doesn't have time to register what's happening. The officers grab him and flip him, face down, onto the floor. He's cuffed with his hands behind his back. One slash of his knife and things get interesting.

Someone starts to read his Miranda rights, but Jeremy tunes it all out, focusing instead on the tight cuffs and knee against his spine. He finds it hard for his chest to rise and fall with the pressure on his back, and he starts to unintentionally hyperventilate as he tries to draw in a good breath. His face rubs hard against the scratchy rug, and when they lift him to his feet, he feels woozy and his cheek burns. He finds himself almost passing out from the sudden movement, his knees buckling unexpectedly. But they catch him before he drops to the ground and then throw him roughly against the wall to search him.

"Still feel like a tough guy, Rose?" an officer whispers in his ear. His breath smells like coffee and cigarettes. Jeremy almost retches as it skates across his nostrils. He doesn't respond, just keeps his mouth set into a look of boredom, anticipating the next move.

He sees them check his hiding spot. They take their time, thoroughly searching it as if he hid something precious in there. He finds himself almost laughing at the earnest way they finally declare "all clear" about a hole in the wall he discovered only a few days ago.

Jeremy is dragged up the stairs. He lets his legs buckle again, just to see them all jump at once to grab him. When they emerge onto the ground floor, he's amazed at how quickly everything erupts into chaos. Only minutes earlier he had been up here, and it was peaceful. It was quiet. Now, various levels of officers cover every corner with guns drawn, and detectives mill about. That's when he spots Philip, chatting with a detective over by the window. His face is serious, and he keeps nodding. When they emerge with Jeremy, his eyes trail over to him.

Before he can say anything to Philip, a familiar voice breaks through.

"Not so smart when the game isn't rigged, huh, Jeremy? Or is it Cal?" Disdain seethes from the words.

Jeremy looks to his right to see the voice belongs to John Leroux. He leans against a chair and smiles from ear to ear. It's an unwelcome sight, turning Jeremy's stomach. But Jeremy gives him a blank stare, refusing to show even a hint of recognition.

They lead Jeremy through the living room, pushing him around like a rag doll, even though he isn't fighting them. The officer holding his cuffs jams him harshly against a wall, making him face it and shoving his forehead into the wood. Jeremy smirks, amused at their pathetic show of toughness.

"You're doing great," Jeremy says sweetly.

The officer grabs him by the back of the neck and slams him hard against the wall again.

"Shut the fuck up, you piece of shit!" he screams into Jeremy's face, spit flying.

It's then that Philip saunters over to Jeremy, and for the first time, there's a private grin on his face. The serious and concerned citizen has vanished. Suddenly, it all starts to make sense.

Philip flicks his eyes to the two officers holding Jeremy. The officers give the briefest of nods. They acknowledge him. They know him. Immediately, Jeremy can feel every bit of rage rise inside of him. His body feels as if it is popping with anger. He swears his skin will begin to boil.

The officers turn away knowingly as Philip leans closer to Jeremy's face. He keeps a grin plastered on and whispers, "There was never any danger for me. You know that now, right?"

Jeremy stares into his eyes, despite the storm that rages inside him. He doesn't say a word, just lets his eyes bore back into Philip's.

"This is my territory you stumbled into, my friend. This is my world to conquer. You unknowingly had the complete disadvantage."

Jeremy scoffs, letting the smile return to his face, but refusing to speak.

This seems to piss off Philip. His smirk drops slightly and he inhales sharply. But after only a second of a slip, he's back to grinning like a hyena in heat. He gets as close as he can, whispering so only they can hear, "Come on, Jer. Did you really think I would be stupid enough to leave the body where we buried her? Did you think I would leave that thread for you or anyone else to pull?"

This confession genuinely shocks Jeremy. His eyes widen slightly and his mind races. Philip moved Morgan Davies's body. He went back to the hearth in the woods—where so many years ago he had cried and carried on like a wounded doe—and he moved her. That's why he agreed to everything. He knew they would never find his secret because he made it unfindable. "Leaving my ID on her was a nice touch, asshole."

The one thing Jeremy never anticipated was that Philip would grow into his own instincts. He never anticipated that the anxious pastor, the son of the beloved judge, would find his own darkness and harness it. But then again, he saw it today when Philip killed Richard. He saw the calmness, the fascination in Philip's eyes as he watched Richard struggle to breathe as paralysis consumed him. It wasn't as if he was losing a piece of himself in that moment, it felt as if he was nurturing something already there. Because Jeremy has had such a singular focus, he ignored what he was seeing so clearly.

What else has Philip done? The two friends had parted ways, unable to overcome what had happened that night when they were young. Philip claimed he couldn't recover from it. He had to remove Jeremy from his life to move past the trauma he claimed Jeremy caused. Now Jeremy can see the reality was that Philip had to give himself space to explore his own malevolence. He had to find a way to preach piousness while bathing in sin. Jeremy thought he had all the chess pieces, but instead, Philip changed the game altogether.

None of it mattered. None of the blackmail was real. The power Jeremy felt was not earned.

Philip continues, never letting his face drop, "What church do you think all these fine officers belong to? Who do you think baptizes their babies?" He glances around briefly, confirming that all the officers around them are ignoring their interaction. "You know who my father is," he whispers. "This police department isn't clean."

Jeremy sucks a breath in and licks his lips. "You'll live to regret this," he finally says.

Philip chuckles, looking him in the eyes. "Too bad you won't."

CHAPTER 33

*T*HAT DAY, OFFICER GRAHAM *guarded Wren in the car, while officers stormed her rental home right in front of her eyes. She asked to be let out. She didn't want anything between her and Richard when they brought him outside to her. She was convinced he was going to be okay, left as an injured piece of bait in Jeremy's stupid little game.*

Officer Graham had warned her they didn't know what they would find inside, but Wren insisted it was nothing she couldn't handle. Staying behind Graham, Wren had inched closer to the front door, waiting for the crescendo to come.

It didn't. Officers walked out the front door calmly, telling them no one was in there. They found a broken candle and Richard's phone. Richard himself was nowhere to be found and neither was Jeremy.

She was wrong. She called it wrong. To further her confusion, the officers on the scene don't seem surprised that Jeremy wasn't there. They took it stoically. Too stoically for Wren's understanding.

After confirming no one was inside the rental home, Wren had next watched in shock on body camera footage as they found Jeremy hiding in a shit-covered hole somewhere else. She watched them drag him up the stairs of a house and she watched them read him his rights. It was a strange moment filled with a chaotic mixture of relief and confusion.

She learned Jeremy was found in Philip Trudeau's—Pastor Philip's—home. It was Philip who informed police that Jeremy had forced his way into Philip's home, threatening his family if he didn't let him stay. Philip claims he complied out of fear, but after only one night, he couldn't take it and called the police. Leroux didn't believe Philip's story. He said it looked as though Jeremy had been there longer, but the cops insisted that was nonsense.

Before Wren had even a minute to process what was happening, the word came over the radio that the other team of investigators, the team sent to the location in the woods off Chapel Road, had found the body of an adult male in his thirties. As the physical description unfolded, Wren knew her entire universe would never be the same.

She fell to her knees, heaving and screaming into the fallen leaves beneath her feet. It was a pain that she had never experienced before. It was a physical ache that felt like a wild animal had burrowed through her chest and into her stomach, ripping everything apart as it moved.

Jeremy had left Richard's body near an old fireplace in the woods, just as the text from Richard's phone had said. She should have known that just when she thinks she has Jeremy figured out, he becomes more incapable of dissection.

Again, she screamed, her palms digging into the dirt. She tried to tear the earth apart, anger and sorrow merging into a poisonous union inside her.

Wren couldn't think of anything else but pain.

"The autopsy report is done, Dr. Muller." The voice shakes her from her nightmarish daydream. Anytime she has found herself alone, which isn't often, she slides back into that moment and relives it over and over again. It's a tortuous exercise of pain that her mind plays on repeat, and she always hopes it will end differently. It's been weeks, and although she has received the preliminary results of her husband's autopsy, she has been anxiously awaiting the complete report.

She sits up from her reclining position in the morgue office chair and holds out her hand. Mark, a newer technician who happens to be on shift today, has gotten the dubious task of delivering this atomic bomb to his new boss. He places the folder into her hand, then walks quickly out of the office.

"Thanks, Mark," she says to no one, slapping the folder down on the desk and rubbing the space between her eyes. A tension headache moved in days ago, and it seems to have set up shop for good.

She isn't ready to look at it. She hasn't ever been ready to see his name on this kind of paperwork. It's like a never-ending punishment that she loops herself into every day, every hour. It's like what she felt while Jeremy was on the run. She feels raw and open, controlled, and afraid almost all the time. Any minute could bring another fresh hell, a new barrage of emotional turmoil to suffocate her.

She hasn't stopped moving since it happened. She demanded they allow her back to work, and no one stepped in her way this time. Somehow, it's been easy for everyone to understand that this is what she needs, or maybe she didn't give them a choice. To remain at home, in that empty home they built together, would be a death sentence. It would be like throwing her headfirst back into that bayou and letting her perish.

She hasn't been home alone since it happened. A constant stream of friends and family have stood watch over her, as if she were a ticking time bomb that they might need to detonate at a moment's notice. She finds herself right back in that fragile place, only this time no one expects her to heal. Pity is painted onto her in thick, globby layers. Although people mean well, it's bothersome and unwelcome, like a coat of paint that will never dry.

She will never be ready to look at this autopsy report, but something gnaws inside her, telling her that there is more to this. She refuses to allow Richard's legacy to be that of another Bayou Butcher victim. For weeks, ever since Jeremy was arraigned on charges in Louisiana, Wren has felt as if there is more to Richard's murder.

Unfortunately, she seems to be alone in this. Jeremy won't talk. Suddenly, he's tight-lipped, making investigators do all the work without the benefit of a confession.

Interestingly, it was a bartender who linked Jeremy with the dead woman in the fairgrounds, as well as a missing man from Virginia. He claimed a man in glasses with dark hair was heavily pursuing the fairground victim at his bar the night she went missing. He felt something was off about the guy, just didn't like the feeling he was getting from him, but when he asked for identification, he had a legitimate one that said his name was Tom. Not convinced, he quizzed him on his birthday, and he rattled it off : July 5. It was when he overheard Tom tell the victim he was a Capricorn that the alarm bells got louder, since July 5 would make him a Cancer.

The bartender was reluctant to come forward at all. He thought it was a waste of time to tell police—he just thought the guy was a little predatory and he didn't know his zodiac sign. He figured the whole thing wasn't close to a smoking gun, but he ended up being incredibly helpful with his instincts, because he came forward to police with his gut feeling and was able to identify the man he saw that night in a photo lineup.

Jeremy had brutalized that girl, sending her out in the fairground to be hunted down slowly and methodically in a game he rigged to win. Hearing the details of it were shockingly triggering for Wren. It was like reliving her entire situation again. It still disturbs her to think that he was able to find another playground and other victims to act as his prey.

She thought his arrest would make it better, but it just made it different.

Now, he's found a new way to torture people, even with his hands and feet shackled. He smiled in court for his arraignment, constantly blowing a stray piece of hair off his forehead, catering to a demographic of hybristophiliacs that everyone will needlessly have to contend with. He's the perfect monster and he's perfectly aware of it. Someone like Jeremy Rose doesn't squander an opportunity to hurt people, even when another step is added. He takes incarceration as a challenge for how creative he can get.

She opens the folder and immediately shuts it again. Just seeing the word *deceased* is enough. She isn't ready.

As she enters her home, Lindsey is there. She rises from the couch as soon as Wren enters, immediately gesturing to the pizza and gin and tonics on the coffee table, set up with lit candles.

"Welcome home, you beautiful bitch. Your feast awaits."

Wren drops her bag, allowing herself a faint smile. "You are such a welcome sight," she says. "Let me quickly shower and I am ready to dive in."

Lindsey throws her arms in the air triumphantly, knowing how hard it has been to wrench a smile from Wren lately.

"I have *The Craft* cued up too," she reveals.

"Oh, I need that. Be down in a few minutes." Wren jogs up the stairs, heading for the bathroom. For a moment she feels the emotion of comfort. She feels how excited she would have been to have pizza, a cocktail, and a *Craft* movie night with one of her best friends. She can touch that emotion for just a second, but as soon as she lifts her face to see her reflection in the mirror, it all falls away. She touches her puffy eyes and chapped lips. She sees the markings of her sorrow right there in the looking glass. It brings her immediately back to the place she can't escape, the place of unimaginable sadness.

She steps into the shower, making it hotter than normal. It leaves her skin red, blotchy, and angry.

After slipping into the small comfort of some sweats, she makes her way to Richard's closet. It feels as if it's radiating something, but she can't tell if it's trying to keep her away or draw her in. She pushes forward, regardless of the intentions. When she steps inside, the smell of him overwhelms her, and her knees buckle. She grabs a shelf to steady herself. When she puts her weight on it, the entire thing falls, sending shoes tumbling down with her to the carpeted floor. For a moment, she sits and softly cries, quietly chastising herself for even coming into the closet to begin with.

Quickly, her cries turn into anger. She had warned him of his shoddy installation and had been vocally concerned that one day it would tip over onto him.

"Richard, I told you this would fall!"

Sitting on the ground in just sweatpants and soaking-wet hair, she kicks one of his sneakers away.

When she looks down, she notices the corner of the shelf gave her a good slice on her arm, not deep, but enough to lightly bleed. When she sees it, the anger is gone. Replacing it is nothing that can be accurately described, but she begins to laugh. She laughs from her belly, leaning back into the closet wall and burying her face into a pair of pants that fell in the crash. She laughs louder and harder than she can remember doing in years.

"Wren!" Lindsey runs into the room, responding to the sound of the shelf falling. "Are you okay, what happened?" She crouches down, grabbing Wren's arm. "Oh my god, you're bleeding!"

It takes her a second, but she soon realizes the sounds she is hearing are not sobs, but giggles. She is confused, but within a few seconds, she is laughing too. Together they laugh until tears roll down their faces, neither truly knowing why. It's like an exorcism for Wren.

When she catches her breath, Wren grabs one of his well-worn T-shirts and throws it over her head. It's a Tom Petty shirt and the fabric is soft and cool. The smell is comforting and overwhelming at the same time, fresh and clean, with the scent of him embedded in it.

"I told him to fix this shelf," Wren says, smoothing out the shirt and standing up with Lindsey's help.

Lindsey puts a hand lightly onto Wren's back. "He's laughing his ass off right now," she says.

Wren chuckles, shutting the door behind her and throwing her hair into a messy bun. "You're absolutely correct."

"Let's get you a bandage for that scrape."

Together they walk down the stairs.

The evening is quiet, with moments of relief. Laughter, nostalgia, and comfort ebb and flow with numbness and pain. She feels lighter somehow, despite it all.

"Remember when we tried to call the corners, like in the movie?" Wren says, taking herself back to a better time.

Lindsey laughs. "Yes! Didn't we use your hermit crab?"

"Dr. Mayberry. Yes, yes we did."

"Was he the third or the fourth?"

Wren takes a sip of her drink. "He was the fourth. Very distinguished."

"Well, he didn't help us call any great power down. I was planning on turning so many traffic lights green." Lindsey grins.

Wren laughs. "Or maybe he called it down for himself. He lived like fifteen more years! Remember? My dad had to take over his maintenance when I went to college."

Lindsey doubles over, letting out another hearty laugh. "Wren, shut up, I totally forgot that. Pour one out for Dr. Mayberry."

Just as she is about to respond, there is a sharp knock on the door. Both Lindsey and Wren freeze, turning their gaze at it. It's silent in the room, with the heaviness of anxiety settling in. Wren can see Lindsey's face is etched with fear. She's sure there is a certain amount of expectation that danger or unsavory characters may follow Wren around, considering everything that has happened. She can't fault Lindsey for being cautious.

Wren walks toward the door, stopping next to it and peeking out the window, onto the porch. The light is off and it's dark, but there is a figure standing there, motionless. She always leaves the light on.

"Get behind me," she orders in a hushed whisper.

Lindsey does as she's told, hunching behind her and clutching an umbrella as a weapon.

"Who's out there?" Wren asks, using an authoritative voice and slipping her phone from her pocket to dial 911.

A moment passes with silence and then the person on the other side of the door finally speaks.

"Muller, it's John."

It's as if someone let the oxygen back into the room, and the two women almost collapse on each other in relief. Wren swings the door open for Leroux.

"Why the fuck would you just cold-knock?!" she yells, pulling him inside.

"I texted you first to let you know I was on the way."

She attempts to argue, but a glance at her phone proves his story is correct. She has three separate texts from Leroux telling her that he's coming over, telling her he's on the way, and then letting her know he was standing on her porch. Color rushes to her cheeks and she hugs him.

"I'm sorry."

He pats her shoulder. "Hey, I'm glad you're having a night where you could stay away from your phone."

"Come on in," she says walking back into the living room.

"Yeah, come join our witchy evening of carbs and alcohol," Lindsey says, plopping back onto the couch but still holding her umbrella weapon.

"Wait, why are you here?" Wren suddenly realizes this is strange for eleven p.m.

Leroux rocks on his heels. "Yeah, that's the thing. Can I chat with you for a second in the kitchen, maybe?"

A familiar dread fills Wren's stomach. "Yeah, is everything okay?"

"Yes."

He doesn't elaborate and his eyes tell her not to question him further.

"Lindsey, I'll be right back."

Lindsey nods, holding her umbrella up. "You got it."

They walk in silence to the kitchen.

"Do you want anything? Water?" she asks, stopping to spritz water on her rescue fern.

He shakes his head, pacing a bit. "No, thanks."

She sits, expecting he'll do the same, but he keeps pacing. He stops now and then to play with a magnet on the fridge and wrings his hands a lot.

"Okay, please tell me whatever the hell you are here to tell me," Wren says impatiently.

He stops, finally looking at her. "I haven't wanted to bring anything up to you lately. This is a situation that none of us is prepared to deal with, and I want you to know I wouldn't come to you unless I felt very strongly about what I was coming to you with."

She feels her heart begin to pound in her chest and she scratches her fingernail into the wood on the kitchen table. "What is it?" she asks softly.

He sighs, finally slipping into the seat across from her. "Wren, have you looked at the complete autopsy report yet?"

The words hit her like a tidal wave, and she blinks. "No. I have it. But I didn't look through it yet." The night feels as if it comes crashing down around her. Even the mention of the documents sends her right back into her nightmares. She squeezes her eyes shut and shakes her head, trying to clear it from her mind.

He notices her warped expression and sighs. "I'm so sorry, but I think we need to look at it together. Right now."

Wren looks up, crinkling her brows together. "John, spit it out."

Leroux pauses, looking as if he is searching for the solution before sharing the problem. He takes a shaky breath before looking into Wren's eyes. "I don't think Jeremy killed Richard alone."

Wren can feel the heat rise to her cheeks, making them feel as if they will burn away. She sucks in a breath, scratching the table harder and bringing pieces of wood up and under her nail. She feels nothing and everything all at the same time. "John, you better be damn sure of what you are saying right now."

Feeling her ire, he stands, beginning to pace again. "I know you don't want to hear this. I know that."

She blinks rapidly, shaking her head in silence.

He stops, looking at her with desperation. "We need to talk to Jeremy."

A series of panicked thoughts make their way through her mind. She shifts in her seat, trying to force her system to calm itself. "Tell me more." The words come out soft and measured.

"I believe Philip Trudeau was present when Richard was killed."

She puts a hand over her mouth, leaning her elbow on the table and closing her eyes. She tries to focus, to make sense of what she is hearing, but everything feels as if it's caving in around her. Her mouth goes dry, her stomach heaves, and she can feel a cold sweat begin to form on the back of her neck. "John, you know I trust you."

"I know this is a lot, but you know that I would never steer you into something unless I was absolutely sure."

She looks into Leroux's eyes, searching them for doubt. All she sees is her friend. "I am barely alive right now, John. I am *barely* alive."

"Wren, we have to talk to Jeremy."

She shakes her head, not understanding the false finality of it all. She thought it was over.

"Listen, other than his lawyers, he has one other name on his approved visitors' list."

Suddenly everything comes into focus. Her breathing calms and her stomach stops churning. She darts her eyes around her kitchen, their kitchen.

The thought of seeing Jeremy face-to-face again repulses her, but she has never run from that feeling before. She isn't going to run from it now. Rubbing her hands over her face, she takes a couple deep breaths before looking back at Leroux, eyes filled with resolve.

"I'll do it."

ACKNOWLEDGMENTS

When I am writing, I truly become some sort of mythical nightmare creature. Clad in worn-out sweatpants, consuming only coffee, whatever my current hyperfixation snack is, and a steady stream of carefully crafted playlists, I no longer exist on this plane of reality. But when I do come up for air, emerging from my writing room like a goblin, there are many people that carry me through to my next transmutation. Thank you endlessly:

To my John, once again you have given me the gifts of time and endless support to get this book finished. Without you, none of it would be possible. I don't just mean this book, I mean everything. You are wonderful, beautiful, selfless, and incredibly creative. Philip became what he did because of your brilliant input. Thank you for just being you. You are everything. I love you more than cookies, coffee, and caramel. The three Cs . . . you beat 'em.

To Mom and Dad, I will always thank you for everything I ever do. You are magnificent and top-notch, as far as parents and humans go. Forever your "ghoul."

To Karen, who created one of my all-time favorite humans and is one of the most selfless people in the universe. You are outrageously appreciated.

To Ash, who knows my entire soul. Thank you for creating so much cool shit with me. I appreciate you more than I could ever express. You are magic. Pure, chaotic, beautiful, hilarious, loving Gemini magic. Never, ever change.

To Mikie and Dave, who are some of the most wonderful people in the galaxy. I appreciate you both so much, it is beyond words. You are creative, kind, and perfectly hilarious.

To Sabrina, who is my literary agent but has become my friend, partner in crime, and frequent receiver of my anxious texts, you are incredible. I am so fortunate to know you and to have you in my corner. Let's take over the world together or something, okay? I'll bring the Chex Mix.

To Marissa and Seth for always encouraging my madness and for always being in my corner. LFG!

To Dinesh for being a true friend, an encouraging pal, and a comforting chum, and for bringing that beautiful Luna Moth Sheena into my life.

To my editor, Hayley, Molly, and the rest of my Zando family for continuously believing in me and this story. You are dreamweavers.

To my WME badasses Suzy, Florence, and Sylvie, you are continuously an amazing part of this journey and even took it international! I am so thankful for you.

To the Berkshires for giving me all of my favorite childhood memories and most of my adult ones too. Thank you for being my forever happy place.

To all my eagle-eyed readers, I'm sorry to report that as of 2024, Lafayette Cemetery is closed to the public for tours.

ABOUT THE AUTHOR

ALAINA URQUHART is the *New York Times* bestselling author of *The Butcher and the Wren*, which was published internationally in more than twenty languages. Drawn to the spooky, haunting, and fantastical at a young age, she's thrilled to finally share with readers all the stories she has filed away. When she isn't writing, she is the science-loving cohost of the chart-topping show *Morbid*. An autopsy technician by trade, she offers a unique perspective from deep inside the morgue. Alaina hails from Boston, where she lives with her husband, John, who is the human of her dreams, along with their three magical daughters, two labs (Blanche Devereaux and Sidney Prescott), and a forever ghost Puggle named Bailey.